THE *ALFA'S* FISH KEPT COMING, PINGING HARD.

Damn, Boxer cursed to himself. That *Alfa* skipper is good. The Soviet hunter-killer sub was holding its ground, guiding her remaining wire-guided torpedo at the sonar image that the fleeing American sub was producing.

Boxer maneuvered the *Manta* hard left and dove, but the enemy torpedo was too fast.

"Prepare to take a hit," Boxer said into the MC as the blip closed.

The torpedo exploded against the sensitive shaft plates, and the *Manta* began to spiral downward, a popping sound coming from the stern hull as the sea began forcing its way in.

Then the *Manta* touched the bottom with a crash, bouncing once before settling on its keel.

Under two thousand feet of ocean.

ACTION ADVENTURE

SILENT WARRIORS (1675, $3.95)
by Richard P. Henrick
The Red Star, Russia's newest, most technologically advanced submarine, outclasses anything in the U.S. fleet. But when the captain opens his sealed orders 24 hours early, he's staggered to read that he's to spearhead a massive nuclear first strike against the Americans!

THE PHOENIX ODYSSEY (1789, $3.95)
by Richard P. Henrick
All communications to the USS *Phoenix* suddenly and mysteriously vanish. Even the urgent message from the president cancelling the War Alert is not received. In six short hours the *Phoenix* will unleash its nuclear arsenal against the Russian mainland.

COUNTERFORCE (2013, $3.95)
Richard P. Henrick
In the silent deep, the chase is on to save a world from destruction. A single Russian Sub moves on a silent and sinister course for American shores. The men aboard the U.S.S. *Triton* must search for and destroy the Soviet killer Sub as an unsuspecting world races for the apocalypse.

EAGLE DOWN (1644, $3.75)
by William Mason
To western eyes, the Russian Bear appears to be in hibernation — but half a world away, a plot is unfolding that will unleash its awesome, deadly power. When the Russian Bear rises up, God help the Eagle.

DAGGER (1399, $3.50)
by William Mason
The President needs his help, but the CIA wants him dead. And for Dagger — war hero, survival expert, ladies man and mercenary extraordinaire — it will be a game played for keeps.

#11 HARBOR OF DOOM

—— BY IRVING A. GREENFIELD ——

ZEBRA BOOKS
KENSINGTON PUBLISHING CORP.

ZEBRA BOOKS

are published by

Kensington Publishing Corp.
475 Park Avenue South
New York, NY 10016

First printing: April, 1989

Printed in the United States of America

This book is respectfully dedicated to Mr. Michael Bergman, whose technical and editorial suggestions made it possible.

Irving A. Greenfield

Chapter 1

"Conn, sonar," Hi Fi Freedman's voice crackled through the MC intercom system. "Enemy sub off our stern, skipper. Target bearing one seven zero degrees . . . Range nine thousand five hundred yards and closing . . . Speed three five knots . . . Depth one zero zero feet."

Admiral Jack Boxer, commander of the super-submarine *U.S.S. Manta* looked at his exec and ordered, "Battle stations."

Capt. Mark Clemens triggered the diving klaxon and repeated the order. "All hands, battle stations. Prepare to dive."

Bathed in the red glow of the control room, Boxer took his position at the COMMCOMP, the computer brains of the attack center, and activated a series of switches and dials. A bank of LED lights went from red to amber to green. All systems go. He quickly found the image of the Soviet sub on his tail on the UWIS screen, and realized that time was running out. "Dive . . . Dive," he commanded. "DO, diving planes at one five degrees. Dive to four zero zero feet, Whitey."

"One five degrees, aye, aye, sir. Going to four zero zero feet." Amos White, the senior chief petty officer aboard the *Manta* was the chief of the boat, or Cob, as he was known to the crew, as well as the diving officer. Whitey pushed forward on the diving yoke. The *Manta* responded instantly, and nosed downward at a forty degree angle, dropping like a stone. The men in the attack center braced themselves.

"What about the men we left behind on the ice cap, skipper?"

Boxer's face turned grim. Clemens's question triggered flashes in his mind of their mission, a simple evacuation of a team of Russian scientists from the American ice station Omega, at the Pole. A mission gone wrong almost from the start. The Ruskies got there first.

Now, his commando force led by Major Rolly Jones and his Rangers, and Capt. Dick Dickerson and his Snow Troopers, was being cut down by their Soviet counterparts. Both sides were being decimated in a struggle for control of a patch of ice and a weather station, America's bleakest and most remote outpost in the northern hemisphere.

If the *Manta* didn't survive this attack, neither would his ground forces, and Boxer knew it. He said, "They'll have to fend for themselves, Clem. If we survive, we'll go back for them. Right now, we've got an enemy sub on our tail trying to bugger us, and they will unless we shake them."

"Sorry, skipper. I guess I knew the answer to that before I asked it."

Boxer watched the image of the Russian sub gaining on them, a blip on the UWIS a mere five miles back. He keyed the MC. "EO, ahead full. Bring us up to flank speed."

"Aye, aye, skipper. Full ahead. Going to flank speed."

Boxer sensed that the captain of the Ruskie sub was good, damn good. He decided to try a ploy. He signalled the aft torpedo room. "ATO, conn. Prepare to launch the drone.

"Aye, aye, skipper." The torpedo officer punched some commands into his electronic console, and a sleek, black torpedo-like projectile that projected the sounds of a full size SSN sub, slipped into one of the aft launch tubes. "Ready to launch drone, sir."

The fire control officer was seated behind his equipment in the attack center. Boxer told him, "FCO, launch drone."

"Launching drone, aye, aye, skipper."

Boxer heard the sound of a hatch opening and the hiss of compressed air that sent the decoy on its way. Then he ordered, "Helmsman, hard right rudder. Come to zero nine zero degrees."

Mahoney, at the wheel, turned the rudder over hard right, and repeated the command as the *Manta* responded immediately to the helm.

Boxer breathed a sigh of relief. "That ought to do it."

"Conn, sonar," Hi Fi reported. "Target bearing one six nine degrees, skipper. Range eight thousand five hundred yards . . . Speed four zero knots . . . Depth three five zero feet."

"Roger that, sonar." Boxer noted his exec's worried face. "They didn't buy the decoy, Clem. That Ruskie skipper knows his business."

"Skipper, two new targets on the same bearing, range four five zero zero yards . . . Speed five five knots."

"Torpedoes," Boxer cursed. "Whitey, one five up on the planes."

Whitey pulled back hard on the yoke. Clemens blew the forward ballast tanks to the sounds of compressed gas escaping. The *Manta* nosed upward.

The first fish passed thirty feet below the *Manta*'s

9

hull, a close miss. Too close, Boxer realized. The second torpedo caught the stern at the point of entry of the propeller shaft. The *Manta* was hurled ass over end, spiraling downward out of control. Boxer struggled to hang on.

Clemens stared at the UWIS screen. The Soviet sub was closing in for the kill, and the terror showed on his face.

Boxer looked back at the diving officer. Whitey was desperately fighting to control the slide. At six hundred feet, the *Manta* finally levelled off.

Boxer keyed in the forward torpedo room. FTO, load one and four."

"Loading one and four, aye, aye, skipper."

Boxer glanced at the UWIS screen and watched the Ruskie sub closing in for the kill. "FCO, prepare a firing solution."

FCO repeated the command as he fed coordinates into the CIC computer.

"Conn, sonar. Two new targets heading our way. Two more fish," Freedman said, and read the coordinates.

If these two torpedoes found their mark, Boxer realized, he and his men had less than three minutes to live. Desperate times call for desperate measures. He said, "FCO, slave in on the two fish. Prepare new solutions."

"Aye, aye, skipper." In a few seconds, he was ready to fire.

Clemens watched Boxer calmly switch on the mike and bring it to his mouth. To him, it seemed as if the skipper was almost smiling.

Boxer said, "FCO, fire at will."

"One and four away, skipper."

The ensuing explosion rocked the two opposing subs

10

and sent them careening out of control, and sent shock waves out over hundreds of miles of Arctic sea.

Boxer held tightly to a grabhold on the COMPCOMP console. Fortunately, he was still strapped into the bolted down commander's seat. He fought off the immense feeling of pressure crushing him and caught a glance at the depth gauge on the bulkhead over his head. Twelve hundred feet and still dropping. The immense explosion that saved the *Manta* from certain doom had hurtled them out of control into the deep, icy waters beneath the polar ice cap. All those aboard the *Manta,* or the Soviet supersubmarine, who were not rendered unconscious by the blast, sat or lay there too dazed to think, too stunned to question their fates.

In the eerie faint-red glow of the attack center, Boxer strained to find his executive officer, Mark Clemens. Clem was climbing back to his seat against the thirty degree pitch of the deck. CPO Amos White was still secured into the diving officer's seat, holding his ears. Boxer paged him on the MC mike. "Whitey, you okay?

No reply.

"Whitey, are you alright? This is Admiral Boxer. Over."

The COB shook the ringing sound from his head and with a weak smile, gave a thumbs up sign. "Aye, aye, sir. Got an awful headache, though."

Boxer made a pull-back motion with his hands, and said,"Whitey, bring the diving planes back to null. We're sinking like a stone."

Still slightly dazed, Whitey nodded his head, placed his hands on the wheel and pulled back on the yoke that controlled the planes. "Aye, aye, sir. Diving planes coming to null," he responded simultaneously.

11

Boxer watched the image of the *Manta* level off on the DDRO, and verified it with a check of the diving bubble coming to the null position on the depth gauge. The submarine seemed to break its fall and level off. Boxer began to feel that perhaps they were safe for the moment.

"Conn, sonar. Conn, sonar. Can you read me, skipper? Can anybody read me? Conn, sonar . . ."

Boxer could barely make out Hi Fi Freedman's weak voice. He spoke into the mike. "Roger that, Hi Fi. Boxer here. Over."

Freedman breathed a sigh of relief. "There's an enemy sub on our tail, skipper. Target bearing one nine five degrees . . . Range nine thousand yards . . . Speed three zero knots . . . Depth one one zero zero feet. He's pinging us, skipper."

"Helmsman, hard right rudder. Come to zero nine zero," Boxer commanded.

Boxer waited for the confirming response. None given. "Helmsman, hard right rudder," he repeated. "Come to zero nine zero. Over."

"Mahoney's down, skipper. I'll take over the helm." Clemens stepped over Mahoney's prostrate body and climbed behind the ship's wheel.

"Conn, sonar. Target bearing one nine five degrees . . . Range seven thousand five-hundred yards . . . Speed three zero knots . . . Depth one one zero zero feet. Hey, wait. Jesus, skipper, two new targets on the same bearing closing in at seven zero knots. Killer darts."

"Roger that, sonar." Beads of sweat began to appear on Boxer's forehead. He wiped at them with a shirt sleeve. "Helmsman, hard right rudder. Come to zero nine zero. DO, dive. One zero on the planes. Take us

12

down to fifteen hundred feet."

"Aye, aye, skipper," both men chorused, and repeated the commands. In seconds the *Manta* dove deeper and to starboard.

After a tense moment that seemed like an eternity, "Conn, sonar. Killer darts passed over us."

Boxer watched the twin images on the UWIS barely missing their stern. It had been much too close. He keyed his intercom. "EO, what's the problem in there? We almost took a hit."

The engineering officer knew, as did Boxer, that the *Manta* might not be able to withstand another blow. "Sorry, skipper. We've got a malfunction. The shaft housing sounds like a coffee grinder. I'd suggest we go to the backup system."

"Damn. DCO, conn. Can you get in there and fix it?"

"Aye, aye, skipper. I'll see what I can do."

"Conn, sonar," Hi Fi began, and called out a new set of coordinates. The enemy was closing in again.

Boxer studied the faces of his most experienced crewmen, Clemens, Whitey and Hi Fi, and read the fear, the certainty of impending death. The Ruskie sub was closing in fast. With the damaged power train, Boxer felt helpless to stop it. One more desperate try. He keyed the aft torpedo room. "ATO, arm tubes nine and ten. FCO, prepare a firing solution."

"Aye, aye, skipper. Arming nine and ten."

Clemens looked across the control room at Boxer. He sensed that they were close enough to blow themselves up with the same explosion used to destroy the Soviet sub. So this was it. He started to sweat.

"Sorry to bother you, sir." Charlie Andrews, head of the rescued Omega weather station team, stuck his head into the control room, oblivious of protocol. All eyes focused on his impertinence at a time like this. "That Ruskie bastard's creating quite a muck back in there. Guess he senses we've about bought it, and he's screaming bloody murder how he demands to . . ."

"Pisanya."

"What . . . ?"

Boxer's face lit up. "Quickly. Have that KGB bastard brought in here under guard at once. And bring along one of the Ruskie scientists. We might need an interpreter."

"Uh, yes, sir. Right away, Admiral Boxer."

Andrews darted forward into the living quarters and returned at once with two of Rolly's Rangers dragging a protesting Ivan Pisanya along with them. Natasha Scharnovsky followed closely behind.

"Hi Fi, can you raise the Ruskie sub on the ship-to-ship radio?"

"I'll try, skipper. If they'll tune in, I'll try to raise them."

"Use the lady here. Miss, would you please help that man send a message to the Russian submarine trailing us? He'll tell you what to say."

Natasha nodded her head and took her place at Hi Fi's side. In a moment she was conversing with a radioman on the Soviet sub.

"Tell him to get his captain. That we have some of his people aboard."

A tense moment went by before the voice of the Russian commander was heard. Hi Fi turned up the volume.

"This is Admiral Igor Borodine, captain of the *Sea Demon*. You have some final words to say before you

14

die?"

Boxer smiled and took the headset from Natasha. He cleared his throat and spoke to his old friend and sometime nemesis. "Comrade Admiral Jack Boxer here, Igor. We are holding your Comrade Ivan Pisanya of the KGB, and two Russian scientists. You wouldn't want to be responsible for their deaths by sinking us, would you, comrade?"

"I should have known it was you, Jack. Who else could have overcome the odds by destroying two of our *Alfas,* and nearly doing the same to the *Sea Demon.*"

Pisanya began to shout in Russian and gesture menacingly. The two Rangers struggled to keep him under control.

"I think Comrade Pisanya has something to say to you, Igor."

"Roger that, Jack. Patch him through, please."

Boxer nodded to the two Rangers. "Sit on him, and slip this on over his head. He wants to try to save his ass."

The Rangers obeyed. Pisanya lay on his back, hands secured behind him, with the headset on, the two-hundred pound bulk of a Ranger pressing him to the deck. He began shouting at Borodine in Russian. Natasha brought her hands to her mouth and gasped. She looked at Boxer and said, "He is demanding that Comrade Borodine cease firing, and to let us get away. He also ordered Comrade Borodine to have our families rounded up to trade for him." She was pointing to herself and Misha Schmendrakova, the other scientist.

Boxer took back the headset. "Well, Comrade Igor, what is your decision?"

"Lucky for you that you have the scientists aboard,

Jack. Otherwise, I'd be tempted to send that bastard to a watery grave."

"Then you agree to a cease-fire?"

"You have my word. And you?"

"A cease-fire, then. I propose we surface and pick up our ground troops. If anyone survived the fighting, they will surely die if we don't rescue them."

"Agreed. We will get our people back through diplomatic channels. This time you are holding the trump cards."

"We must put our respective country's ideological differences aside for now, Igor, so we may live to fight another day. I suggest that we surface at our former positions and announce our cease-fire to our ground troops."

Borodine realized that Boxer made good sense. A glance at the relieved face of his EXO, Viktor Illyavich, confirmed this. "As you say. Goodbye for now, comrade."

"Roger that, comrade." Boxer began a series of commands to maneuver the *Manta* to the surface. A horrible grinding sound echoed throughout the boat.

"Conn, engine room."

"Go ahead, EO."

"Situation is very serious, skipper. We've got to repair the shaft housing or we stand a good chance of burning it out."

"We can't risk a leak at this depth."

"Yes, sir. We can do without water coming into the people compartment."

"DCO, conn. Report on the damage."

"We need to open the housing and replace and repack the bearings, skipper. We'd have to surface to do it."

Boxer looked at Clemens and shook his head. "We need to surface to fix the drive train, but we need the drive train to surface. Without it, we can only go straight up or straight down. A classic *Catch 22*."

The two of them stood there staring at each other momentarily, each of them pondering a solution to their dilemma. The silence was broken by a anxious message over the intercom.

"Conn, sonar. I just received a Mayday from the Ruskie sub."

"Roger that, Hi Fi. I'll be right there." Boxer rushed back to the tiny sonar room.

Freedman tossed him a spare headset, then replied to the disabled submarine. *"Sea Demon* this is the *U.S.S. Manta. Sea Demon* this is *Manta.* We read your Mayday. Over."

"Manta, this is Admiral Borodine, commander of the *Sea Demon.* Please patch me through to Comrade Admiral Boxer. Over."

"Come in, Igor. Boxer here. What's the trouble?"

"The explosion has ruptured our compressed air system. We can't blow our ballast to surface. In fact, we are slowly sinking."

Boxer rubbed his salt and pepper beard, his brow furrowed in deep thought. "What do you propose, comrade?"

"Well, I hate to impose," Borodine managed a bit of levity, "but allowing as how you have proposed a temporary truce, perhaps we could find a way for your sub to tow us to the surface."

The mental image of the *Manta* towing the Ruskie sub through the deep brought a smile to Boxer's eyes for a brief moment. "I wish it were that easy, Igor. Our propulsion system is down. We can surface, but we can't maneuver. Over."

"Perhaps if I could bring the *Sea Demon* close enough to you we could raft the two subs, and surface together."

Boxer shrugged, "Possible. Give me your depth."

"Four hundred meters," Borodine replied.

"Roger that. I'll place us at the same depth. Can you maneuver around to our port side?"

"Of course, comrade. I could bugger your sub with this boat if you'd like."

That drew a laugh from Boxer and Freedman, and helped ease the tension. "Negative, Igor. Our port side will be close enough, thank you." He could hear the sounds of amusement coming from the Russian sub.

In three minutes, the 3-D image of the *Sea Demon* came up on the UWIS. As the sub came about to position itself on the *Manta*'s port side, Boxer ordered a small amount of ballast eased out of the tanks and they floated up alongside it.

Clemens watched the two submarines park next to each other, port to starboard, on the UWIS, and marvelled at the great skill displayed by both skippers. What a shame that world politics caused them to be pitted against one another. He shook his head at the thought.

"Comrade Boxer, we need to lash the two boats together."

"Roger that, Igor. But we're too deep to send divers out. They'll freeze to death."

"Forgive the impertinence of the question, comrade, but is your boat equipped with the mini-subs that you have used to such great advantage over me in the past?"

"The *Manta* carries one mini, Igor. It's equipped with a grappling arm. That just might do the trick. I'd have

18

to lash a cable around both our boats fore and aft. If that works, then you can maneuver us into position near the ice station, and I'll try to lift us to the surface."

"Excellent. Thank you, comrade. And good luck. If this plan succeeds, Jack, I have an excellent bottle of hundred-proof Russian vodka to celebrate."

In spite of the danger they were about to face, Boxer managed a smile. "That will be just fine, comrade. It will give us something to look forward to."

Chapter 2

Clemens ran his fingers through his unruly mop of red hair. "I'd like to volunteer for the mini-sub detail, skipper. I've already qualified on it back in Connecticut."

Boxer rubbed his beard. No doubt that Clem was the best man for the job, but the mini had never tested out in waters this deep and this cold. Mark Clemens just wasn't expendable. Yet . . . he studied the look of determination in his exec's eyes and made his decision. "Alright, Clem. You've got the job. Slip into a drysuit. At least that'll give you some protection against the cold."

"Aye, aye, skipper. I'm your man."

Clemens headed for his quarters, and returned in five minutes suited up in a bright orange one-piece head to toe coverall, looking as if he were about to enter outer space.

Boxer gave him his orders. "Clem, you'll have to hitch up both subs with one-inch Kevlar cable, stern to stern, bow to bow, and then some."

"No sweat, skipper. I was a good Boy Scout many years ago. What we need is a series of good timber hitches to do the job. I'm up to it."

Boxer looked at Clem a little dubiously. Timber hitches? "I hope so, Mark. I'll instruct Borodine to pull as close to the *Manta* as possible. Good luck."

Clemens called back, "Thanks, skipper," and headed for the aft torpedo room where the mini-sub, dubbed the *Minnow,* was being set down into the launch bay. Clem strapped himself in and gave a thumbs up. The crew sealed him in by dogging on the cockpit cover, and left him alone. Clemens listened to the hydraulic sounds of the bay being flooded. When he was completely submerged, he keyed Boxer on his radio. "Conn, *Minnow.* Ready to launch, skipper."

"Roger that, *Minnow.* Launch time T-minus ten . . . nine . . . eight. . . ." The hatch beneath the mini-sub opened and Clemens eased the steering yoke forward a bit. ". . . three . . . two . . . one . . . launch."

Clemens goosed the accelerator with a touch of his foot, eased the diving yoke forward just a bit more, and gracefully slipped out of the launch bay beneath and behind the *Manta.*

It was pitch black. Clemens activated the high intensity beam centered on the bow and aimed it at the two subs floating together like mating behemoths. He switched on the miniature version of the UWIS, its tiny size an engineering marvel, aboard the *Minnow.* It gave a graphic representation of the area illuminated before him.

He knew it would require some fancy maneuvering on his part. He eased his craft ever so slowly toward the two giant submarines, trailing the Kevlar lifeline behind him like an umbilical cord. He was beginning to feel the chill of the frigid waters, in spite of the drysuit. Time was of the essence. Well, Mark, old boy, he told himself, time to make like a Boy Scout.

Clemens eased the *Minnow* very precisely and slowly,

perhaps three or four knots, around the sterns of the two giant submarines, circling their aft quarters with a length of line. Then he hove to abaft the *Manta* and used the claw-like pincer arm to weave the Kevlar cable between the two subs and around again.

Clem felt he was finally getting the hang of it, and repeated his performance three more times to strengthen the lashing. Then he proceeded forward and worked his magic with the line around the bulbous bow of the *Sea Demon* the more conical bow of the *Manta*. The work became a bit more tricky, as the *Manta* was a good fifty feet shorter than the Soviet boomer.

Clemens finished up with several turns around the conning towers and a wrap around the beams, and headed back to the launch bay of his mother ship.

The task took over an hour. Finally, Clemens signalled the *Manta* that he had finished and was ready to return. "*Manta*, this is *Minnow*. Do you read me?"

"Come in *Minnow*," Hi Fi answered. "Reading you loud and clear."

"*Minnow* coming home to mama. Please ready the launch bay."

"Yes, sir, Mr. Clemens. I'll let the skipper know." He forwarded the message on to Boxer who made the appropriate commands. The wide hatch to the launch bay yawned open.

Boxer watched the proceedings on the UWIS. "Steady as she goes, Clem," he offered, and helped guide the mini-sub into the flooded chamber.

Clemens made a perfect return. After the seawater was forced from the launch area, and Clem was helped out of the mini-sub, he detached the end of the Kevlar line from the *Minnow* and attached it to a nearby stan-

22

chion.

"Good job, Clem," Boxer told him. "Now let's test the lines." Boxer ordered Hi Fi to get Borodine on the ship-to-ship radio. In a moment, he was speaking to his Russian counterpart.

"Comrade Admiral Borodine, we appear to be secure. Kindly increase your speed and we'll put the tether to the test."

"Roger that, comrade. Excuse me while I give the necessary commands." Borodine ordered his engineering officer to bring them up to ten knots. Then he said to Boxer, "I have ordered ten knots, Jack."

"Ten knots, aye, Igor."

Aboard the *Manta* they could feel the vibrations from the Soviet submarine a few feet from their hull. The *Sea Demon* shuddered, the *Manta* in turn, shuddered, and then both subs did a dance macabre to the hum of the *Sea Demon*'s reactor, circling to starboard arm-in-arm. Borodine realized his error and ordered the engine revved down. He said through the radio, "My apologies, comrade. That clumsy maneuver is not one that I have much practice with."

"My fault, Igor. I should have used some back rudder. Shall we try again?"

"Roger that. This time, you can be sure that I'll have my EO be a bit more gentle on the throttle."

The next several attempts went a little smoother, albeit with little forward progress. Then, Boxer got an idea. He radioed his Russian counterpart. "Comrade Borodine, I would suggest that you have your helmsman repeat his orders through a headset to Natasha Scharnovsky, who will in turn call them aloud to my helmsman."

"That just might work, Jack," Borodine replied. "At least it's worth a try."

Boxer set Natasha to work repeating commands in English to Mahoney, who was now back at his station sporting a newly bandaged head.

This time the two lashed-together subs moved as one. The vibrations of the *Sea Demon*'s power plant could be heard aboard the *Manta* as they moved toward the scene of the bloody fighting at the Omega Ice Station.

Viktor Illyavich navigated the course, Borodine gave the required orders to his crew, and Boxer followed suit from the command center of the *Manta*. The rafted submarines trudged ponderously through the sea at a depth of twelve hundred feet, barely making a good seven or eight knots. It took ninety minutes to reach an area of thin ice near the Omega weather station.

Boxer signalled Borodine aboard the *Sea Demon*. "Igor, let's keep the radio lines open as before, with Natasha acting as interpreter. I'm going to attempt to bring us to the surface, now."

"Roger that, comrade. Please proceed whenever you are ready."

Boxer gave the appropriate commands. "Clem, blow some ballast. Whitey, five degrees on the diving planes."

"Five degrees, aye, aye, sir."

"Releasing ballast, skipper," Clemens replied.

The *Manta* rose at the bows, the fifty thousand ton *Sea Demon* stayed put, and the resulting torque caused the rafted pair to rotate to port, flipping over backward with the dead weight of the *Sea Demon* as the fulcrum. The sudden thrust sent any crew not strapped down crashing into bulkheads and equipment.

Boxer sent a quick apology. "Perhaps a thrust from

your engine would help," he suggested to Borodine.

That did the trick. Working together, the two giant submarines drifted awkwardly to the surface. When they were just below the ice layer, Boxer suggested, "Igor, we must coordinate our efforts to break through the ice. I will count down from ten to zero. At that moment, have your EO give it everything you've got, while I clear my ballast tanks. With some luck, we'll break clear through the ice pack. If not . . ."

"Then I wish you good luck, comrade. My engineer is standing by. Please begin your countdown."

"Roger that, Igor. T-minus ten and counting . . . nine . . . eight . . ." Clemens stood by the controls of the air compression system ". . . seven . . . six . . . five . . ." Whitey set the diving planes at four five degrees ". . . four . . . three . . . two . . ." The whine of the *Sea Demon*'s power plant reached feverish pitch "one . . . Now," Boxer ordered.

With a great roar from the *Sea Demon*'s engine, and a tremendous hiss of compressed air forcing all water from the *Manta*'s tanks, the two subs bobbed to the surface throwing ice in all directions. They settled down with a monumental thump, the Kevlar lashing burst apart with a resounding snap. Startled commandos, Soviet and American alike, caught their breath and ceased firing.

Chapter 3

It took a few moments for Maj. Roland Jones to realize that the *Manta* and the *Sea Demon* had surfaced together. And that a few hours ago they had dived, the Soviet sub intent on the destruction of the *Manta*. And, for whatever reason, the *Sea Demon* was now within his firing range. He tapped Sgt. Mean Gene Greene, his senior squad leader. "Get the fucker," he shouted, and then added, "Be careful not to hit the *Manta*."

Mean Gene in turn shouted a order to a few of his men and grenades flew at the Soviet craft. One . . . two . . . three explosions rang out. The *Sea Demon*'s conning tower sustained some damage, as well as the forward machine gun turret. Shards of twisted black metal spewed forth from the hit sites.

Things fared as badly for the *Manta*. Boxer cursed the damage that the Soviet ground force was doing to his sub. He ordered Hi Fi to radio Borodine. "Comrade Admiral Borodine. Together, we must call off this carnage and demand a cease fire."

"Agreed, comrade. You announce to your side, and I'll order our troops to desist."

In a moment, loudspeakers blared orders in both languages to the ice-bound commandos. "Cease-fire," each skipper announced. "Lay down your weapons. We have declared a temporary truce." They went on to explain

26

that their respective submarines would have been destroyed and all aboard lost had they not come to each other's aid. Each side was to retreat to his own mother sub, maintaining the status quo.

The firing ceased. No one made a move toward the black, hulking towers that separated the two warring camps. Too many good men already had died fighting over this barren patch of ice with its few expendable buildings and the lofty radio tower that linked the Omega weather station with the outside world.

Sensing the mutual distrust of the combatants, Boxer and Borodine decided simultaneously to make an appearance atop their sub's sail bridges. White flags went up first, then cautious heads, then the fully uniformed figures of the commanding officers of each boat. "Hold your fire, Rolly," Boxer shouted into a bullhorn. "This cease-fire is for real."

Borodine gave a similar order to the commanding officer of the elite Arctic Wolves commandos. Reluctantly, both sides edged around to their respective subs, never for a moment taking their eyes or aim away from their enemies.

"Hatches open. Deck details topside, on the double," Boxer barked. In moments, a boarding party was helping the survivors aboard the *Manta*. Not more than forty, Boxer noticed grimly, including the wounded. Almost sixty good men had died trying to defend the Omega weather team and the Russian scientists whom they had rescued. Not very good, he hung his head. Not good at all.

"Uh, skipper?" Rolly Jones said, now at Boxer's side on the outside bridge. "We ain't gonna leave that for the Ruskies to take over once we're gone, are we?" He was referring to the remains of the weather station.

"Good point, Rolly. You can be sure the Ruskies will be back just as soon as weather permits. We'd better take it out. Will you do the honors?"

Rolly Jones smiled sardonically. "You bet, skipper. I'll set up a rocket launcher."

Boxer watched from his lofty viewing stand as Rolly and Mean Gene knelt on the forward deck, hand held rocket launchers poised on their shoulders. "Fire," shouted Jones and twin rockets found their marks. The cement block radio building exploded in flames, sending debris everywhere. The radio tower was ripped apart at the base and toppled to the ice with a thud.

The political officer aboard the *Sea Demon* stuck his head over the bulwark and shook a clenched fist at Boxer. "Stop that. I, Captain Boris Zukor, political officer of the Soviet Navy Submarine Fleet, demand that you cease the destruction of that property. I further demand the release of the Soviet citizens that you have taken prisoner aboard your boat.

Boxer caught the ironic expression on Borodine°s face. Boxer smiled. The old sea dog knew what was to come. "Forget it, Zukor. The two scientists were your prisoners. They are my guests. And Deputy Director Pisanya will be my guest until we get to the safety of our home port. I'm certain he'll be traded back to you for some prisoners of conscience, perhaps the families of these scientists who have been left behind."

As Zukor began waving his fist and shouting, Boxer continued into the bullhorn. "Besides, your Comrade Pisanya has admitted he likes our food better."

The political officer sputtered, as Borodine struggled to keep a straight face.

Boxer continued. "Comrade Admiral Borodine. I suggest we make repairs to our boats and clear out of here. The storm seems in no hurry to clear up."

"Roger that, comrade."

Boxer had to clear the aft ballast tanks while maintaining slight negative buoyancy toward the bows in order to enable his damage control team to make the repairs to the propeller shaft housing. It was after midnight when the *Manta* was again running properly, and Boxer ordered the decks cleared and hatches dogged closed for descent. He noticed the Soviets still hard at work on the *Sea Demon,* illuminated by the never-ending midnight sun.

"Dive," Boxer ordered. A klaxon siren sounded and the black hulk of the *Manta* slipped once more beneath the ice. "Take us down to one zero zero, DO. Zero five on the planes. Nice and easy, Whitey." Boxer wanted to test the repairs under easy conditions before deep diving and heading flat out for Alaska's arctic coast.

"DCO, report."

"She sounds real good, skipper. No sign of a leak. The drive train's humming like a kitten."

"Roger that, DCO." Boxer smiled at Clemens, who was pacing nervously around the control center. "Let's go home, Clem. This is one mission I'd just as soon put behind me."

Clemens stopped pacing. "That makes both of us, skipper."

Boxer called to Whitey at the diving station. "DO, dive to four zero zero feet. One zero on the planes."

"Diving to four zero zero, aye, aye, Sir. Planes set at one zero."

Mahoney brought the helm amidships to facilitate the

dive.

"EO, go to four zero knots," Boxer said into the MC.

"Aye, aye, skipper. Going to four zero."

"Passing through two zero zero," Clemens called off, keeping one eye on the DDRO while he adjusted the ballast tanks. "Passing through two five zero," he droned on in a monotone, and continued with a sounding until the sub levelled off.

"We're at four zero zero feet, skipper," he announced.

"Diving planes at null, sir," Chief White said. He was the only one aboard the *Manta* that still referred to Boxer as sir, instead of skipper, as Boxer preferred. Boxer realized that some routines die hard, and Whitey was close to putting in his thirty and out. Boxer would gladly endure being called sir in exchange for having the best diving officer around.

"Helmsman, make good course one five seven."

Mahoney turned the wheel to port and adjusted his course to one five seven, knowing that was in a direct line to Point Barrow, Alaska. They were going home.

When they were safely underway, Boxer called the medic into the control room. "I'd like a report on the wounded, Doc."

Doc Calahan replied, "Well, the sick bay's filled to capacity, skipper. Major Jones's and Capt. Dickerson's boys took a beating. A few of them will need to be hospitalized when we get back to base."

Calahan scratched his head and continued, "I've done what I can to make the men as comfortable as possible, skipper. We really don't have the facilities aboard to treat this much . . ."

"I understand, doc," Boxer cut him off. The *Manta* was built as a fighting boat. Not a floating hospital.

Nobody's faulting you."

Calahan smiled sheepishly. "Thanks, skipper. Most of the commandos are sacked out already. They've been through a lot." Then he added, "All of the guys in our crew who were able gave up their bunks to them."

Boxer's face beamed with pride at his men's act of kindness.

"Some of the previously wounded are up and around, now, skipper. Oh, and Lieutenant Carson's awake, and she's been asking for you." Dr. Calahan averted his gaze, not wanting eye contact with his captain "If you don't mind my saying so, skipper, you look as if you could stand a break yourself."

Do I look that bad, Boxer asked himself? He had been awake and at the conn for at least the last thirty hours that he could remember. He could feel the strain in his eyes, he had a pounding headache, and the muscles of his neck and shoulders were all knotted. In short, he felt like shit. "Roger that, doc," he admitted. "I suppose I could stand a quick shower and then catch forty."

Taking his cue, Clemens moved into the control room. "Clem, you've got the conn. Have me awakened in three hours."

Boxer went into the head, stripped off his uniform and took a two minute Hollywood steam shower, a vast improvement of Kit Carson's over the old-fashioned submarine shower. He padded to his quarters with a towel wrapped around his waist.

He stepped through the doorway and was greeted with the sight of Lt. Kathleen "Kit" Carson sitting up in his bed, scratched and bruised, but still looking beautiful. "Oh, I'm sorry," he blurted out. "I can come back. I

31

forgot you're still convalescing."

"No," she stopped him. "Please don't go. You need the rest more than I do. You look like you've been through hell."

Maybe I do look that bad, Boxer mused. He was nursing a nasty bruise on his right shoulder, the same one that had been shot through last year. There were dark circles under his eyes, and his shoulders were scrunched from muscle spasm, the results of the torpedoing they'd received.

Carson noticed the perplexed look on Boxer's face. She smiled and said, "We'll share it, then." She held out her arms to him, and the blanket fell down to her waist, revealing her full, though firm, pear-shaped breasts.

Boxer's face melted. "Perhaps you're right. Maybe we should share the bed. There's not enough bunk space to go around, you know."

Boxer removed the towel and tossed it on a chair, then slipped under the covers alongside of her. As her arms wrapped around him, he said, Mmmm, you feel good."

"That rest I got did me some good. I feel a lot better. Here, let me do something for those knotted muscles."

Boxer was too weary to fight it, and let her work her magic fingers into his neck and shoulders. Ten minutes of that, and he was feeling more relaxed.

Carson's fingers moved down his rippling back muscles, as she kneaded them back into shape. Boxer was sinking into sleep, so she slid her hands down lower until she found what she wanted.

Apparently, what he wanted, too. He immediately became rigid in her hands.

"Is that any way to treat your commanding officer?" he asked her.

"Did you want me to stand at attention, too?" she smiled back.

Boxer held her in his arms and pressed her to his chest, kissing her parted lips.

"Make love to me," she whispered.

Exhausted though he was, Boxer didn't need a second invitation. He positioned himself over her as Carson slid her body beneath his. Soon, they were moving with a singular rhythm, he entering her in long, easy strokes, she pushing back against him, meeting each other halfway. They were soon consumed in a frenzy of lovemaking. And then, his head went back and his back arched just as she moaned, "Oh, oh . . . oooohhhh."

Boxer gently let his weight down on her as they held each other tightly, their bodies joined as one. They kissed, and Boxer rolled off of her, his head resting on the pillow beside her.

"Thank you, darling," Kit said softly, but Boxer didn't hear her. He was already asleep. She caressed his brow, and pulled the covers up over them, then snuggled in close alongside him. "Sleep, my lover," she whispered. And then she closed her eyes and slept, too.

Chapter 4

The trip back to Point Barrow was uneventful, fortunately, for all aboard the *Manta* were in need of rest. Boxer kept the shift rotations short, and the workloads light. They arrived at the Naval Research Station around midnight, though the sun had only partially dipped below the horizon because of the high latitude.

Captain Eric Dawson, the station's CO, was awakened and on hand to greet Boxer and provide medical attention for those who needed it. He watched Ivan Pisanya being manhandled off the sub by two tough looking Rangers, followed by two very nervous scientists.

"This man is our prisoner, Captain," Boxer explained. "He's a high-ranking KGB officer whose actions caused the destruction of Omega Weather Station, and the loss of sixty good men."

Dawson nodded as he watched the ragged remnants of a once proud commando group disembark.

Boxer said, "I intend to speak to CIA Director Tysin himself about transferring him to a more secure location."

Dawson looked a little surprised. "It is my understanding that Tysin is no longer running the Company, Admiral. It seems he disappeared."

"Hmm," Boxer rubbed his beard. "Who's in charge?"

"The acting director, I believe. I'm surprised you

34

didn't know about it."

"I guess they had their reasons. There has to be some kind of need to know requirements." They probably figured I'd go after the bastard myself, Boxer thought. And they'd probably be right. "Oh, and please make these two people feel at home, Captain. They are Soviet scientists who have come back with us on their own volition, and may seek political asylum in our country. They've been through hell, so please treat them as our guests."

"Aye, aye, Admiral." Dawson turned to his aide, a young lieutenant with a blond crewcut. "Meade, take these people to my quarters and make them very comfortable. Get them some breakfast and some clean clothes, anything they want."

Lt. Meade saluted crisply and replied, "Aye, aye, sir." And to the Russians, Natasha Sharnovsky and Misha Schmendrikova, he smiled and said, "Won't you please come with me, folks?"

They looked to Boxer who gave them a go-ahead nod, and followed the lieutenant to the CO's quarters.

Dawson offered, "Looks as if your sub took some damage, Admiral. It's looking a little worse for wear."

"That's correct, Captain. We'll need to put in to drydock for some repairs as soon as we get back to Norfolk."

Dawson cleared his throat. "I have a message for you from the CNO, Sir. He'd like you to call him at 0730 for new orders."

Boxer turned to watch the last of the wounded being carried off the *Manta*. The rest of his crew was either in the mess hall for mid-rats, or hot-bunking a few hours sleep. He pushed his cap back and ran his hand over his

35

weary eyes. "In that case, Captain, I'd better grab some z's. Something tells me that this may turn out to be a very long day."

Half a world away, a weary former CIA Director stepped off an Alitalia 747 at Da Vinci Airport, easily cleared customs due to his new beard and tinted contact lenses, and of course, the phony ID. The CIA had no lack of phony identification papers, and Tysin had been in the Company long enough to acquire his share, as well as safe houses and secure bank accounts in a dozen cities, worldwide. Rome was one of them. He hailed a yellow cab, and gave him the address of a department store on the Via Veneta, about a mile from the American Embassy.

He got out and walked to a pay phone, wasting no time in making his contacts. He gave his name and some other pertinent information, and waited inside the store. In fifteen minutes, a big, black Mercedes Benz limo pulled up in front, stopping in a no parking zone. Tysin walked out to the car as the darkly tinted rear window slowly lowered.

"Ah, Señor Tysin. Your own mother wouldn't recognize you."

"Open the door, Julio. Quit jerking around."

The uniformed driver went around and opened the rear door for Tysin while Julio Sanchez slid over to the seat on the street side. As the driver pulled the big sedan out into traffic, Sanchez said, "Tsk, tsk, quite a temper for a man who is no longer in a position of power, my friend."

Tysin scowled. "Don't fuck with me, Julio. I could

have had your balls on a platter many a time if I chose to, so don't take me lightly."

Sanchez cringed at the thought of his balls on a platter. Ball would be more specific, thanks to that bastard, Bruno Morell. He had tortured Julio, cutting off a testicle to make him talk. "So, what can I do for you, Senor Tysin?"

"I'm on the lam, Julio. My secretary was murdered, and I'm being framed for it."

Sanchez's eyebrows went up. With people like Tysin, it's always someone else who does the dirty work.

Tysin went on, "I'd been having an affair with the young lady, lovely thing she was. We were good for each other. I helped her along with her career, she gave me what I couldn't get at home from Vivian."

"I see," Sanchez replied, nodding sagaciously. He could understand all that, very well. The old tit for tat, as old as Adam and Eve.

Then Tysin's face fell. It seemed to Julio that the man's entire body drooped as he continued talking about it. "And then it happened," Tysin continued. "The girl, Lori-Ann was her name, was married to a chap who worked for the State Department. He turned traitor on us, and it became my duty to have him arrested. And then she changed."

Julio kept nodding. People don't change, he knew. Just our perceptions of them.

"She tried every sexual trick she knew to stop me from turning in her husband. Not that she really gave a shit about the jerk, but because it would make her look bad. You see, the guy had a boyfriend. She couldn't bear the thought of *that* being splashed about all the news media. She wouldn't be able to show her face in town, and D.C.'s a very big town."

Sanchez shook his head. How foolish some men are when it comes to women. Even the high and the mighty manage to succumb to a piece of ass. But never Julio Sanchez. He always showed the woman who was boss.

"So, she tried to blackmail me. Me! The Director of the CIA and this cunt tries to blackmail me."

Sanchez smiled. So, now the sweet, lovely young thing is a cunt. The worm turns.

Tysin was in a rage, now, squirming in his seat, gesturing animatedly, his voice rising so loudly that Julio put a reassuring hand on his arm to settle him down. "So, this *cunt* has all these videos of us fucking on the sofa in front of the TV. And she threatens to send a copy to Channel Three if I don't forget about the problem with her husband. Threaten the Director of the CIA."

"So, you killed her," Julio Sanchez said matter-of-factly.

"No," Tysin almost shouted. "I slapped her around a little, and took her precious video tape of us. And she laughed at me, told me she had more copies and that if I didn't leave her alone she would send them to the newspapers and the TV stations no matter what I did. And then she told me she hated having sex with me, that I was an old fool to think she cared about me." Tysin's face became serious, then. "That's not true, of course. She just told me that to hurt me. I know she really loved making it with me."

Sanchez sat there trying not to stare into Tysin's face. So, the old boy's really lost his marbles, he thought. Better try to humor him a bit, then drop him off somewhere. "So, who killed her, then?"

"I don't know. After I left her apartment, our apartment, really, I was in a rage. I took a long walk to calm down. Stopped in a local bar and put down a few scotches, and decided to go back and try to fix things up between us. You know, tell her I wouldn't turn her husband in if we could go back to the way things were between us." Tysin shrugged, "You know, I could always have someone else take him out later, anyway. No skin off my teeth, as they say. But when I got back to the apartment, she was already dead."

Sanchez's face dropped. "What? So soon?"

Tysin nodded his head. "Whoever did it must have been waiting outside. When I left, he, I'm assuming it was a guy the way her neck was broken and the back of her head bashed in, he must have gone upstairs and done the job. Probably figured her murder would be pinned on me when they found out about the two of us, you know. And he was right, the bastard."

Sanchez sat back in his seat. He glanced out his window and barked a command to the driver, who then made the next left turn onto a freeway. Julio said to Tysin, "So, what are you going to do now, my friend?"

Henry Tysin took a deep breath and let it out. "You know, I've made a lot of contacts in my years with the Company. Some of them people like yourself."

Julio's face reddened.

"Don't take offense, Julio. I didn't mean it that way. I just meant that I worked with people outside the law as well as in. I can work both sides of the street. I'm still sharp, I know a lot of people, I've got money in safe banks, and hideouts all over the world. And you even said my own mother wouldn't recognize me."

"So?"

Henry smiled. "So, I think I'm do for a little change in my career. First, I'm taking over Bruno Morell's old network." He held up a forefinger for emphasis.

"You'll have trouble there, señor. The Barberi brothers have moved in on it already."

"Then I'll move them out. With your help if need be," he added.

Nice of him to deal me in, Julio thought to himself, sourly.

"Second," the second finger went up to join the first, "I'm going to find out who killed Lori-Ann and track him down, make him confess on the television, and then kill him. That way, they'll all know I didn't kill her."

Still talking like a madman, Sanchez mused. He's really lost it, but I wouldn't want him for an enemy.

"And then, I'll be in the same business as you, Julio. There's enough work to go around, especially between old friends."

Sanchez realized that Tysin was too dangerous to be left alive. But first, Julio must take the man into his confidence, make him feel comfortable. like old friends. Then have him killed. "So, Señor Tysin, or should I call you Henry now that we are old friends, you will be safe here with me. Let's get you settled in, get a new identity. Then we'll try to find your killer."

Tysin backed against the inside of the car door, as far away from Sanchez as he could get. "I have everything I need here. My own place, my own papers. All I need from you is to get me the police reports from DC. Find out who besides me they think might have murdered Lori-Ann. Then, lend me a few good men, and I'll find and kill the bastard the same way he killed her."

Julio Sanchez knew he had a tough case on his hands.

He'd always thought that Tysin was a bit fucked up, but now he was sure that the former CIA leader was certifiably crazy. All he could say was, "Sure, Henry. Anything you want."

Chapter 5

0730. Boxer held the telephone receiver to his ear while sipping his third cup of piping hot black coffee of the morning; He sat at Capt. Dawson's desk and took in the room while he waited. Nothing spectacular. Cold gray painted cement block walls with a few naval prints. File cabinets, computer consoles and peripherals, the telephone scrambler, of course, with its bank of flashing LED lights, and Dawson's prize trophy, a four-foot-long scale model of the American supertanker, *Manhattan,* the first to prove the commercial feasibility of the fabled Northwest Passage. Dawson had told him it had been passed down from the former CO of the base, a gift from the tanker's owners in gratitude for aid given by the Coast Guard.

Boxer chuckled to himself. It took over four hundred years to solve the problem of the Northwest Passage, and the oil companies decide on the pipeline, instead. Well, so much for foresight. Suddenly, a voice spoke to Boxer on the phone. "Admiral Boxer, please stand by, sir. Admiral Mason wishes to speak to you."

"Roger that," Boxer replied.

"Mason here," came the CNO's gravely voice.

"Boxer here," came the mimicked reply.

Mason made a dour face, much aware that Boxer was toying with him. "I understand that you got back with the Ruskie scientists?"

"Two of them, sir. The other two died when their plane crashed near the Pole. We also brought back a ranking KGB man."

"Good," Mason smiled. "Damn good. Then the mission was a success."

Boxer shook his head. "Only if you consider the loss of sixty good fighting men a success, Admiral. And the loss of the weather station."

"Weather stations can be rebuilt, Boxer. And those men knew they were at risk when they went out on that mission. They died for their country. Now, listen, your new orders are to steam for San Diego to have the *Manta* repaired. Your men are to get ten days R & R at the base there."

"San Diego, Admiral? Why not back the Symington boat works? After all, they built the boat."

"Dammit, don't argue with me over everything I order you to do, Boxer. You're going to be needed on the West Coast. When you arrive in San Diego, you are to let me know personally, and then you'll fly back here for a briefing. At that time, I'll make everything crystal clear to you why you're not putting in at New London or Norfolk. Do you understand?"

"I understand what you're saying, Admiral," Boxer said drolly.

"Do I make myself perfectly clear, Boxer?"

Boxer smiled. Isn't that the phrase a former president always used when he garbled a message to the voters? "Is there anything else, Admiral?"

"Dammit, Boxer. Don't get my blood pressure up." The CNO slammed down the receiver. Boxer had anticipated this behavior and couldn't stop himself from

43

laughing as he sat there holding the receiver away from his ear at arm's length.

Boxer thanked Capt. Dawson for the use of the facilities. His able bodied seamen and commandos were filing back on board the *Manta*. The more seriously wounded were airlifted to local military hospitals. At 0900, the *Manta* backed out of her berth and slipped beneath the Beaufort Sea.

"Helmsman, make good course two six zero," Boxer ordered.

"Two six zero, aye, aye, skipper."

The *Manta* sailed at periscope depth until five miles offshore, then Boxer ordered a dive. The two-toned klaxon alarm went off as Boxer called off the commands. "DO, dive to two zero zero feet. EO, make four zero knots."

"Aye, aye, sir. Going to two zero zero," Whitey replied.

EO responded, "Aye, aye, skipper. Going to four zero knots."

Boxer followed their progress on the charts being monitored constantly by Clemens, and by Lt. Carson, who insisted she was well enough to perform her duties again. They were going to slip through the Bering Straits, the narrow expanse of water separating the USSR from the westernmost part of the continental United States. The waters here were usually swimming with Soviet vessels bent on defending the vast submarine bastion in the Sea of Okhotsk. Boxer's aim was to steer clear of the enemy and make a straight run southeast to San Diego.

They passed by St. Lawrence Island, a windblown, rocky island about thirty miles from the Soviet Union.

44

Boxer ordered the DO to dive deeper.

"DO, dive to four zero zero feet."

"Aye, aye, sir. Going to four zero zero."

Boxer watched the DDRO and the bulkhead depth gauge while Whitey called out their progress.

"Passing through two five zero . . . passing through three zero zero. . . ."

They were interrupted by Hi Fi's sudden message. "Conn, sonar. I'm picking up a pinging. There's something in the air above us looking for a target."

"Roger that, Hi Fi." Boxer keyed the MC mike. "ATO, release a noisemaker."

"Aye, aye, skipper." The aft torpedo officer loaded a tube with a three-foot-long black cannister, made an adjustment to a series of dials on the aft end of the device and dogged shut the torpedo hatch. The noisemaker was expelled with a whoosh of compressed gas, and immediately began setting off exploding noises designed to fool a sonobuoy suspended from a low-flying plane or helicopter.

"Helmsman, right full rudder. Make course zero nine zero."

Mahoney turned the wheel hard to the right and held it down. "Rudder, full right. Coming to zero nine zero, skipper."

"Target bearing one seven five, skipper. Torpedo heading for the noisemaker. . . . Range four five zero zero. . . . Speed six zero knots."

Boxer knew he had to vacate the area fast. "EO go to flank speed. Give me all you've got."

"Aye, aye, skipper. Going to five zero knots."

"Roger, EO. Sonar, please report."

"Torpedo is going for the bait, skipper. Bearing and

speed the same as previous. . . . Range two zero zero zero and closing."

The *Manta* was four miles away when the air-launched torpedo found its mark, and the noisemaker was blown out of the water. The sound waves carried easily to the retreating sub and sent it bouncing along at four hundred feet. A shaken Hi Fi Freedman reported back, "Conn, sonar. They didn't buy that decoy. The sonobuoy is still searching for us."

"Damn." Boxer keyed his Radar operator. "RO, find out what's up there so interested in us."

"Aye, aye, skipper." The radar officer tuned in the ATI, the aircraft target indicator, capable of tracking and distinguishing up to fifty airborne targets at a time, and coordinating defensive measures against them.

Boxer watched the proceedings from the ATI screen on the COMMCOMP.

"Conn, radar. That's a chopper on our tail, skipper. She's dangling a sonobuoy on a line, fishing for us."

Boxer said to Clemens and Carson, "Let's send up a little present. Clem, arm two SIAM missiles."

Clemens smiled. "Aye, aye, skipper. My pleasure." He went forward into the missile compartment just ahead and starboard of commando force's quarters.

"Carson, work out a firing solution based on the ATI fix. You're going to get a chance to play with one of your own toys."

"Aye, aye, sir," she beamed. She adjusted some dials on the missile control console, and reported, "I have a firing solution, skipper."

"Roger that, Kit. Fire when ready."

Carson studied the image on the screen, set her commands on a numeric keypad, and pressed a large red button. "Portside missile launched, Sir."

For four hundred feet, the submarine to air missile was propelled by the thrust of compressed air in the launch tube. Once it lifted out of the sea, its own engine ignited and surged the twelve-foot-long silver projectile toward the unwary helicopter a hundred feet off the surface. The chopper burst into a brilliant ball of fire that sent flaming debris in all directions.

"Conn, radar. Affirming a hit, skipper."

"Good shooting, guys."

Lt. Carson gave a thumbs up and a smile.

As Clemens returned to the command center, a message came in from sonar. "There's a surface ship trailing us, skipper. Bearing three zero five . . . Range five one zero zero . . . Speed three zero knots."

Boxer scurried to the COMMCOMP and switched on the CIC module. He keyed the sonar fix into the computer and asked for ID.

SOVIET GUIDED MISSILE FRIGATE
GORSKI CLASS DISPLACEMENT 23000 TONS
ASW CAPABILITY: TWO PODS ASROCS 9 PER
PLUS ROCKET-LAUNCHED DEPTH CHARGES
FLANK SPEED 40 KNOTS

"Shit. That chopper came from the frigate." Boxer knew they were approaching an abyssal plain, a severe drop in the ocean floor of three to four thousand feet, and had hopes of racing for it. However, the *Manta* was already at flank speed, so there was little hope of that. The frigate would have to be dealt with here and now.

"Conn, sonar. Multiple targets heading our way. Bearing three zero two to three zero five . . . Range four thousand and closing, skipper. Speed seven zero knots."

"ASROCS," Boxer spat. "Whitey, dive. Go to six zero zero."

"Diving to six zero zero, aye, Sir. Planes at one zero."

On instinct, Boxer headed his sub directly for the Soviet frigate. "Helmsman, come to course three zero five. EO, flank speed."

"Aye, aye, skipper," came the replies.

"Conn, sonar. At least three of the rockets are turning around and coming after us."

"Roger that, sonar. FTO, prepare tubes one and six with Mark 48's."

"Loading one and six, aye, aye, skipper."

Boxer watched the image of the frigate on the UWIS screen and the tiny blips of the ASROCS on his tail. "FTO prepare a firing solution for one and six."

"Aye, aye, skipper."

Just then, three explosions could be felt more than heard behind them. Boxer smiled. The Russian vessel had aborted the three rockets. "They didn't want to risk being hit by their own rockets."

The next explosion came from above, half the distance from them and the surface ship. The *Manta* shuddered. "Depth charges. Dive . . . dive. DO go to one thousand feet. One five on the planes."

Whitey pushed forward on the diving yoke while repeating the orders. Clemens blew out the forward tanks, taking on water ballast.

Several more cans exploded overhead. Boxer chose to pass under the frigate, starboard to port, and well below. Once again, he had successfully negated the enemy's weapons.

"Passing through nine zero zero feet . . . passing

through nine five zero feet . . ." Whitey's voice droned on. The *Manta* levelled off at one thousand feet. They were well off the portside of the surface ship.

Boxer ordered a new fix and firing solution on the frigate. "FTO, fire one."

"Launching number one, skipper," FTO repeated, and followed the wire-guided torpedo on its race towards the Soviet ship. He slaved the fish in on the target using the sophisticated equipment on board until the torpedo was a thousand yards from the ship. Then the homing devices in the nose of the fish took over.

"Mahoney, rudder right full. Go to zero nine zero.

Mahoney repeated the directions and the *Manta* turned hard to starboard.

"Bulls-eye," Hi Fi shouted. The next instant the bow of the Soviet frigate blew apart, leaving a thirty foot hole below the waterline. A secondary explosion sent a five-hundred-foot fireball skyward. They'd hit the ammunition storage.

The officers in the attack center and the sonar room watched the image of the enemy ship settle at the bows and sink in less than nine minutes. Boxer wiped sweat from his brow with a sleeve, and settled back into the commander's chair. "Okay, crew. Good job. Now let's get the hell out of here before we attract the entire Soviet Navy."

Chapter 6

Boxer strode down the corridor of the east wing of the innermost Pentagon building en route to the CNO's headquarters. He was escorted by a Marine corporal as far as the reception office where he was turned over to the young Naval lieutenant on duty. Boxer stood there at attention in his formal summer whites, resplendent with gold, egg salad trim and a chest full of battle ribbons. "Admiral Jack Boxer here to see Admiral Mason."

The Lieutenant saluted crisply and asked Boxer to be seated while he notified the CNO of his arrival. Boxer was made to wait a half hour before being admitted to Mason's office — Mason's way of paying back Boxer for constantly goading him.

"Admiral Mason will see you now, sir," the young Lieutenant told Boxer, and held the door for him, then quickly ducked outside as Boxer stepped inside.

Boxer saluted his CNO. Mason gave a perfunctory salute and told Boxer to sit. Boxer pulled up a leather upholstered side chair from in front of the massive teak desk that filled up a large portion of Mason's private office. The United States flag and the standard of the United States Navy stood on poles behind and on either side of the desk, while an original oil of "Old Ironsides" took over the richly panelled back wall.

Mason removed a long, thick cigar from a humidor shaped like a sea chest and removed the wrapper. He carefully clipped the tip with a pen knife and lit up, pushing the cigars towards Boxer. "Smoke?"

"Thanks, Admiral. I'll stick with my pipe if it's alright with you."

"Suit yourself," Mason replied, blowing a cloud of smoke toward the ceiling.

Boxer fished an old meerschaum-lined briar from his pocket and soon had an ash glowing just right. The "old man" seemed to be loosening up toward him just a bit, it seemed. It's about time, he thought.

Mason cleared his throat, flicked an ash into a crystal ashtray on his desk. "I want to comment on your just completed mission." He folded his hands on the desk in front of him. "You retrieved the two surviving Soviet scientists you were sent out to pick up, thus denying the Ruskies the use of their services. What's more, they've decided to defect, and we're doing all we can to get their families out of the U.S.S.R."

The CNO was actually being considerate of him, Boxer noted. I could sure get to like this, he thought.

"Furthermore," Mason continued, "Deputy Director Pisanya is the highest ranking KGB officer we've captured to date. A good move on your part."

"I took him along as insurance against being attacked by the Ruskies, Admiral. I . . ."

"Don't interrupt me when I'm commending you, dammit. This isn't easy for me."

Boxer suppressed a smile. "Yes, sir," he said.

"On the down side, you expended five Mark 48 torpedoes at a cost of $3.8 million each, plus you sustained damage to the *Manta* in the neighborhood of twenty-five, thirty mil. Wait, hear me out without comment. On the plus side, you bagged two Ruskie *Alfas* and a guided-missile frigate, and damaged their newest super-sub. Not bad."

Not bad, hell, Boxer said to himself. But coming from Mason, he'd take it as a compliment.

"I realize you lost a lot of good men, and contrary to what you may think of me, I abhor the loss of lives of our servicemen, even though at times there is no other way around a situation. Which brings me to the point of this meeting."

Boxer sat up in anticipation. Mason was sure beating around the bush with him.

Mason took a long pull on his cigar, savored the smoke and let it waft towards the ceiling. Then he took his time, and asked, "What does 7 December mean to you?"

Boxer felt the short hairs on the back of his neck prickle, and a chill go up his spine. "December seven Nineteen forty-one—a date which will live in infamy," he responded somberly, quoting former President Franklin Roosevelt. "The bombing of Pearl Harbor." Boxer let the words hang there.

"This year, seven December Nineteen ninety-one, marks the fiftieth anniversary of the Japanese raid on Pearl, and President Spooner has invited all the nations of the Pacific theater, as well as many of our World War II allies, to a remembrance ceremony in Hawaii. The Japanese will be there, of course, as our guests, to demonstrate the benefits of peaceful coexistence with the U.S. over a war-like stance. We're hoping the Ruskies and their allies get the message."

"A noble thought, sir. The Japanese gave up their military priorities and became one of the foremost industrial nations on the planet. If we could all turn our swords into plowshares, the world might be in better shape."

Mason cleared his throat. "Yes, well, the President wants you and the *Manta* in on the security detail. There've been threats made by some of the terrorist groups against the ceremony."

"Whew, that's a tall order, Admiral. Hawaii receives over six million visitors a year. It's impossible to screen out everyone who may hold a grudge against us."

"Your job will be to prevent an attack by sea. There is a large enough military presence on Oahu to handle any trouble on land."

"I haven't been to Pearl in years, since I was in training. It will be nice going back, I hope."

"If all goes well, Boxer, you and your men may get to spend the holidays in paradise."

Boxer smiled. "That's nice of you, Admiral. The men will appreciate it."

Mason got up from his seat and began pacing behind the desk. "Well, then, your first assignment will be to meet with delegations from Japan, the U.S.S.R., and Australia in San Francisco. From there, you head out to the islands."

Boxer took his cue and rose from his chair, grabbing his cap from the desk and placing it back on his head. "Is there anything else, sir?"

"That's it for now. Go back to your ship. You'll receive your orders from the base commander in San Diego. Dismissed."

0845. The ancient Japanese man remained behind the crowd of mostly American tourists at the *U.S.S. Ar-*

izona Memorial. He stood reflectively in front of the massive marble wall bearing the names of the more than eleven hundred American servicemen who lost their lives aboard the battleship during the bombing of Pearl Harbor that fateful December morning in 1941. He had been aware of the enmity of several of the Americans who stared at him as if he had personally sent these brave souls to their deaths. In point of fact, he had.

As a young naval aviator assigned to the Imperial Navy's carrier, the *Kiryu,* he flew on the first wave to attack the harbor in a *Kate* torpedo bomber. The young ace pilot scored a hit on the *Arizona* mere minutes before a huge bomb entered the old battleship's forward powder magazine and caused an explosion that sent a tremendous fireball skyward, and the *Arizona* to its death with over eleven hundred men aboard.

He had spent the last forty some-odd years feeling remorse for the act that he had gloried in at the time. He had gained a reputation as a fearless fighter, been promoted through the ranks during the war, and been instrumental in helping build Japan's awe-inspiring position as a leading merchant sea power. As an old man, upon his retirement, he'd had the honorary title of admiral bestowed upon him by his admirers.

It was with a very troubled heart that Adm. Hoshi Mako waited on this stark and solemn monument that he was, in part, perversely responsible for. He stood there in his black business suit, his back to the park ranger directing the first tour group of the day back toward the shuttle launch, and the second group into the far end of the memorial.

Adm. Richard Stark, U.S.N. Retired, former CNO of the United States Navy, stepped off the launch along with the others in group two, neatly dressed in a white jacket atop gray slacks, incognito in civilian garb, as he'd been asked in the letter. He paused inside the entrance, stepping aside to let the crowd pass by, craning his neck for a glimpse of the man he'd travelled over half the world to meet.

Stark ventured further along, caught up in the crowd peering out either side of the center of the structure, through cavernous slices in the white structure to allow viewing and picture taking of the rusting remains of the once formidable hulk lying below. Not much to see except a decaying gun turret and barnacle encrusted wreckage.

As the second group departed, Stark spotted the wispy ancient Japanese mariner, still at his position before the memorial name wall. Hoshi Mako. Stark moved closer and quietly cleared his throat. Mako's concentration was broken. He turned his head to see his wartime nemesis and later peacetime friend, Admiral Stark.

Mako bowed slightly. Stark extended his hand. "Admiral Mako."

"Admiral Stark. How good of you to meet with me. A load has been lifted from my shoulders."

Stark gripped Mako's bony hand with both of his. "It's good to see you again, my friend." Stark's gaze fell on the wall of names beyond Mako. "I lost a lot of friends that morning," he whispered.

The old Japanese man followed Stark's gaze. He looked very sad when he nodded, and replied. "I, too, felt a loss that day. My brother was among our few casualties of the raid, shot down by anti-aircraft fire before my very eyes."

The two of them stood there for several minutes, not

saying a word. Finally, Mako broke the silence. "I asked you to meet me here today in hopes that an incident such as happened here never takes place again."

Stark was surprised. "Could it? Your country hasn't the means nor the inclination to wreck havoc such as this today."

The old Japanese closed his eyes and slowly nodded his head from side to side. "There are those who would have otherwise."

Stark didn't know what to say. Then, a young woman in a park ranger's uniform came up to them and very politely said, "Excuse me gentlemen. We'd appreciate it if you'd return to the main exhibit on this shuttle to make room for the next tour group." She couldn't have been more than twenty-one or twenty-two, and smiled sweetly at the two elderly gentlemen in their seventies at least.

Had Admiral Stark been in uniform, no one would have dared disturb him. Yet, in their civies, to this young thing, they were just two old men overstaying their visit. Well, so be it, Stark thought. For now. This is the way Mako had asked for the meeting to take place, to keep a very low profile, not cause an incident. He took his elderly friend by the elbow and helped him along toward the exit. They took the five minute boat ride back in silence, turning from time to time for a last look at the white concrete structure.

"I'll get a cab," Stark said, indicating the line of taxi's in the parking area beyond the park entrance. Already the line of visitors had queued several blocks along the sidewalk leading to the site.

"That is very kind, but I have a car waiting," Mako said, and ushered Stark to a black Rolls Royce with darkened windows idling alongside the curb. As the two old seamen approached, a young Japanese man in black chauffeur's livery jumped out and ran around to open the rear door for them. As they slid into the plush back seat, Mako said, "I maintain a home here on Oahu. I hope you will join me there for tea."

"My pleasure," Stark replied.

The driver got in front and asked through an intercom, "Where to, Grandfather?"

Mako smiled at Stark's surprise. "Home, Yoni."

"Yes, Grandfather," Yoni put the Rolls into gear and headed off on the half-hour drive to Diamond Head.

Chapter Seven

"So you see," the aged Japanese seaman told Stark, "There are those in my homeland who are now in their seventies and eighties, very wealthy, powerful men who still yearn for Japan's return to the military ascendancy which dominated half of the world through the last war. They are going to die soon. They realize that. They are obsessed with this folly, for they see themselves as having nothing to lose."

"And what do they hope to gain?"

"Their place in history. Ah," the old man smiled. "Our tea is here."

A beautiful young woman, in traditional Japanese garb and a mountain of raven colored hair piled upon her head with lacquered combs, carried a tray bearing an antique china tea service and several covered bowls. She smiled and bowed to Admiral Stark, and then toward Hoshi Mako. "Shall I pour for you and your guest, Grandfather?"

"Thank you, Lotus Blossom."

Stark smiled back. A man measures his riches by the number of grandchildren who dote on him, he thought. Mako is very rich, indeed, then. As Lotus Blossom poured the tea and uncovered bowls of steaming rice and elegant cookies, Stark reflected on his forty-year marriage that ended with the death of his wife, Vivian, who had never borne him a child. And upon his brief love affair with Boxer's mother that bore him another man's son that he could never claim as his own.

When his granddaughter had left them, Mako sipped his tea, and scooped rice from a lacquered bowl into his mouth with chopsticks. Admiral Stark drank his tea and munched on a cookie. "Then they have not learned the lessons that history has taught. Your homeland is much more prosperous in peace than it was at war. Your industrial giants have set the standards for the rest of the world. Their place in history is secured."

Hoshi cleared his mouth with a sip of tea. "For some, total world domination is the only goal that is acceptable. Remember, for centuries, our leaders were Shoguns, omniscient warlords. There are those among the surviving warlords of the Great War who would be Shoguns today."

Stark blotted his lips with a red linen napkin. "So, you're saying that some of the old gang are looking for one more try at it?"

Mako used his napkin and set it on the table. He pushed back his chair. "Come, let us take a walk in the garden. It's good for the digestion."

Admiral Stark followed Hoshi out the rear door of the twenty-room mansion and into a formal garden, the jewel of his palatial estate at the base of Diamond Head crater with a view of the sea. A gardener tending a Bonsai tree bowed as his master approached, and withdrew, leaving the two aged seamen alone. They walked through the garden, stopping occasionally so that Mako could stoop and savor the fragrance of the hibiscus or frangipani flowers that lent brilliant flashes of color to the greens of the tropical plants and the natural hues of the rock gardens and statuary. They paused before a pagoda-like shrine. Hoshi suggested they sit and rest a while.

Stark took all this in. Surely, Hoshi Mako counted his riches in more pecuniary ways as well as familial. He must be incredibly wealthy, very powerful, while at the same time appearing very humble in Stark's eyes.

"To answer your question," Mako continued, "yes. There is an elite clique consisting mainly of World War II era military leaders and a few industrialists and politicians who would like nothing better than to turn the world's clocks back to Nineteen forty-one. And as you put it, to have another try at it."

Stark ran his fingers through his full head of white hair. "This has something to do with your asking me to meet you here on Oahu?"

"This has everything to do with why I asked you here." Mako sat there on the bench, leaning forward towards Stark, palms planted firmly on his thighs. "These old men have the desire, the finances, and the military and industrial expertise to again rule the Pacific theater."

Admiral Stark shook his head. "All they need is someone to bomb Pearl Harbor all over again."

"Exactly."

Stark looked directly into his counterpart's eyes, taken aback by the seriousness in the old man's tone of voice.

"Are you familiar with the Red Army?"

Stark said, "I assume you're referring to the band of Japanese terrorists rather than the Soviet Army?"

"Precisely. I have been privy to some inside information, some very good information leading to the conclusion that the industrial-military clique has joined forces with the Red Army and their allies for the purpose of recreating the destruction of Pearl Harbor."

A fist-sized knot formed in Stark's gut. He swallowed hard. "You're serious, aren't you?"

"I would not lie to an old friend. The Red Army bandits have joined forces with the Italian Red Brigade, the remnants of the Beider–Meinhof gang, and the most radical splinter groups feeding off the PLO and others. Their aim is to cause massive destruction. The clique, who are known as the Shogun Society, will provide the financing and expertise. In just over three months they are going to attempt to deal a mortal blow to the combined fleets present at your Pearl Harbor anniversary celebration."

"They couldn't succeed. They . . ."

"Please don't underestimate these fanatics. They may succeed if we don't stop them." Mako's voice rose in pitch and volume. The old man leaned far forward in his seat. "We must stop them. We must."

Admiral Stark leaned forward and placed a hand on Hoshi's shoulder. "Then I must take whatever evidence you have to my President to get him to beef up security."

Hoshi Mako looked very somberly at Stark, and sighed deeply. "That is the problem, my old friend. It is all hearsay. These men are experts at the clandestine, of hiding the truth. Unfortunately, there is no hard evidence."

The giant American Airlines 747 touched down at San Francisco Airport at 1130 hours. Boxer pulled his bag out from under the seat in front of him, gathered his garment bag from the hanging locker, and headed for the exit. A young Coast Guard ensign in summer dress whites caught his attention. The officer held a small sign in front of him with the words ADM. BOXER written with a black marker.

Boxer walked up and stood in front of the man. "I'm Adm. Jack Boxer."

The ensign studied the fortyish well-built man with salt-and-pepper hair and trimmed beared. He was wearing a navy blue blazer with a crest on the pocket, some kind of nautical design with Thomas Williams, Co. embroidered into it. Not exactly what he'd expected an admiral in the United States Navy to look like.

"Well, son, are we going to stand here all day?"

The ensign gulped, saluted, and made a clumsy attempt to extract himself from his predicament. "I'll take your bags, sir. I have a car waiting out front."

"I can manage fine," Boxer said, heading for the exit. The young officer held open the rear door of the government issue gray Chevy Celebrity sedan for him. "What's your name, son?"

"Mullins, sir. Ensign Edward Mullins."

As they drove around the maze of feeder roads onto the highway, Boxer noticed, "Quite misty."

"It's like this almost every day, sir. Mist rolls in off the sea and envelops the bay and the land on either side. You get used to it."

They took the interstate to the city proper and wound their way to the Presidio, a park-like compound of military and private buildings on San Francisco's northernmost quarter, at the foot of the Golden Gate Bridge. They were greeted at the gate of the Coast Guard station by a sentry who recognized the car and driver and let them pass.

Mullins took Boxer directly to the C.O.'s quarters. Capt. Earl Van Peebles stood up and saluted. Boxer returned the salute and they exchanged greetings. "Ah'm delighted to have you as our guest, Admiral. Please feel raht at home here, sir. And Mullins, take the admiral's bags, will you? Show some respect for the admiral."

Boxer shook him off. "I'm fine, Captain. I'd like to go to my quarters and prepare for my meeting tonight."

Van Peebles smiled. "Have you eaten yet?"

Boxer said, "If you call a bag of peanuts on the flight over eating."

"Well, whah don't we chow down first and then I'll see you to your rooms mahself. We've got some first class food at the officer's mess."

"Sounds good to me, Captain."

"Ensign Mullins, take the admiral's bags to the VIP guest building."

"Aye, aye, sir."

Van Peebles took Boxer to the nearby mess hall, where they took seats in the officer's wing. A steward stood by to serve them. "How're the crabs, today?" he asked the waiter.

"Couldn't be better, Captain." The waiter went into the kitchen and returned with a pile of red and white crabs eight to ten inches across.

"Dungeness crabs, the local catch," Van Peebles told Boxer. "Dig in, Admiral. They're sweet as can be."

Boxer broke off a claw and scooped out some of the meat, dipped it into the cup of drawn butter, and popped it into his mouth. He closed his eyes and savored the taste. "You're right about these, Van Peebles. They're delicious."

"Please feel free to call me Van, Admiral." He fed

himself a forkful of crabmeat. "Food around here's much better than that Yankee stuff we hadda eat when I was stationed at Stapleton, up in New York. Can't even get decent grits up there. Can you believe they don't even know what you're talkin' about when yo'all ask for grits."

Boxer stifled a laugh. "Yes, I can believe it. Stapleton Naval Base on Staten Island was my home port for many years."

"Folks around these parts are a little strange, too," Van went on. "They think stuff like bean sprouts and avocados are vegetables." He shovelled another forkful of the succulent white flesh into his mouth. "But yo'all can't beat these crabs."

The two of them continued to eat, leaving a mound of empty crabshells in their wake. "That was really a great treat, Van. I appreciate it. Now, I've got to be briefed on tonight's meeting. What do we have on the agenda?"

Van Peebles made a face. "The Ruskies, tonight, Admiral. Six-man delegation led by an Admiral Constantin Dezhnev. Then there's a submariner, like yourself, fella named Boromine. And a bunch of KGB types with 'em."

"Boromine?" Boxer asked, "Could that be Borodine?"

Van Peebles shrugged and consulted a small notebook he removed from a back pocket. "You're right. Admiral Igor Borodine. Know 'em?"

"Quite well. In fact we had a recent run-in under the polar ice cap several weeks back. All hush-hush."

"I've never seen anything reported by the media," Van remarked.

"Never will, I hope," Boxer added. "At least I know

64

that one honorable man will be present among the Soviet delegation."

That evening, Boxer stood at the head of a long table in a soundproof conference room at the Coast Guard station. A press of a button brought down a movie screen which filled the wall behind him. An overhead camera projected a 3-D topographical map of the Hawaiian Island chain on the screen.

To his right sat Dezhnev, the group's leader, then Borodine and his executive officer, Viktor Korenso. Across from them sat three representatives from the KGB. At the rear of the room sat Lt. Darby McGee manning the electronic equipment and two enlisted men acting as aides.

In front of Boxer and each of the Russians was a yellow pad and sharpened pencils, as well as drinking glasses and pitchers of ice water.

"On behalf of my President, I want to thank you for your commitment to making our Pearl Harbor anniversary ceremony multinational in scope. It is our hope that the mistakes of the past will make themselves evident to all and prevent a recurrence of that kind of nightmare."

Boxer activated a clicker device and Lieutenant McGee zoomed in on the island of Oahu, which now filled the entire screen. Evident was the mountain range that slashed diagonally through the northeast sector and at the northwest quarter, formed by the very volcano that created the island. Also evident were the numerous military bases and reservations taking up perhaps a tenth of the total area.

Another click and the camera once again zoomed in, this time on Pearl Harbor and the adjacent area along the southern shore from Ewa Beach to Diamond Head. After discussing the various facilities available, Boxer suggested that the Soviets tie up their fleet at the East Loch, well within the confines of the roughly hand-shaped harbor.

"Nyet," came the reply, six voices speaking as one.

"Totally unacceptable," Dezhnev spat. "Obviously, you have a very short memory," he told Boxer. "Our ships would be sitting ducks, to borrow one of your phrases."

Borodine spoke up. "Admiral Dezhnev is correct, Comrade Admiral Boxer. There would be no way to defend our ships against an attack by air or by sea, or even by land. Your government allows much too easy access to such an important military asset. And, it will be my job to provide security for them."

The senior KGB man, Alexyi Kozhevnikov, rose from his seat. His voice was cold and hard when he addressed his colleagues. "Comrades, it is obvious to me, as it should be to you, that the Yankee imperialists would like nothing better than to make us easy prey. How easy for an experienced submariner, such as this man before you, to launch an underwater attack against our ships. And how easy for this government to blame it on some third party, to point a finger at some unknown terrorist group. Are we going to risk the destruction of our flagship, the *Archangel,* to participate in this Yankee ceremony? Are we going to subject ourselves to the imperialist's lies and treachery?"

The others shook their heads.

"The answer should be obvious to you, comrades. I say we withdraw from this fiasco at once."

The two other KGB men rose at once and shouted their approval of their leader's suggestion. The naval officers remained seated.

Boxer raised his voice to be heard over the ruckus. "Gentlemen, please. Comrades, please listen to reason. We are not trying to trick you into a trap. That position would offer our security forces the best opportunities to defend and protect your fleet. If that is not favorable to you, then suggest an alternative."

"He lies," Kozhevnikov shouted.

"I do not lie, comrade. Ask Comrade Admiral Borodine here. He knows I speak only the truth."

The head of the delegation, gray haired Admiral Dezhnev, turned to Borodine for a reply. Igor cleared his throat and stood up. He held up both hands to quiet the KGB people, who were still grumbling to themselves. "I know this man. We have fought frequently. At times we have nearly sunk the other's submarine. And yet, we have fought side by side to save the other's life. We are enemies, due to our national and political differences. Yet, on a personal level, we are very much the same. I give you my word, Comrades, that this man speaks the truth."

"Maybe so," snarled the senior KGB man, "but his political leaders speak only lies. How can we trust them. I say we withdraw."

"Wait," Boxer implored them. "Think about it overnight. We can meet here again tomorrow morning to iron out our differences."

The senior Admiral stood up and looked across at the KGB people, then at Borodine and Viktor. "We will meet again tomorrow." That was all, the meeting had been abruptly terminated.

As the Russians filed out, Boxer called Borodine aside. "Igor, I was hoping that you and Viktor might have dinner with me tonight. San Francisco has hundreds of fine restaurants."

Borodine looked to Dezhnev for approval. The old man nodded his head and followed the KGB men out of the conference room.

Borodine explained to Boxer that he temporarily commanded an *Alfa* class sub, now that the *Sea Demon* was back at Polyarnyy for repairs. The *Murmansk* was at this very moment moored off the San Francisco coast in a restricted area, with his crew and guard detail aboard. So far, the Coast Guard was doing a good job of keeping inquisitive eyes averted. It was now only 2000 hours. He and Viktor would not be expected back til midnight.

"What I could go for would be some good home cooking," Viktor said.

Boxer thought about it for a moment. "There's a good Hungarian restaurant not far from here, down by Fisherman's Wharf. I think you'll like it."

And like it they did. *Paprikas Fono* served them up steaming kettle-cooked *gulyas* soup, a delicious chicken strudel, and of course, beef and veal paprikas. They also ordered several loaves of *langos,* a fried peasant bread served with cloves of raw garlic, which they rubbed on the hot bread before dipping it in the sauces and eating it. All this they washed down with a rich, red Hungarian Cabernet. The talk centered mostly on families left at home. The evening was a time of good food, good wine, good friends, and good will. Boxer felt sure he and the Soviet delegation would come to a better understanding of the situation in the morning.

Chapter 8

So far, everything had been working out even better than Seshu "Niki" Nikimora had hoped. Exploring the Presidio Park area in his stark black business suit, he looked every bit the photo-hungry Japanese tourist snapping his Nikon at everything in sight. Driving about in a rented Toyota Corolla, he got his obligatory shots of the Golden Gate Bridge, the massive red-bricked Civil War fortification, Fort Point, and of course, the fifty–foot tower of the submarine parked offshore in a restricted zone.

Strange, there were no markings on the conning tower, yet not so strange to Niki Nikimora. After all, one wouldn't want to advertise to all the world the presence of a Soviet *Alfa* class sub and have the tourists and the media all over it. This suited him perfectly.

When the three comrades went ashore in a tender dressed in light blue jumpsuits, it took Niki a moment to recognize the captain with his salt and pepper beard and hair. The lean blond man and the toad-shaped grunt that were framed within Nikimora's telephoto lens were no doubt a high ranking ship's officer and the boat's political officer, respectively. So much the better, Niki figured. A bear without its head is so much less of a foe.

As night darkened the waterfront, Niki had his sentries posted to intercept the three high-ranking Russian officers should they return to the submarine too soon. He checked the luminous display of his chronometer. 2030 hours precisely. Now. After three months of preparation and countless hours of drill, it was time for him to put the master plan in motion.

He produced two quick clicks on a tiny transmitter imbedded in one of the buttons of his business suit. The signal was received by his lieutenant, Sunni Akima, who acknowledged and replied in kind. A pair of inflatable boats were pushed off a nearby beach and rowed silently northward, blending perfectly with the night. The inflatables and the five men aboard each were encased in black rubber.

Nikimora drove the Toyota Corolla just under the speed limit along Lincoln Boulevard, the coastal route down the Presidio's west side. Suddenly, the car sputtered to a halt within shouting distance of the MP's attending the checkpoint for the off-limits area of the beach.

The three guards on duty first heard the rantings and cursing, and played their searchlights in the direction of the noise. What they saw was a fortyish Japanese man wearing a black business suit getting out of a Toyota and opening the hood. They watched him open the hood, and heard his screams when hot steam and smoke bellowed from the front end.

It was all they could do to contain the man howling curses at the car, his wife crying and imploring him to stop beating the car and seek medical attention, and the short, round mama-san shouting at her no-account son-in-law for his stupidity and incompetence, and at her daughter for marrying the idiot. Soon, flames from the engine could be seen by the three Soviet seamen on deck-detail aboard the *Alfa*.

The sergeant in charge of the guard detail radioed for a wrecker and a firetruck. The two vehicles arrived with lights flashing and sirens wailing, adding to the cacophony that already existed. Two firemen extinguished the apparent grease fire with extinguishers. The tow truck driver pulled around to the rear of the Toyota and backed the tow bar up against the car's bumper.

It was all anybody could do to calm down the screaming trio and sort out the why's and wherefore's of the mess. Reports had to be filed, and someone had to pay the driver of the wrecker, or that piece of shit Toyota could stay right where it was, he told them.

Aboard the *Murmansk*, two of the deck crew craned their necks for a better view of the ruckus taking place on shore not far from their position. The sight of the flames against the night sky caused them to chide their third member to see what the stupid Yankees were up to. The third seaman, Nikolai, with the most seniority of the deck detail, caught a glimpse of activity on shore and told the others to shut up and pay attention to their work. That was answered with an obscene gesture behind his back.

The two lower ranking seamen shared a knowing look and continued to stare at the fire on shore, trying to figure out what was going on. When they turned to see if Nikolai was still checking on them, it seemed as if he was suddenly doing a graceful backflip off the deck. His AK-47 flew from his uplifted and outstretched arms, and he seemed to follow it backward into the icy sea. Before they could figure out what had happened, a knife found its mark in one seaman's throat. A second and third knife cut the remaining deck guard down. One of the blades lodged in his heart, killing him almost instantly.

Five black-clad forms climbed onto the *Alfa*'s deck from the seaward side of the submarine. Their leader, Akima, motioned with hand signals, and the two slain Soviet seamen were deftly removed from the deck and pulled onto the inflatable raft alongside the body of Nikolai.

The second five-man team boarded the *Murmansk*, and headed toward the stern. Akima climbed the conning tower while directing the rest of his squad toward the forward hatch. At his signal, four of his men dropped black canis-

71

ters, about the size of a soup can, down into the sub, and closed the hatches. Akima dropped two cans down through the hatch in the conning tower and kicked the hatch shut.

They needed two minutes for the gas to do its deadly task. The *Murmansk*'s cook was the first to notice that something was amiss, and the closest to the forward hatch. He was having difficulty breathing. Air, I've got to have air, his brain kept telling him. He pushed against the heavy hatch. What's the matter with those fools on deck. He tried to get out the words—Get off the hatch, stupid. Now what. The sonar officer, and a *michman,* an NCO, were at his feet, clawing at him. Got to get out.

The cook heaved his two-hundred-pound bulk against the hatch. It gave. Shoving with a forearm, he pushed the hatch up and back. He kicked at the hands pulling him down by his feet. Stupid bastards, he cursed silently. He hauled himself up onto the deck, his lungs bursting, his face purple. Fresh air at last.

A black rubber-clad arm wrapped around the cook's neck and lifted his jaw up and back. A knife pierced the cook's neck from the right, blade edge forward, and drove through to exit from the left. With one forward slice the cook's throat was slit completely through, severing the carotid arteries, the jugular vein, and the trachea all at once. Silent and deadly. The cook was tossed aside.

The SO was next to claw his way out to the deck, the next to die in the same manner. The *michman* died from the gas before he could climb the steel ladder to the outside.

Akima gave the signal. Gas masks went on over the faces of the ten Japanese commandos. They dropped below and systematically swept through the hull insuring that every last man aboard the Soviet sub was dead. A third inflatable raft was paddled alongside the sub and eight new black-clad figures emerged. Satisfied that the carnage was complete, Akima slapped one of the new men on the shoulder and said, "Tomi, she's all yours. Get us out of here, Captain, nice and slow, nice and easy."

Tomi Saburo was not new at this. While the dead guards and the now deflated rafts were hauled aboard and dragged forward, he had his skeleton crew rev up the engine, cast off the mooring lines, and the *Murmansk* slipped slowly out to sea, gently settling to periscope depth.

"What the fuck's going on with the Ruskies, sarge?"

"Look, sir," the sergeant was explaining to the irate Japanese man kicking the steaming front end of the tan Toyota. "The driver's not going to remove your vehicle if you don't pay him."

Nikimora shouted back, half in his native tongue, half in pidgin English, that he was not going to pay to have a rental car towed, that they could come to take the piece of garbage, and his mother-in-law, too, for all he cared.

"Sarge," the guard continued, "What gives with the Ruskies? Looks like they've moved their sub."

"Huh?" He glanced behind him, watching the tower slip lower into the sea. "Prob'ly trying to get some peace and quiet." He returned his attention to Nikimora. "Now, sir, please calm yourself down," he implored.

Then a Nissan Sentra driven by another Japanese man pulled up alongside the burned out car. The driver called out something to the Niki, who then became very quiet and polite, and began bowing, as did his wife and mother-in-law. The three of them got into the Sentra, which drove off, leaving the MP's staring at the Toyota dangling from the rear of the tow truck. The MP's looked at each other. The wrecker driver asked them, "Who's goin' to pay for this, I wanna know?"

Aboard the *Murmansk,* the air scrubber system was blowing the last remnants of the poisonous gas out of a blow-hole atop the sub's sail. Akima produced an instrument that looked like a rubber bulb at the end of a dial. Satisfied with the reading he got, Akima removed his gas-mask. He took a small, careful breath, his mask ready to be put back on if need be. It needn't. The air didn't smell all that good, but it was pure. He nodded to the others and they all removed their masks as well.

Akima looked around his new domain. A Soviet *Alfa* submarine. Unbelievable. He shook his head and began to laugh. A few of his men nearby looked at him oddly, they'd never even seen him smile before. Was he going crazy? That was something that would have to remain to be seen. None of them would dare risk his life asking that question out loud.

Chapter 9

"Daddy, Daddy, you came back."

Boxer beamed. He held out his arms. Has it been this long? His son seemed to have grown a foot since Boxer had last been home. "John."

The boy jumped into Boxer's grasp, clinging tightly to him. Boxer hugged him and hoisted him up until they were face–to–face. The freckled face had Gwen's fine features, the tawny hair was hers too. But the eyes are mine. Yes, there was no mistaking those steel gray eyes. "I missed you, son," he managed.

"I missed you, too, Daddy. I love you."

Boxer held the boy tighter. It had been almost two long years. "I love you, John."

"Take it easy, John. You'll mess your father's uniform."

Boxer glanced up, cast a hard look at her. Gwen was still beautiful. Lustrous, long golden hair flowed over one shoulder to the deep, V-neck of her royal blue jumpsuit. Her full breasts strained against the silky fabric, threatening to burst free if the front zipper were to inch downward ever so slightly.

But she had to know that he'd gladly trade a wrinkled uniform for a minute more holding his son.

Gwen averted his icy stare. When the boy led his father into her uptown apartment, she merely said. "Hello, Jack. It's been a long time. Did you forget you still had a son?"

Bitch. In front of the boy. Boxer merely said, "Hello,

Gwen. Let's try to make this a pleasant visit, this time, okay?"

Gwen said nothing.

"Well, I thought I'd take the two of you out to dinner, tonight. Anyplace you'd like," he told her.

"We already have plans for the evening, Jack. I'm sorry."

"Sorry? What the . . . what do you mean, you're sorry. I haven't seen my son in almost two years, and you tell me you have other plans? How . . . ?"

"I'm getting married, Jack. Frank and I are going out to dinner. John's going to the babysitter."

Boxer's face reddened. He watched the eight-year-old boy standing behind his mother, tears welling in his eyes. "He'll stay with me. I'm still his father."

"Ready, dear?"

Boxer watched the tall, dark haired man step out of the bedroom, his bedroom, once, dammit. He was wearing at least twelve, fifteen hundred dollars in designer clothes, and a smug expression when he saw Boxer.

Boxer watched Gwen smile at him, her lover, no doubt, by the expression on her face. An expression, Boxer reminded himself, once reserved exclusively for him.

She said, "In a moment, darling. My ex-husband was just leaving." She gave Boxer that look, dismissing him, making him the fool in the eyes of his son. As the tall man got closer, she said, "Jack, this is Frank Gold, my fiancé. Frank, Jack Boxer."

Frank held out his hand, flashed a big, white-toothed smile.

Boxer ignored him. "Why are you doing this to me, Gwen? Have I ever denied you anything? Have I ever missed a rent or alimony payment? Have I ever been late with the child support? Have I ever . . . ?"

"Have you ever so much as called in the last two years?" she fired back, her face turning cold, the smile gone, now. "Have you shown even the slightest attention to your son during that time? Some father you've been. And now, you think you can walk back into our lives, just like that, take us to dinner, and all is forgiven? Just go right back to the way things used to be? Not a chance, Jack Boxer. And when we get married next month, Frank is going to apply for adoption of John. And considering your desertion of your family ties, the judge is sure to. . . ."

That did it. Boxer tried to suppress the anger boiling up inside, tried to be pleasant, give her the benefit of the doubt. But this was too much. He squared off with the larger man, feet slightly apart, hands balled into fists at his side. He bent his knees, slightly, weight a bit forward, ready to spring. "That's enough, Gwen. Frank or anyone else will adopt my son over my dead body." He glared menacingly at them both.

"The kind of work you're in," Gold said, "that may be sooner than you'd like to think, Jack."

Stars went off in Boxer's head. He sprung forward toward the big man.

Gwen tried to move between them, knowing they'd gone too far, knowing a fury that her new lover would be no match for had been unleashed.

Not quick enough. Boxer's left hand reached around past Gwen, grabbed a handful of Frank's seventy-dollar tie just below the knot, and twisted it. Frank didn't respond in time. He gagged as Boxer applied pressure, yanking him to the floor. He winced as Boxer dropped his weight onto him, knees crushing his chest, the pressure on his throat ever present, choking out his life.

Gwen screamed, "Get off of him, Jack." She was on her

77

knees beside him now, her long nails digging into his face. "Jack Boxer, you stop that. Get up . . . Get up. . . ."

"Get up, sir. Please, Admiral Boxer, please wake up. It's urgent."

"What the . . . wha. . . ?"

More banging at the door. Boxer shook his head, trying to separate his thoughts, trying to decide what was a dream, and what was real.

"Admiral Boxer, please, sir. Captain Van Peebles has to see you right away. He say's it's urgent, sir."

Boxer's eyes adjusted to the dark. His pillow lay twisted in his grasp, his broadcloth pajamas soaked with sweat, his own personal nightmare now over. He looked at the red LED figures on his alarm clock — 0300. He'd slept a little under two hours. Boxer got out of bed. "Coming," he called out to the messenger behind the door. "I'll be right there." Grabbing for his robe, he wondered. What could possibly have gone wrong in that short a time? He would soon find out.

Van Peebles was sitting at his desk, his hair and uniform slightly disheveled. He, too, was roused from his sleep because of the message from Washington. He saluted when Boxer walked into the office, and pointed to the scrambler phone. "Cultrain wants you to call him back immediately."

Boxer walked to the phone, his mind now alert. Everett Cultrain wanted to speak to him at three in the morning, 6:00 A.M. D.C. time, Boxer calculated. Wonder what got the acting Director of the CIA up so early? He picked up the phone, dialed the number that Van had written down for him, and waited with the handset against his ear. After a moment, a voice asked him to ID.

"Admiral Jack Boxer here," he said into the mouthpiece, and gave his serial number. Boxer knew that regardless of who he said he was, he was being voiceprinted at the other end of the line.

"ID checks positive, Admiral Boxer. Go ahead, please. Director Cultrain is on the line."

Cultrain's voice came on harsh and demanding. "Boxer, what the fuck's going on out there?"

"Sir?"

"We sent you to San Francisco to meet with the Ruskies, to work hand in hand with them on the security of the Pearl Harbor Day ceremony, to make peace with them, at least until the show's over, and what do you do?"

Boxer said, "I don't know, yet, sir. The meeting didn't get off to a rousing start, but . . ."

"You totally fucked up, Boxer, and you tell me you don't know anything about it? How the fuck . . ."

Boxer looked at the receiver, and hung up. It seemed to him that the CIA directors all played the same record. Kincaid, Tysin, and now Acting Director Cultrain. The phone rang again.

Boxer looked at the phone, then at Captain Van Peebles. Van shrugged, and looked back at Boxer. Not me, man. You're the one who hung up on the old man.

Boxer picked up the phone and said, "Boxer here."

"Dammit, Boxer, what the f . . ."

Boxer hung up again.

The phone rang again.

Once more, "Boxer here."

"Boxer, you hang up on me again, I'll have you arrested and court martialed. I'll have you busted down to ensign, and thrown in jail forever. I'll . . ."

Boxer's voice got hard. "Why don't you just tell me what

you called to say, and skip all the bullshit, Cultrain."

"Dammit, I . . . Now wait, Boxer. Don't go hanging up again."

Boxer smiled, caught Van Peebles's attention, and winked. "Go ahead, Sir."

"What the hell happened to the Ruskie sub?"

That caught Boxer off guard. All he could say was, "What did you say?"

"The Ruskie *Alfa* that was moored off the Presidio has disappeared. You really didn't know about it, did you?"

Boxer shook his head. "I'm hearing about it for the first time from you right now, sir. And I was out to dinner with the sub's skipper and exec up until a few hours ago."

"That's part of the problem," Cultrain continued. "While you were out on the town, someone made off with the goddamn submarine. Borodine and his exec have been arrested by the KGB, and they're demanding your head for conspiring with them to steal the *Murmansk*. The Ruskies really think that the U.S. is responsible for the disappearance of their sub."

Boxer let out a long, low whistle. "How could they . . . ? Someone had to be watching our every move. Maybe, maybe someone on board the sub commandeered it, knowing that Borodine and Viktor were going to be out for several hours."

Cultrain didn't like the idea. "I think you're groping at straws," he told Boxer.

"Think about it for a moment. You and I know we didn't steal the sub." There was silence on the line. "Cultrain," Boxer demanded, "we both know the U.S. isn't responsible for what happened, don't we? I have to know the truth."

"It wasn't us, Boxer."

Boxer was pacing the floor, now. "Well, if we didn't have

anything to do with it, who could possibly steal a nuclear submarine? Not many people, I'll tell you. You'd need an experienced skipper, and at least a skeleton crew just to move the sub out to sea. Somewhere along the way, they'd need the remaining crew to join them. And if they did get that far, they'd have to hide the damned thing. Not something your run-of-the-mill highjacker gang could pull off."

Cultrain was chain-smoking Marlboros now, lighting the next with the last. A cloud of thick smoke shrouded his upper body in spite of the air purification system in effect, and to the consternation of his closest staff members. He said, "Something of that magnitude would have to be pulled off by a combined commando force of some other nation, one with a grudge."

Boxer nodded his agreement. He was fishing in his pocket for his pipe. Van Peebles gave him a hand, packing a plug of aromatic tobacco into the meerschaum-lined bowl, and holding a flame to it while Boxer drew in the sweet smoke. "Grudge against the Ruskies?" Boxer asked, blowing a smoke ring toward the ceiling. "Or us?"

"Or both, for that matter," Cultrain added.

Boxer scratched his head. "Terrorist group?"

"Who?" the Director asked, "IRA? PLO? They couldn't find their ass with both hands."

"There's no lack of terrorist groups that would like nothing better than to embarrass us and deal a blow to the Soviets at the same time. Or vice versa. Has there been an investigation at the scene yet?"

"Not enough time. Apparently, you're the first out there to know about this. The Soviet ambassador was on the phone to the White House at 4:00 A.M., Eastern. The President woke me, and I woke you. Now find out what happened last night while you were out entertaining your

Ruskie friends, and report back to me by 1400. I have to have something to tell the President. And, I don't have to remind you, Boxer, that both our asses are on the line."

"No, sir, you don't. I'll call in at 1400."

Cultrain said, "You'd better. And don't be late." But Boxer had already hung up.

Van Peebles was downing his fourth cup of black coffee. "What now?" he asked Boxer.

"We investigate. You got any more of that coffee?"

Van got up and poured a cup for Boxer. "Milk and sugar?"

"Black will be fine, thanks. First, I'd like to speak to all the people involved in the security detail last night. We'll start with them, see if we can flesh out a story." We'd damn well better, Boxer told himself, or a lot more than our asses will be at stake. The implications of what had happened were not lost on him. The very future of the world might be at stake. Boxer tried not to think the unthinkable. We could be looking at the very start of World War III.

Willy Braun waited at the side of the narrow serpentine roadway, concealed by the density of the underbrush, waiting patiently behind a spruce tree for just the right moment. Patience, he told himself, for the hundredth time that day, is a virtue. He checked his Swiss chronograph. 2055. Five more minutes. Willy's stomach churned, betraying his outward calm. He ducked his head behind the spruce's trunk, lest his men see him, and popped two antacid tablets into his mouth. Damn stomach.

At two minutes to nine, the receiver in his pocket squawked a warning. "They're here."

They're early, Willy muttered to himself. He was a very

precise person. Patient and precise. He disdained the lack of either of these traits in others. He stuck his head into the open and whispered, "Now."

Two heavy logs toppled across the road. The roadblock was now complete. Willy signalled his men to stand by. One minute, he gestured.

Two truckloads of sailors returning to the submarine base in Kiel, a shipbuilding town in the north of West Germany, overlooking the Baltic Sea and neighboring Denmark. The first truck braked to a stop just a few feet from the fallen tree trunks blocking the road. The second vehicle barely missed crashing into the first.

The driver of the lead truck stepped out to see what was the problem, followed closely by the backup driver who was riding shotgun. The two of them approached the roadblock, cursed their luck, kicked at the heavy logs, and made a feeble attempt at moving them. Not a chance. The driver turned to call for help. He was blindsided by a baseball bat to the head, and dropped like a stone in his tracks, the back of his head crushed. His backup driver was just straightening up when he was struck from behind. He died instantly, never knowing what hit him.

It happened so swiftly, that no one within the canvas-covered troop carriers was aware that they were under attack. The driver and assistant driver of the second truck had opened their doors and were just stepping down when they were grabbed, pulled to the ground and beaten to death by more of Willy's men. Willy checked the time. 2103. Excellent. So far, so good.

Twenty-four men wearing the trademark black outfits of the Beider-Meinhof gang quick-stepped to the sides and rear of the troop carriers. At a signal from their leader, Willy Braun, they threw open the canvas flaps which covered the rear of the trucks and protected the "A"-crew of the SSN *Dusseldorf,* back after a weekend pass while their boat was being refitted.

The sailors found themselves staring down the barrels of UZI machine pistols and various other automatic handguns. No one moved. They sat there, mesmerized, not used to any type of military action on land. After all, there were submarines.

"Out. Out. Get out, all of you. Now." Commands were barked, and one by one, the sailors were pulled down from the trucks and lined up along the roadside, single file, hands on heads. Willy Braun checked his chronograph again. 2112. It was going too slowly. He resisted the urge for another antacid tablet, though his stomach churned, and acid burned the already ulcerated lining.

"Strip," he ordered his prisoners. "Now. Take off your uniforms. You, there, I told you to strip." He kicked one reluctant sailor in the ass, really sent him flying. The others started to remove their uniforms.

"Faster, faster," he shouted. The stripping took place at what seemed to Willy to be a snail's pace. When about half of the submariners had removed most of their clothing, Willy's self imposed patience began to run thin. They were running way behind schedule. He signalled his squad leaders, then he began the carnage. He used a silenced revolver to shoot the first six men in the head.

The other prisoners, realizing the fate that awaited them, panicked and began to run into the woods. The Beider-Meinhof's began shooting.

"Be careful," Willy Braun yelled to his men. "Try not to shoot through the uniforms. Quick, there," he shouted to one of his men. "Take off his pants before he soils them. Unless you want to wallow in shit for the rest of the night."

One squad of six commandos pulled the roadblock logs off the road using portable hoists they had brought along for the task. The other three squads massacred the remaining submariners, chasing some of them into the woods, dragging a few, weeping and begging for mercy, to the side of the road where the hapless sailors were bludgeoned to death and robbed of their uniforms.

Willy took a quick count. Sixty-four dead: sixty submariners plus two drivers from each truck. Good. Though the lack of cooperation of the victims had cost him an extra fifteen minutes. He called his men together. "Quickly, change clothing. Find something your size and put it on. Then, into the trucks. We're running late."

It took five minutes for the commandos to dress as submariners. Another ten minutes for the dead sailors to be dragged into the brush cover alongside of the road. The roadblock was already removed, the new drivers got in place, and the two vehicle convoy headed for the naval base.

2140 hours. Willy Braun, riding alongside the driver of the lead vehicle, ordered them to a halt near a densely wooded area a short ride from the base. He whistled two short, shrill blasts, and twenty men already dressed as submariners stepped onto the road alongside the trucks. Willy smiled at the tall, blond bearded man who approached him. "Well, captain, how goes it?"

"You are late, Willy."

"Trouble," Braun muttered. "Get your crew into the rear vehicle. Tell my men to get into this one."

Captain Erich Heinze, West German Navy, retired — actually given medical discharge against his wishes — replied with a Nazi salute and marched to the second truck. In minutes they were off again.

As they approached the sentry post guarding the entrance to the base, Willy ordered his driver to pull ahead, let him talk to the guards while the second troop carrier held back. He held the proper paperwork for the group. Better not to get the others involved until he cleared the checkpoint.

Willy had killed the first mate, a very likable, popular guy, and taken his uniform. It was one of the very few mistakes that he made that day. He showed the papers to the sentries, and he was waved through. "Park over there," the guard told the driver. The truck was parked in front of a row of low cement block buildings which housed the troops. A PX was at the end of the first row, a short distance from Willy's truck.

Meanwhile, the second truck, bearing Erich Heinze and his crew, had just been waved into the yard. Willy told his men to dismount, then stood back and watched the progress of the second vehicle. Very good, Willy told himself. No incidents. We are almost home.

"Krupps. Otto Krupps," a voice called out.

Willy looked up to see who was calling. A slightly tipsy submariner was being given a lift to his quarters by two burly MPs in a jeep.

"Krupps," he called out again. "Hey, you're not Krupps. What happened to Krupps? What did you do with him?"

"You must be mistaken," Willy told him. "He's been drinking again, hasn't he?" Willy said to the MPs. "Of course, I'm Otto Krupps. Mustn't drink so much, mate."

"No, you're not. I swear, he's not Otto Krupps," he told the guards, now becoming wary of the truckload men disembarking from the troop carrier. "Krupps is the first mate. I'd know him anywhere. What's my name, then?" he challenged Willy. "Go on, what's my name? See," he told

86

the MP, "He doesn't know who I am. That's not Krupps." The sailor shook his head to clear it. "Then who is he? Who are those men?"

"Good question," the MP answered, leveling his carbine at Willy Braun. "You, there. Step over here real slow. The rest of you don't move."

The second MP, the driver of the jeep, picked up the radio and began calling for reinforcements. A siren went off from the sentry bunker. Immediately, several jeeps raced to cut off and surround the other troop carrier. Erich Heinze realized that his luck had just run out. Sitting there next to the driver, he removed the Walther PPK automatic from its holster and placed it on his lap.

"That's not Otto Krupps," the drunken sailor parroted. "I told you it wasn't him."

Someone stepped from behind Willy's truck and emptied his UZI at the MP covering Willy. Willy drew his revolver from its holster and fired four shots point blank into the man who betrayed him. The Beider-Meinhofs behind Willy opened fire on the security forces that converged on them. Their automatic weapons proved deadly, cutting down the MPs and anyone else unlucky enough to try to capture them.

Barney Maguire, the sergeant in charge of the previous shift, was wakened by the commotion, and raced to the guardhouse in just his skivvies, T-shirt, and helmet. "What the hell's going on?"

He was quickly brought up to date. He ordered the occupants of Heinze's truck arrested immediately. Then he asked why Willy's commandos still had the upper hand.

"We are trying to capture them, but they have automatic weapons. We cannot get close."

"Capture?" He grabbed the guard's sleeve and tugged.

"Come with me." They raced to a jeep with a rocket launcher mounted in the back. "Let's go," Maguire ordered. "You drive."

"Right." The guard started up the jeep.

"Get as close as you can, then veer off sharply. I'll try to get off a shot."

They headed directly for the parked troop carrier, now with Willy's men using it for cover to shoot up everything in sight. Willy spotted them coming and ordered his men to concentrate their fire on the approaching jeep with the crazy guy standing in the back in just his underwear.

Bullets whizzed past them, some careening off the steel frame, some cutting up the earth in front of them. "Now, turn away," Maguire ordered.

The driver veered hard left, giving the sergeant a clear shot at the vehicle. More shots were fired. "I'm hit," the driver yelled, losing control of the jeep.

Another round tore through the flesh of Maguire's thigh, but not before he fired his single rocket. With a thunderous roar, the troop carrier exploded, sending fire and twisted steel and twisted bodies everywhere. Willy Braun never knew what hit him.

Captain Erich Heinze watched his dreams burst into flames in front of him. He watched his crew step down from the rear of the vehicle under armed guard. He watched his driver step out of the cab with his hands above his head. Cowards. That was not a fitting ending for Captain Erich Heinze. He placed the barrel of the Walther into his mouth and pulled the trigger. The din outside was so loud that no one even heard the shot that took his life.

Chapter 10

Boxer saluted the Marine corporal standing guard at the door to Van Peebles's quarters. The room had been set up with a table and three chairs placed on a wooden platform at one end of the small room. Two of the chairs were occupied by a stern-faced Marine colonel, Bart Trenton, and an equally resolute Van Peebles. Trenton appeared to be a bit shorter than Van, but very trim and wiry, with a heavy beard that Boxer guessed he had to shave twice a day, and a very short crewcut.

Boxer took his seat between them. There were pads and pencils for note taking, and carafes of ice water and steaming coffee in front of them. Boxer learned that Van and Trenton had already interviewed the towtruck operator, and came up with very little. An Oriental man, presumably Japanese, had stiffed him on the towing fee, the car rental company had reported the vehicle stolen a few days previously, and had refused to pay until the wrecker operator threatened to sell their Toyota for scrap and parts.

Sgt. Lewis Donaldson, arms handcuffed behind him, was marched past the other two MPs on duty when the *Murmansk* disappeared, and shoved roughly into the hearing room by his Marine escort. The look of impending disaster on his fellow detainees was not lost on Donaldson. He too, felt like a condemned man, his stripes and pension surely lost because of his error in judgement

89

the previous evening. His entire body began to sag under the weight of his dishonor.

"You're at attention, Sergeant," Colonel Trenton barked.

The sergeant self-consciously straightened himself out.

Boxer took a sip of ice water. "Guard, remove the prisoner's handcuffs."

The Marine guard glance at his colonel for guidance, and when none was offered, he unlocked the handcuffs. Trenton glared red-faced at Boxer and the prisoner, but said nothing. Boxer was the senior officer present, and as such, in charge of the proceedings.

Boxer ordered, "Tell us what happened last night, Sergeant. Try to remember as many details as you can."

"Well, Admiral, it was just after dusk, you could barely make out the vehicles up on the road, just their road lights. Of course, if they turned down toward the beach, our checkpoint was very well illuminated."

"Go on, son."

"Well, sir, you see, this car up on the road, the Toyota, it turns out, starts to sputter and make all kind of grinding noises. And then you hear all this yelling and carrying on up there. So naturally, we grab our searchlights and go have a look-see."

Trenton blurted, "You left your post, Sergeant. On who's orders?"

Sergeant Donaldson wasn't bearing up well to the pressure his colonel was pouring on. "It . . . it was my own decision, sir."

While Trenton glared him down, Donaldson continued his story, trying not to make eye contact with the colonel. He looked directly at Boxer. "You see, Admiral, we were supposed to man the checkpoint. We had the road barricaded and concertina wired. Anyone trying to get down to that submarine would still have to get past me and the boys, plus the roadblock." The sergeant kept slipping into a less rigid stance as he gave his report, and then had to snap to attention as he caught Colonel Trenton's icy expression out of the corner of his eye.

"And then what happened?" Boxer coaxed.

"Well, we went up to see what the trouble was, still keeping the barricade between us and the submarine. And this Japanese guy was cursing at the car, kicking it. I mean *really* letting go and kicking dents into it. Smoke was coming out of the hood, and when he opened it, it looked to me like he might have gotten scalded himself by the steam that sprayed up."

"Excuse me, Sergeant," Van Peebles interrupted. How can you be so sure he was Japenese? The towtruck driver just identified him as being Oriental."

"Begging your pardon, Captain," Donaldson replied, I spent a tour of duty on Okinawa a few years back. I know Japanese when I see it and hear the lingo. They were Japanese."

Satisfied, Van sat back and sipped at his coffee. "Go on, Sergeant."

"Well, sir, you see, the guy's still making a big fuss, then his wife and her ol' lady start mouthin' off at him. We're getting traffic backed up, and I decided to call for a tow truck and have the lot of them removed from the road, which we did. And by the time we got back to the checkpoint, we see the submarine almost completely underwater, kinda slipping away."

Colonel Trenton said, "And why didn't you report it to your superior immediately?"

"Well, sir, I figured, it's the Ruskies' sub, they can move it if they want to. Besides, there was no indication of any wrongdoing down there. Nobody got passed us, I'm sure of that. And Ivan had his own guards on deck detail. I didn't hear any complaints from them."

Boxer glanced at Trenton and Van Peebles. "Anyone have any further questions for the sergeant?"

Van shook his head, no. Colonel Trenton started to say something, then just shook his head.

Boxer said to the prisoner, "Sergeant, you're dismissed. For now, you'll be confined to your quarters. I'll call you back if I need you again." He flicked his head, and the Marine guard escorted Donaldson from the inquiry room.

Colonel Trenton took a drink of ice water, and crunched an ice cube between his molars. Tough as nails, Boxer thought, watching him.

"We haven't come up with a suitable punishment for that soldier, yet. I recommend death by firing squad, or at the very least, a long stint in the brig, plus a dishonorable discharge."

"For what reason?" Boxer challenged the Marine colonel.

"Discipline. Set an example."

"How much punishment do you think that soldier will receive if he's dead, Colonel? I'll leave my recommendation with Van."

Trenton stood up, his face red, flushed with anger. "As you like, Admiral. But that sergeant ever steps out of line one hair, and his ass is mine. Good day, sir." He turned to Van Peebles. "Captain."

Salutes were exchanged and Colonel Trenton departed.

Van watched the door close behind the colonel and told Boxer, "I've never seen him so pissed. He's used to getting his way."

"Too bad. Personnally, I don't think the MP's were that far out of line. After all, they were trying to protect the Ruskie submarine from a landbased attack. The Russian sailors were supposed to be watch outs for any trouble by sea. They've got all the sophisticated listening equipment aboard. They'd have to know it if any other boats were approaching too closely."

Van shrugged. "So what do you suppose happened? Mutiny?"

Boxer shook his head. "On a Soviet *Alfa?* Not a chance. Perhaps on one of ours, someone other than the skipper could drive it. My exec, Mark Clemens, sure could. Once, one of my former officers, a Captain Bush, just freaked out. Killed a few men and took over a nuke. Nearly started the apocalypse."

Van Peebles looked at Boxer, intent on his story.

"But on a Ruskie? No way. Borodine's exec, Viktor Korenso, could run the *Alfa,* no problem. But the Soviets split up the jobs so no one man knows too much, especially the rates. Their noncoms, they call them *michmans,* run all the routine jobs, and their officers know about as much as some of my better seamen. They put in their tour of duty and they're out. Very little re-upping. No, Van. It wasn't an inside job."

"Who then?

"Well," Boxer continued, "someone was very clever, and very well organized to have pulled a fast one on both our MPs and the Ruskie sentries aboard the *Murmansk.* And for starters, I'd guess the Japanese."

"The Japanese? But why? They're not at war with either us or the Soviets."

"Good question, Van. That's what I hope to find out."

Both of them got up to leave. There was a knock on the door.

"Yes?"

It was Ensign Mullins. "Excuse me, sir. A message just came in for Admiral Boxer."

"Thank you Mullins," Van Peebles said. "That will be all."

Mullins saluted and retreated.

"I've got a hunch I've just gotten my new orders, Van. Barring another catastrophe, my bet is I'm off to Hawaii."

Captain Tomi Saburo thought he was in heaven. In fact,

a Soviet *Alfa* was the closest thing to heaven that a submariner could ever hope for, up to the emergence of the super-subs from the *U.S.S. Shark* and the behemoths that sprang from that prototype on both sides of the Iron Curtain. She was capable of forty-five knots, powered by liquid-metal cooled power plants, built with a titanium alloy hull capable of withstanding depths of a thousand meters, fully computerized and heavily armed. And most important to Saburo, it only required a small crew, comparatively.

His dozen submariners had been well trained by the very nation whose boat they stole. Speak about biting the hand that feeds you, Tomi Saburo smiled. Well, the Soviets had trained the Libyans and the Cubans, who in turn were always eager to train any group willing to prey on their enemies. True, his training had been aboard the *Viktor* class subs and older types, but he'd learned enough about the *Alfas* to do at least a credible job. Consider this a practice run, he figured. And, when comes the revolution, he'd be ready.

Now steaming west at forty knots at a depth of one hundred meters, course two four zero, he was heading for the Hawaiian chain. Three hundred miles off the coast of California, the *Murmansk,* now renamed the *Kaga,* after one of the carriers that took place in the 1941 attack on Pearl Harbor, made its first contact.

The sonar officer raised Saburo on the ship's intercom. "Captain, I have a target."

The captain smiled. "Good work, SO. Please commence with the bearing, range, and speed." Always the patient teacher to his rather inexperienced crew.

"Yes, Captain. Target bearing zero three five degrees . . . Range . . . " The SO did a quick calculation. " . . . Ten miles . . . Speed one-five knots."

Ears perked up in the control room. They were less than fifteen minutes from a possible target on which to practice their recently acquired skills. "I copy that, sonar. Engineer, keep up the speed until I order a change."

"Yes, Captain."

"Helmsman, right rudder ten degrees. Come to zero three five."

"Yes, sir. Coming to zero three five, Captain."

Tomi turned the conn over to his next in command and walked back to the sonar station. "What do you make of the target?" he asked his SO.

"Something big and slow, Captain. A merchantman, I think. Too slow to be a warship."

Tomi Saburo took a spare headset and listened intently. "Tanker, I think. Or a freighter."

When they were within five miles of their slow-moving target, the captain ordered their speed reduced to twenty knots, fast enough to catch the merchantman, but slow enough not to betray their existence to any but a warship with sophisticated sonar systems. At one mile to target, Saburo ordered the boat slowed to five knots and raised to periscope depth.

"Search periscope up," he ordered, and had his first look at the target. "Tanker. I was right," he congratulated himself. He needed to be sure he wasn't about to fire on his own mother ship. His approach was forty-five degrees abaft the beam. He could easily read the thick, white letters of the American re-flagged Kuwaiti tanker, *Newport News,* on its way to Oahu with a load of high quality oil. Well, now for some practice for the torpedo crew and fire control team.

"Torpedo room, arm one and two."

The five men in the bow torpedo room, two submariners supplemented by three of Akimo's commandos, slipped torpedos into tubes one and two. "Ready, Captain. One and two are loaded."

"Stand by." He walked the short distance to the fire control computer and asked the FCO to prepare a firing solution. He checked the calculations and ordered the torpedoes slaved into the coordinates. At the short distance away, Saburo knew it would be a duck shoot. He took his place at the periscope. "Fire one."

"One away, Captain."

Saburo watched the wake of the silvery torpedo streak towards the belly of the huge tanker. He spotted several figures on the stern rail pointing to what he guessed to be his periscope. He increased the magnification and homed in on them. Their faces reflected surprise and fear. Now one of them was pointing down at the trail of his torpedo, skimming just below the surface. They started to scamper, but to where? They must know that they were about to die.

"Bulls-eye," the captain reported. The men cheered. A direct hit amidships. The huge tanker listed to port. A geyser of seawater shot two hundred feet in the air. And then . . . nothing.

"Fire two," Saburo ordered.

"Two away."

The second torpedo hit just under the waterline, below the superstructure. This time a fireball ripped over six hundred feet in the air, breaking the tanker in half, fuel oil spreading over the deck and surrounding seas, catching fire and raging out of control.

Tomi Saburo watched several dozen men dropping lifeboats over the side and letting themselves down on ladders to board them. "Shit," he snarled. He couldn't afford any survivors bearing witness to his attack. "DO, surface. Deck detail, prepare to man the cannon and machine guns. There are to be no survivors. Repeat, no survivors."

Sunni Akima smiled. He was glad the captain had the balls to do what needed to be done. He and his men stood ready to climb on deck as soon as they surfaced, and finish the job. It would be just like a shooting gallery.

"Maintain present speed and course," Boxer ordered. He was glad to be back aboard the *Manta,* with the majority of his crew still with him, manning their stations. Gone was Lt. Kit Carson, back in Norfolk on light duty, a temporary desk job until she was fully recovered from the trauma she suffered under the Arctic. Also missing was his entire strike force. Double Dick Dickerson was back in Alaska, training a new platoon of Snow Troopers. Rolly Jones and his Rangers were recuperating from their ordeal and rounding out their membership at Paris Island.

So far, he was pleased with the performance of his boat. The repairs seemed to restore the *Manta* to a condition every bit as good as it started out. His plan was to approach Oahu from about two hundred miles to the north, where he could test out the integrity of the double-walled hull in a series of deep dives in that very deep area of the North Pacific.

The *Manta* was at two hundred feet, travelling west southwest, about two hundred and fifty miles off the coast of San Fancisco when Hi Fi Freedman summoned his captain to the sonar room. "Skipper, I'm picking up a Mayday from about a hundred miles south and west of us."

Boxer picked up a set of headphones and listened in with one ear. He looked for the origin of the signal on Hi Fi's computer console.

"Signal's kinda weak, skipper. Sounds like it may be coming from a non-military vessel. It lacks the clarity and power that a fighting ship's radio would output."

Boxer knew the *Manta* was trailing a mile long antenna line behind her, capable of receiving radio signals within a hundred mile radius. Whatever was sending the Mayday was probably at the outer perimeter of that range. "Can you get a fix on it?"

"I'm trying, skipper." Hi Fi turned up the volume control. He did a quick calculation on the computer, and pointed to a weak flashing blip on the console. "I make it 135° 15′ West Long by 32° 57′ North Lat." The coordinates were displayed on the screen above the blip.

Boxer walked back to the control room and took over the conn from Clemens. He picked up the MC mike and gave instructions to the crew. "Helmsman, left rudder ten degrees. Come to course two zero seven degrees."

"Rudder left ten," Mahoney responded. "Coming on two zero seven."

"EO, full ahead. Bring us up to flank speed."

"Aye, aye, skipper. Full ahead. Going to five five knots."

They were heading for a disaster at sea, or a hard two hour sprint at best. Would there be any survivors, Boxer wondered? The radioed message was garbled. *We're hit. We're on fire. Taking on water. Listing heavily.* What had actually happened to the tanker that identified itself as the *Newport News* out of Kuwait, during it's desperate call for help, three hundred and fifty miles from anywhere? From nowhere.

Ninety minutes later, Hi Fi heard the final report from the *Newport News.* They were being fired on by another ship, as yet unidentified. Who would do such a thing? Kuwait was not at war. And the Iranians were not known to venture with its naval forces much beyond the Gulf. Who, then?

After that, Boxer homed in on the satellite signals beamed by the disabled vessel's emergency transmitter. And finally, those signals ceased as well.

"Skipper, I have a target bearing two seven degrees . . . Range over twenty five miles, and skipper, get this, the sound signature is a Soviet *Alfa.*"

"Can you be sure from this distance, Hi Fi?"

"Skipper, I hear that sound in my sleep. My skin gets goose bumps when I hear it. Yes, sir, I'm damn sure."

"Roger that, Hi Fi. Good work." Boxer rubbed his beard. "Hi Fi, send a message to San Diego. Ask them to check for any friendly subs within a fifty mile radius of these coordinates."

Freedman prepared the message and encoded it before sending it to headquarters via satellite, a micro-second bleep that he hoped wouldn't be picked up by their target.

The reply came back shortly. "Negative, skipper. San Diego reports no friendlies."

Boxer removed his cap, ran his fingers back through his salt-and-pepper hair, then replaced the cap. So the hunt was on. So be it. He keyed the MC. "EO, cut speed to one five knots."

"Aye, aye, skipper. Reducing speed to one five."

As the submarine slowed, the engine noises aboard the *Manta* became noticeably quieter. Quiet enough, Boxer hoped, to sneak up on the *Alfa* without being heard on their sonar.

"Skipper, I have a second target, this one a surface vessel, though I'm not getting a clear picture. Bearing is three four two . . . Range four thousand yards . . . Speed zero. Repeat zero. New target is dead in the water."

Dead in the water. If the target was the stricken tanker, Boxer hoped that the expression didn't hold true. "Mahoney," he ordered, "come to three four two."

"Aye, aye, skipper, coming to three four two."

"EO, all engines stop," Boxer ordered when they were one thousand yards from the surface target, and the *Manta* drifted on its forward momentum almost directly below the still blazing wreckage of the Kuwaiti tanker, *Newport News*.

Torn between going after the submarine that undoubtedly torpedoed the tanker, and surfacing to check for survivors when there wasn't a prayer of anyone surviving the blazing inferno, Boxer ordered the *Manta* to surface. Just below periscope depth, Boxer ordered the ascent halted. The fiery oil spill on the surface had caused the surrounding sea to warm up thirty degrees, even at this depth. Boxer shook his head and ordered the Manta moved to a safer vantage point.

When they finally broke surface, Boxer had to avert his eyes from the glare of the flaming sea. Then, through a filtered scope, he realized that no one could survive that inferno. No way.

As a matter of routine, Boxer played the scope over a three sixty azimuth to see what he could see. He was stunned by what he saw. About two-fifty, three hundred yards beyond the *Manta*'s position, ten men clung precariously to a partially swamped six-man life raft. And beyond them, Boxer could just make out the telltale dorsal fins of a pair of sharks building their courage enough to test the nearby flaming seas in search of the easy prey that their primitive senses assured them was close by.

"Damn. Survivors." Boxer signalled the crew to stand by to surface. A bell rang out five chimes. Men ran to man their stations. Boxer ordered, "DO, surface."

"Aye, aye, sir," Whitey replied, and blew the ballast while bringing the planes up five degrees.

The *Manta*'s bow broke surface first. As the sub levelled off, Boxer ordered his deck detail topside as soon as they had decks awash. "I want two inflatables out to those men, now," he said. "Have sharpshooters aboard each raft, and men in the water to help those survivors aboard. We have to get to them before those sharks do."

Two life boats were popped from their cannisters on deck and inflated as they hit the water. While a crew of scuba divers went to rescue the surviving members of the tanker's crew, two seamen activated the hydraulic system that raised the *Manta*'s forward heavy machine gun. They took aim at the prowling sharks, determined not to let them within the well-defined perimeter deemed necessary for the rescue operation.

As the rescue team approached the swamped life raft, they could hear the moans and cries and prayers of the survivors, all in Arabic. The rescued men were half-drowned, half-burned, exhausted beyond belief, and over-whelmingly happy to be saved.

They had clung precariously to life, the more fortunate still holding on when Boxer spotted them. They had watched helplessly as some of their mates, more battered or less tenacious, slipped into the sea.

One by one, the survivors were handed aboard the lifeboats. To make room, several of the scuba divers swam alongside back to the sub.

"Look, there." A deckhand pointed to the sharks. One of them disappeared, only to resurface mere feet from the two returning vessels.

"Shoot," the other urged.

"Can't. The son-of-a-bitch is right between the two lifeboats. Can't risk hitting them." He yelled to the returning rescue team. "Ahoy, behind you. Shark."

The shark bumped the lead raft, and dove. Petty Officer Nelson Horne, Nellie to the guys he worked with in damage control, slipped away from the second inflatable, drew his knife, and followed the silvery form below. He was ready.

The shark hit the gunwale of the lead raft again, this time more forcefully, this time gouging the tough rubber skin with his teeth. The outer wall made an audible pop and started to lose air.

Nellie Horne struck with his weapon. He just missed the eye, instead tearing a gash into the flesh around it.

The shark dove.

Nellie sought protection on the lee side of the raft. The shark would not be in a good mood when it arose again.

This time, the sharpshooters aboard the second raft were ready. This time, the shark was hit three, four times, head shots. The two lifeboats struggled back to the safety of the *Manta* before the second shark decided to join his mate, and found it turned to chum.

The surviving tanker crew turned a few noses as they were led forward to the sick bay. Those in the worst shape were placed on the four available cots. The walking wounded did the best they could, huddled in whatever space they could find on the deck. Burns and wounds were dressed, they were bundled up to ward off hypothermia, shot up with antibiotics, given sedatives, and treated for shock.

Meanwhile, Boxer continued his chase south and west, following the last known bearing of the mystery sub. Hi Fi could find no trace of the submarine on sonar, so Boxer ordered a sprint-and-drift maneuver-sprinting at full speed to close the gap, then drifting at five knots to allow the sensitive passive sonar to hear what was out there. Still, nothing on the sonar screen, nothing on the UWIS.

Damn. Boxer figured she had to be within earshot of the *Manta,* even with a two hour headstart. He ordered an active sonar search on a one-eighty azimuth, confident the enemy sub hadn't slipped behind him.

Hi Fi cringed. He hated to use the active sonar. Its pinging sounds could pinpoint their position to the enemy as easily as it could find them.

Boxer dreaded using the damned active sonar, but he was sure the mystery sub was at least aware of his general vicinity, yet he hadn't any idea where it was.

"Target bearing one eight zero, skipper. Range forty thousand yards . . . Speed one-five knots on the surface on course two six zero. Its a big one, skipper."

"Roger that, sonar. We're on our way." Boxer ordered the *Manta* to approach the new target at flank speed, lest it also fall prey to the marauding submarine.

At five thousand yards, Boxer brought the image of the target into sharp focus on the UWIS. He asked for ID on the CIC computer.

TANKER . . . 655,350 TONS
LENGTH 1659 BEAM 240
POSSIBLE IDS:
1. ICHI-BAN/TORA FLT JAPAN
   END SEARCH

So, Boxer said to himself. There's only one ship in the world with those characteristics, the *Ichi-Ban,* Japanese supertanker, star of the Tora fleet. Boxer knew the Tora shipbuilding conglomerate. They had been considered for building the *Tecumseh,* the supertanker that housed the *Shark* on its maiden voyage, a floating safe port out at sea. Quite a novel idea at the time. But the President wanted to buy American. Couldn't blame him, what with the huge trade deficit with Japan already.

"Hi Fi, try to raise that tanker. I want to warn her about the mystery sub. They may be its next victim."

"Aye, aye, skipper." Hi Fi worked out a transmission signal, using the Universal Maritime Code. When contact was made, Boxer asked to be patched through to the tanker's captain. Captain Nagatama assured Boxer that his ship's sophisticated listening gear had detected no submarine activity in the area prior to picking up on the *Manta*'s sonar signal a half hour back.

Son-of-a-bitch, Boxer frowned. He didn't like it one bit to be made by a merchantman homing in on a sonar fix.

"We have injured aboard," Boxer told them. "Taken from the *Newport News.* Do you have facilities aboard to treat them?

"Negative, *Manta* Suggest you return them to shore yourself. We're on a tight schedule."

"Copy," Boxer fumed. He was toying with offering them an escort to the supertanker, what with that submarine in the vicinity, but with an attitude like that, not a chance. "Out."

Boxer stormed out of the radio room, pissed at the lack of cooperation on the part of the *Ichi-Ban's* captain.

"But how could he pick us up on sonar, and miss the maurauder completely?" Clemens asked him. "And to have registered surprise at the sinking of the *Newport News?* It just doesn't make sense," he added.

Boxer thought about that for a moment. No, indeed. It just doesn't make sense at all.

Chapter 11

The delay cost Boxer a half day's travel time after waiting for the Coast Guard cutter, *Santa Cruz*, to split the three hundred odd miles of sea between them, and the time consuming transfer of the tattered remnants of the tanker crew from the *Manta* to the cutter. From the sparse hard data that could be drawn from the *Newport News* survivors, it seemed that they were attacked without provocation by an unknown submarine, which torpedoed them at least twice. And then the bow and stern sections of the tanker refused to sink by virtue of being constructed of watertight compartments, the submarine crew finished the job with deck-mounted rocket launchers.

Boxer understood that was standard procedure, the cost of Mark-48 torpedoes, or the equivalent, was in the neighborhood of three to four million dollars each. Rocket shells were infinitely cheaper, and much more expendable.

Boxer became more and more sure over the course of the three-day journey to Oahu, that the stolen Russian sub was responsible for the destruction of the Kuwaiti tanker. There were, however, too many unanswered questions: Why, for instance, would anyone want to attack a vessel of a neutral nation on the high seas, and destroy its precious cargo? For what gain? And, who? His nagging feeling was that it may very well have been a Japanese crew responsible for all the trouble, which, once again, brought up the question, why?

At 1800 hours on the third day, after having sailed for

eighty hours at forty knots, the *Manta* arrived off the southern coast of Oahu. Boxer signalled CINCPAC headquarters of his arrival, and was given clearance to enter Pearl Harbor as night fell upon the islands. He brought the *Manta* into a berth at the sub base and reported immediately to nearby CINCPACFLT headquarters, for a meeting with the old man, himself, Admiral Charles Willis.

An MP was dispatched to pick up Boxer and drive him the short distance, into the palm shaded courtyard, pulling up under the white portcochére, labeled in foot high brass letters, COMMANDER IN CHIEF UNITED STATES PACIFIC FLEET. Two sentries at the entrance quickly ID'd Boxer and provided an escort to Willis's quarters.

Willis extended his hand. "Boxer, I hear good things about you. Mostly good, that is." CINCPACFLT was smiling. "Personally, I don't believe half the crap I've seen in your file. My sources tell me you're okay."

Sources like Admiral Stark, no doubt, Boxer thought, as he shook the old man's hand. Unlike the CNO, Chi-Chi Mason, Willis earned his current position the hard way, coming up through the ranks and proving his superiority in every task given him, up to his present command. Boxer felt that he wouldn't mind at all if Willis were to become the next CNO. "Admiral Willis, a pleasure to meet you. Admiral Stark has always spoken of you with the highest regard."

"Have a seat, Jack. Could you use a drink? I was getting ready to settle down with some twelve-year-old Glenlivit when they notified me you had arrived."

Boxer seated himself in the leather upholstered chair opposite the big mahogany desk and nodded. "Wouldn't want you to have to drink alone, sir. I'd be happy to join you."

Willis got up and walked to the dry bar to the left of the American flag behind this desk, and produced glasses, an ice bucket, and the bottle of Glenlivit. "Scotch okay with you? I've got some very smooth Kentucky bourbon, if you like."

"Vodka is my usual drink, Admiral, but the scotch will be just fine. Neat, please."

Willis poured two fingers of scotch for Boxer, with a splash more for good measure, then filled his own glass with ice and the liquor. "Well," he said, handing Boxer his drink, "what shall we toast to?"

Boxer held up his glass. "To the men who lost their lives here at Pearl Harbor that December morning in Nineteen forty-one."

They clinked glasses. "Yes, to those who died," Willis replied, and took a long pull on his scotch. Boxer noticed a tear form in the admiral's eye. From the hit of whiskey, or from the memory, he wondered.

"You'll be quartered at the sub base, Jack. Feel free to make use of all the facilities here at headquarters. If you ever need anything . . ."

"Thank you, Admiral. I'll get settled in and meet with you first thing in the morning to work out a game plan, if that's alright with you."

"Roger that, Jack. By the way, Admiral Stark paid me a courtesy call the other day. He's staying on the island with a friend. He asked that you get in touch with him when you got here."

Boxer reached for a slip of paper that Willis handed him. On it was simply the word, Stark, and a local phone number.

"Oh, and Director Cultrain is sending over his best agent to assist you with the security for the ceremony. You'll have that to look forward to, tomorrow, as well."

"Nice of him," Boxer said, tongue in cheek. He'd bet the Company man was there as much to spy on him as to help. That'd be just like Cultrain, cast in the same mold as his predecessor, Kinkaid. He downed his drink, and placed the empty glass on the desk. "Well, thank you for your hospitality, Admiral. I'd better be getting back to my men."

Boxer was back at CINCPAC headquarters at 0630, anxious to get started on his new assignment. He was offered coffee and a danish by Willis's secretary, and told that the admiral would be with him in a half hour. Like Boxer, Willis did with little sleep, and was already being briefed by his Fleet commanders, and by his intelligence people.

At 0700, Boxer was admitted to the inner sanctum. What he'd failed to appreciate the previous evening was the series of prints and oil paintings of boats and ships on the wall behind the official flags and office equipment. They ranged from a World War II PT-Boat steaming through a rough, choppy sea; to a series of destroyers, frigates, the battleship *U.S.S. New Jersey;* and in the place of honor, alone on the right hand wall, a four-by-six oil of the carrier, *U.S.S. Rickover,* the newest and most prestigious ship in the fleet.

After saluting, Boxer made a comment about the paintings. "My commands," Willis told him. "It's been quite a wonderful experience, Jack. The *Rickover,* there's the queen of the U.S. Navy. My personal favorite, before they kicked me upstairs, to head the Third Fleet. And now this. I'll tell you, son, I really miss being at sea. Unfortunately, my responsibilities don't permit much of that, anymore, except for a few inspections each year. Not really necessary, you know. Just an excuse to give an old man a chance to regain his sea legs, and to breath the salt air mixed with the smell of machinery oil again. Nothing like it."

Boxer really liked the man. Here was an executive who worked his way up through the ranks, and when he got to the top, still remembered his roots, and didn't rub his subordinates faces in his success. Quite a difference from the CNO, Mason, who used politics and ass-kissing to claw his way up, a pompous ass whom Boxer disliked from their first meeting.

"Well, I can see that you're anxious to get started, Jack.

Let me fill you in on what's happened so far." Willis paused as his secretary knocked and entered with a tray with fresh coffee and sweet rolls. "Thanks, Marie. Please help yourself, Jack," CINCPACFLT said, popping a pastry into his mouth.

"Coffee will be just fine, sir." Boxer noticed the admiral's waistline—it looked as if this was a favorite part of his daily ritual.

"Well, Jack," Willis went on. "You are, of course, aware of the disappearance of the Soviet *Alfa*. At first, we didn't know what to make of it. Thought maybe, you know, the Ruskies were trying to provoke an international incident on the eve of our Pearl Harbor Day fest. Be just like Ivan to try to steal our thunder." He paused to sip some coffee. Boxer noticed he drank it black, but with at least three spoons of sugar. The man really had a sweet tooth.

"My best guess was that a Third World terrorist group figured out a way to steal the sub right from under us, and the Ruskies, Admiral. I am well acquainted with the skipper of that sub, Admiral Igor Borodine, and his exec, Viktor Korenso. We've dueled a dozen times over the past ten years, and saved each other's asses as many times."

Willis nodded, and took another bite out of a cinnamon danish. "I'm well aware of your relationship with Borodine, Jack. It's all in your file, right up to dinner together the night his sub was stolen."

Boxer looked up from his coffee, surprised; hell, pissed. Had he no privacy at all? "That's correct, Admiral. In fact, Borodine assured me that everything was secure when he and Viktor joined me for dinner and a tour of San Francisco. He told me most of his present crew had been with him almost two years, a long time by their standards. He said it was a pleasure commanding them, a matter of mutual respect."

"The thing that gives credence to your theory, Jack, rather than a mutiny on the part of the crew, is that the

Ruskies have arrested Borodine and his exec, and are planning to try them for treason for conspiring with you to have the U.S. steal the sub out from under him. Our intelligence people report that he's being held in Vladivostok until December, when he's to be tried and executed."

Boxer's face reddened, his jaw muscles twitched from the tension. "Sorry, sir. It's my fault he's in this mess. Had he been on board that night, the same fate that had befallen his crew would have been his, too."

"There's no such thing as due process in the U.S.S.R. Too bad about Borodine, I agree, but nothing that you or I can do about it, son."

Maybe. Maybe not, Boxer thought. I've got to find a way to get Igor off the hook, to save him.

Willis continued. "Jack, almost simultaneously with the disappearance of the *Alfa* there was an aborted attempt to steal a West German sub out of the Kiel shipyards. And," he added somberly, "a successful hijacking of a NATO sub out of Sicily. One that we built for the Italians, by the way."

"A nuke?"

"SSN"

"Sounds like an organized attempt to create a small fleet of subs in a hurry. Who could be responsible?" Boxer asked him.

Willis sipped his coffee and said, "Any number of hostile Third World countries have the capacity to make off with one of the subs. But I can't think of any that could handle all three. I think we're dealing with an organization that transcends national boundaries. These incidents are international in scope, taken together. And that's the conclusion I have to come up with."

Boxer rubbed his beard. An international terrorist organization? Sounds like something out of a James Bond novel. SMERSH? SPECTRE? All we need now is the Man from UNCLE to stop them, Boxer mused, to himself, of course. "Who then, Admiral?"

"That is for us to find out, Jack. Or should I say, for you to find out. That's job one. I believe the people behind these incidents may be looking to stir up more trouble before they're through. And we'd be a likely target, don't you think?"

The more Boxer thought about it, the more he came to believe it. "Well, let's prepare for the worst, Admiral. And hope you're wrong, sir," he added.

There was a knock on the door, and Marie stuck her head inside. "The CIA agent is here to see you, Admiral."

Willis noted Boxer's look of annoyance, and simply said, "Show her in, Marie."

A beautiful native Hawaiian woman wearing a blue cotton dress with a red hibiscus flower print walked briskly into the room. She nodded perfunctorily at Boxer's wide-eyed stare, and handed Willis her orders. "Special Agent Ona Kamanawanaleia," she announced. "Director Cultrain has put me in charge of security for the big event." She looked directly at Boxer. "I hope you'll have no trouble working for a woman, Admiral Boxer."

Boxer's mouth fell open. The audacity of this . . . this, what, maybe twenty-eight, thirty year old woman trying to pull rank on him. "I'm afraid you've got it turned around, miss. A pretty face just won't be enough to do the man's job that's ahead of us." Get in the quick jibe, Boxer. Damn. He was almost embarrassed by his cheap shot. She'd set him up for it, he was sure.

"My credentials are in order, Admiral Boxer. You can see for yourself. That is, if you can see past your own male chauvinism."

God, she was so beautiful, Boxer thought, taking in her trim, sleek body with its narrow waist, strong legs, and large bosom for a woman as petite as she was. But what a bitch. He wanted to say something, but thought better of it. Instead, he got up and said to Willis, "Well, if you'll excuse me, Admiral, I've got work to do."

111

Willis held up his hand. "Not so fast, Jack. Both of you will have to work with each other for a while, and on an equal footing, so no more bickering. Understood?"

Boxer's face turned red with anger. He merely nodded.

Ona placed her hands on her hips and said, "But Director Cultrain gave me . . ."

Admiral Willis stared her down with an icy look. She straightened up and snapped, "Yes, sir." Then she added, "But I don't see why . . ."

Again the icy stare. She shut up.

"Fine," Willis said. "I suggest you two brief each other on what you know and work out a suitable plan to secure the harbor during the ceremony." He looked each of them in the eye. "Dismissed."

Boxer saluted and went to open the door for Ona. She raced to beat him to the door and opened it herself in a huff. As she walked through the doorway, Boxer turned briefly towards Willis and shrugged. CINCPACFLT smiled and winked at him, and he followed Ona out into the hallway. Marie went up to them and said that Admiral Willis had designated room 104 as their briefing room.

At room 104, there was another inevitable clash at the doorway. This time, Boxer succeeded by opening the door for her. "That was really presumptuous of you . . ."

"That was a cheap shot you pulled . . ."

They both blurted out at the same time. Finally, Boxer decided. "Look, let's start over again. I'm Adm. Jack Boxer. I didn't catch the pronunciation of your name, Miss . . ."

"Kamanawanaleia. In the Hawaiian language, we pronounce each letter, each vowel is sounded out. But, I'll admit," she had just the faintest beginning of a smile, "It's quite a mouthful. Why don't you just call me Ona."

Boxer held out his hand. "Okay. Ona, then you call me Jack, and drop the Admiral stuff."

She shook his hand. Boxer was pleased to note her firm

112

grip. "I was chosen for this assignment because of my knowledge of the islands. I was born on Maui, but I graduated from the University of Hawaii, right here on Oahu. In fact, I was recruited right out of college by the Company eight years ago."

Boxer said, "I got the job because I've worked with the CIA before, many times, under three directors. In fact, at the start of the super-sub program, back a few years, I was officially resigned from the Navy and working for the Company. In truth, I was working directly for Admiral Stark and Mr. Kinkaid.

"Mr. Kinkaid, yes. He was the director at the time I was sworn in. I've never met Admiral Stark."

Boxer smiled at her. At least they were getting somewhere, without all the hostility. "Well, perhaps you'll have the chance soon. I've been given a message that he wants me to call him."

"Go right ahead," she said. "That phone is secure. I'll wait outside."

In a few minutes, Boxer joined her in the hallway, and they headed outside the headquarters building. She pointed to a second hand tour van, white with yellow and green pineapples, and a rainbow that arched over the words HULA TOURS, and under that, OAHU, and a phone number. "That's my chariot. Pretty neat cover, don't you think?"

"Well," he replied, shaking his head, "it's unique, I'll say that much. I bit gaudy, though, for my taste."

This time she smiled a real smile. "Not for Hawaii. We'll blend in real well in this buggy. Have you had a tour of the island yet?"

"No. I came here by submarine, and I haven't been off the base since I got here."

"In that case," she said, opening the side door of the van, "hop in, I'll give you the Honolulu deluxe tour, only thirty dollars, plus tip."

Ona slid the door closed after Boxer got in, and went around to the driver's seat. She reached into a bag and came up with a red and yellow flower print aloha shirt. "Put this on," she said, tossing the shirt to him. "You'll look like a tourist. In fact, you'll be my first and only passenger of the day."

"Would you mind picking up Admiral Stark? He's staying with a friend on an estate over near Diamond Head."

"Not at all. Just sit back and enjoy the sights. And if you see any couples wearing matching Hawaiian outfits, be sure to point them out so I can give them a toot on the horn."

"I thought you liked these clothes?" he said, pointing to his newly acquired shirt.

"Not bad," she quipped. "But can you imagine two of you together?"

Boxer shrugged, feeling a bit self-conscious in the brightly colored shirt. "C'mon," he muttered. "let's go pick up the admiral."

Chapter 12

The Hula Tours van passed through Nimitz Gate at the entrance of the Naval complex, took the feeder road to the interstate, where Ona skillfully plied her way through traffic. They were soon humming along H-1 with the morning rush hour traffic through downtown Honolulu, finally breaking free and winding their way down to the seaward side of Diamond Head crater.

Boxer showed Ona the address Stark had given him. "Fancy digs," she whistled. "That neighborhood has some of the most expensive real estate in the world."

"I understand that Admiral Stark's friend is fairly well off. His name is Hoshi Mako."

"Mako? He's one of the wealthiest men alive. You might say he's the Onassis of Japan, his merchant fleet is second only to the Tora line."

Boxer was looking out the window at the lush foliage separating the various estates along the meandering road. Homes of the rich and famous. At the mention of the Tora name, he turned his attention back to Ona. "Funny you should say that. We had an incident involving one of the Tora line tankers, the *Ichi-Ban,* a few hundred miles off the coast of California. I was not pleased at all by their behavior."

"Here's our address. Not bad."

They were at an ornate iron gate, bearing a small bronze plaque with Japanese figures. Set into the post

115

supporting the gate was a speaker. Boxer got out and toggled the switch below it. "Jack Boxer here to see Admiral Stark."

A voice cackled back. "Please wait a moment, Admiral Boxer. Someone will be there shortly to assist you."

Boxer stood there for a minute or two, gazing down the shrub-lined driveway that disappeared beyond view. Then an open-topped jeep pulled into view, seemingly from nowhere. Boxer guessed there was a service road running the inside circumference of the estate, out of view of the public eye. A young Japanese man with a thick head of straight black hair was the driver. He waved to Boxer and dismounted to open the gate. He smiled at the beautiful young woman inside the van. "I am Yoni," he greeted them. "Would you follow me, please?"

Boxer hopped back into the tour van. "That young man there has eyes for you," he told Ona.

She blushed slightly, and said, somewhat more brusquely than was expected, "I have no time for such things. Especially while I'm on the job."

A beautiful young woman with no time for romance? Boxer mused. What a pity. "He wants us to follow him in."

Ona put the vehicle in gear and followed the jeep along a serpentine drive. They stopped in front of a large house done in Japanese style, replete with ornate pagoda-style roof line.

Ona watched the two elderly men — one a Caucasian dressed in white pants, navy blue blazer and Panama hat; the other an Oriental in traditional Japanese silk robe — step out of the house and bow to each other, and then shake hands. Mako walked Stark to the van. Boxer had already gotten out to greet them.

Admiral Stark had Mako by the arm. "Jack, I'd like

you to meet my old friend, Mr. Mako. Hoshi, this is Adm. Jack Boxer, a very good friend and the closest to kin that I have."

The two exchanged greetings, and Boxer helped Stark into the van. Stark tipped his hat to the young woman driver and settled into a window seat alongside Boxer. Ona said cheerfully, "Hello, Admiral Stark. I'm Special Agent Ona Kamanawanaleia, CIA. But please call me Ona."

The old man smiled at her. "Pleased to meet you, Ona."

"We can speak freely, Admiral Stark. Ona is sharing the security detail with me on an equal basis. She's one of Cultrain's top guns here in Hawaii."

"If you say so, Jack. I've heard of some very distressing developments from Mako. If what he suspects is founded, we may be in for some real trouble when the Pearl Harbor Day event takes place."

Ona started up the van. "Where to, Admiral?"

"Punchbowl, if you wouldn't mind. I'd like to pay my respects to some old friends while I'm here."

"Yes, sir." She pulled out of the driveway and retraced their steps, getting back onto H-1 headed back towards the naval base. Along the way, Admiral Stark detailed what he'd learned from Mako about a possible international conspiracy to deal another death blow to Pearl Harbor, on the morning of the ceremony. It would be their job, Boxer realized, to stop them.

Punchbowl Crater was the nickname of the National Memorial Cemetery of the Pacific in Punchbowl crater, which commanded a striking view of downtown Honolulu. Ona got off the highway and climbed up the winding road to the top of the crater. She found the visitor's parking area and pulled the van into a space.

117

Boxer noticed a nearby plot covered with multicolored flower leis, a symbol of honor in Hawaii. Stark pointed out that it was the grave of Ernie Pyle, the war correspondent of World War II fame. Then he pointed to a long flight of steps topped by a huge wall bearing a raised sculpture and an inscription beneath. "That's the monument to the unknown soldiers of the Pacific. Won't the two of you join me?"

They walked the distance to the memorial. Stark kept up quite well until they reached the steps, where he slowed appreciably. When they finally rested, both Stark and Boxer saluted the memorial. Ona stood by with eyes closed in silent prayer. "Why don't you two young folks go on back down ahead. I'll stay a little longer and join you after these old bones have rested up a bit."

At the bottom of the stairs, Boxer noticed four young men milling around a white Volvo, pointing towards the monument and arguing in what sounded to him like Arabic. What caught his attention was the striking resemblance of one of them to the former PLO leader, Yassir Arafat, whom Boxer remembered from countless news photos during the turbulent Lebanese civil war during the seventies and eighties. Boxer wished he could understand what they were saying.

He and Ona had returned to the parking space, and were leaning against the Hula Tours van, watching them, when something triggered off a rush of adrenaline. As one of the Arabs opened all the Volvo's doors and started up the car, the others walked quickly towards the stone stairway. Two of them were lugging heavy backpacks. The third kept a hand in his pocket, frequently turning around to see who was nearby.

"Damn," Boxer spat, pointing to the group. "I don't like the looks of that. Let's go get Admiral Stark."

As the three Arabs quickened their pace, Boxer and Ona broke into a run, trying to get to Stark before them.

At the sight of them, one of the Arabs removed a handgun from his jacket pocket and fired off two shots in Boxer's direction.

Two rounds ricochetted off the steps, narrowly missing Boxer and Ona. The other two Arabs began taking the remaining stairs at a gallop. Boxer arose and started up the stairs again when another shot stopped him short. What to do. He had to get to Stark and stop those other two from setting off the explosives that they undoubtedly carried in the packs.

His question was answered in the form of Ona charging up the stairs, firing a small automatic pistol at the Arab gunman. A hit. The guy was going down. Boxer took the opportunity and ran after the two men carrying the explosives, leaving Ona to disarm and handcuff her man.

"Jack, look out," Stark yelled as one of the pair turned to face him, trying to remove a gun from his pocket.

Boxer hit him with a low tackle, just at the knees, bringing the guy down on top of him. Boxer saw the crazed look in the man's eyes, high on something or other. Boxer brought up a knee into the guy's groin, saw him wince in pain. Now. Boxer slammed the heel of his hand up hard against the guy's jaw, snapping the head back. The throat. Boxer went for the windpipe, digging his thumb into the groove along the base of the throat, squeezing the life out of the man atop him who was doing his best to separate Boxer's head from his body.

In desperation, Boxer's opponent jammed his thumb into Boxer's eye and gouged. Boxer cried out, grabbed the hand that tore at his eye, and lost his deathgrip on the guy's throat. With a burst of energy, he swung his leg over the Arab, and used his momentum to come up on top. "Son-of-a bitch," Boxer swore, and pummelled the man's face with a combination of punches. Blood and bits of teeth, and pink stuff dribbled from the guy's mouth.

The third terrorist watched his partner getting creamed while he set up the detonator on the explosive packs he was working on. He stopped long enough to help out his comrade. With a burst of speed, he lunged halfway down the stairs and kicked Boxer sharply in the ribs.

Stark, who'd been keeping out of the way of all this, waiting for an opportunity to do something, seized the moment and made a grab for the explosive packs. Before the terrorist who was kicking Boxer could react, the admiral dragged one pack to the edge of the stairs and tossed it over the edge, into the clump of trees that bordered the stairway. The Arab caught up to him as he wrestled with the second pack.

Stark looked up at his assailant, into the eyes of death, up at the hand grasping a gruesome nine-inch blade about to be plunged into him. And then they both heard, "Freeze or you're dead."

The terrorist took a look at the mere woman pointing a puny pistol in his direction, raised his eyes to heaven, laughed at her, and brought the blade down towards his victim.

Ona's first shot stopped the terrorist in his tracks, a shocked look of disbelief on his face. The second shot, a fraction of a second later, tore that look right off the face, entering through the cheek, splintering teeth and bone, finally lodging in the brain. Admiral Stark pushed the body away and got out from under it.

Ona caught up to Boxer and his opponent still locked in a death struggle on the steps. She kicked the terrorist's jaw to get his attention, and twisted the barrel of her pistol into his ear. "Freeze or you're a dead man," she ordered. "Just like your partner there."

He thought about it for a moment, caught a glance of the woman holding a gun on him, trying to make up his mind. He hesitated too long. When his eyes focused again on Boxer, he saw a fist of fury bearing down on his face, the last thing he was to see for a while. Boxer's blow broke the guy's nose and slammed his head back against the stone steps, knocking him unconscious.

"You okay, Jack?"

Boxer got up, brushed the dirt off his pants, and examined the bloody mess all over his aloha shirt. "Yeah, I'll be alright. Thanks, Ona. You did a great job. I really mean it."

"All I did was what I was trained to do. It took real courage to do what you did, going after those two guys unarmed. And Admiral Stark. He risked his life to get rid of those explosive packs. He's a real hero."

"We'd better go see how he's doing. Can you cuff this one?"

A screech from behind turned them around. The Volvo was screeching towards the steps, the driver leaning out the window, firing shots at them. The rounds worked their way directly toward Ona. Boxer threw his body on her, knocking her aside, sending her gun flying. A slug struck the very spot where she'd just been standing.

Boxer picked up Ona's pistol and ran down the steps, trying to draw off the driver's fire. The driver leaned out into the open and fired one round at Boxer. The bullet struck the flesh of his thigh and gouged out a groove front to back. Boxer went down on one knee and fired off three shots. One round smashed the windshield and came to rest inside the Volvo. The second and third shots slammed into the driver's chest. He was dead before he landed backward on the pavement.

Seemingly from out of nowhere, several military vehicles came upon the scene, sirens wailing, MPs with weapons drawn converging on the memorial steps. What they saw was a dead man laying in a pool of his own blood beside a Volvo with its windshield shot out; two more guys, Arabs maybe, sprawled on the stairway, bloody and handcuffed, and an old man looking down on an apparently dead man laying on some kind of knapsack. And then there was the guy in the fancy shirt sitting down on the steps, blood running from a leg wound, and a girl at his side pressing a cloth against his leg, trying to stem the flow of blood.

A burly MP walked up to Boxer and Ona, his M-16 at the ready, and said, "You folks mind telling me what the hell's going on here?"

"I'm Admiral Jack Boxer, on special assignment out of Pearl Harbor. The elderly gentleman up there in the blue blazer is retired Admiral Stark, the former CNO. This woman's identity is none of your concern for now."

The MP said, "Show some ID."

"What's your name, Corporal?" Boxer asked him.

Somewhat taken aback, the MP replied, "Smith. Corporal Eldridge Smith."

"Well, Smith. I suggest you get on the phone to Admiral Willis at CINCPACFLT headquarters and tell him who you have here. I'm sure he'll tell you how to handle this."

It took about twenty minutes for Willis to get a cleanup crew out to Punchbowl, to gather everyone up—dead and alive—and cart them off to the base. Admiral Stark was shaken up but okay. Ona was too. Boxer was treated for what turned out to be a nasty flesh wound, stitched up, and told to stay off of the leg. Not much chance, Boxer

122

figured, the way things were going from bad to worse.

Boxer and Ona cleaned up and changed into some fresh aloha wear. They were whisked to Willis's office where they were told that the four terrorists were part of a splinter faction of the PLO, but so much more radical that once the two groups fought a bloody battle in Tripoli, with the Syrians taking the rebels' side and driving Arafat's boys out to sea.

They had planned a series of terrorist raids on frequently visited tourist sites in an effort to keep the hundreds of thousands of expected visitors away from the Pearl Harbor Day fest. They almost succeeded. In fact, Willis told them, there was evidence found in the Volvo that they were going to try for a suicide raid on the Arizona Memorial, by air or by boat, of all things. "Good work, both of you," he told them.

Boxer put an arm around Ona. "We were just fortunate to be in the right place that time, Admiral. We may not be so lucky next time."

Willis glanced at his watch. "0430 already. You two may as well knock off for the day."

"Thank you, Admiral. If its all the same, I've got work to do."

Ona nodded. "Me, too, sir. Admiral Boxer hasn't seen much of the city, yet. And tomorrow, I want to show him around by air. I've got a chopper lined up to take us over all the islands."

"Well, with that full day ahead of you tomorrow, I'd better let you get on with your work tonight. Admiral Stark is staying on as my guest for a few days. We're going to swap old war stories."

And a lot more, Boxer thought. A naval officer could learn a lot from Stark, even CINCPACFLT. Boxer saluted and held the door open for Ona. This time there was no protest.

"I'm getting hungry," she said as they walked to her tour van.

"Me, too. Haven't eaten since breakfast. You want to check out the commissary?"

She made a face. "I know a really nice restaurant in Waikiki. Do you like Italian?"

"Sure, sounds good to me."

"Hop in. This time we'll take the scenic route."

The scenic route was Route 92, which skirted the shore-line once they were past the airport. It starts off as Nimitz Highway, picks up the bend around Honolulu Harbor where it becomes Ala Moana Park Drive. Boxer's head turned more than once at the sight of the pretty joggers getting their exercise in the tree-lined park. Then across the canal and around the unused Fort De Russy where they merged with Kalakaua Avenue and into the heavily congested Waikiki Beach area. Ona drove the van through the narrow one-way streets of the resort area dominated by dozens of high-rise hotels. She parked in the loading area of the Sheraton Waikiki. "Let's walk. It's only a few blocks."

The lobby of La Trattoria boasted a montage of photos of the greats and near-greats who had eaten there, all signed and wishing the owner lots of luck. When they were seated, Boxer asked the waiter, Mario, what he would recommend.

"You like veal, Signore?"

Boxer nodded.

"Try the Saltimboca. It's our specialty."

Ona ordered the Fra Diavolo, and they munched bread-sticks and drank Bordeaux until the meal came. They polished off a second bottle with their meal, and topped off their feast with espresso and Sambuca. "Best meal I've had in ages," Boxer told her. "Thanks for the recommendation, Ona."

"Thanks for dinner," she replied, as Boxer paid the tab.

Back outside the restaurant, they walked arm in arm. Boxer breathed in the cool evening breeze. "I guess I could go for a long walk about now, to get my head functioning again."

Ona stopped and turned to face him. "What I could go for right now, Jack Boxer, is your body. The dinner and the wine were nice and relaxing, after what we've been through this afternoon, but what I want is to get laid."

Boxer stopped short. His face broke out in a grin. "Just like that?"

She smiled back. "Just like that. Did I shock you?"

Boxer just said, "I guess I'm still a little old-fashioned. Is romance dead?"

She said, "I already told you, I don't have time for that. The pressures of the job, and all that. Besides, what's the matter with you, sailor? What happened to a girl in every port?"

Boxer slipped his arm around her. "I don't need a girl in every port. But I can really appreciate someone special like you. Shall we get a hotel room?"

"Too expensive, Jack. They're priced for the tourists. Besides, they're probably all booked. It's still in season. I have an apartment in town that I share with another agent. She's away on assignment right now on the Big Island. We'll have the place all to ourselves."

Boxer squeezed her to him, and they walked arm and arm to the van. "I thought you said you lived on Maui?"

"I have a house on Maui, way out near Hana," she answered, holding the door open for him, then sliding it closed. She walked around to the driver's side and got in. "The apartment here is just to crash in once in awhile, and to keep some extra clothes."

They recrossed the canal and headed out toward a more residential area, mostly small homes set off with hibiscus hedges, and shaded by palm trees. She pulled the van into the driveway of one such house. "Well, here we are," she said, getting out. "Home sweet home."

Chapter 13

The house was rather spartan, a small kitchen off the living room and two moderate-sized bedrooms. The furnishings were unpretentious, as well.

"Be it ever so humble," Ona quipped.

Boxer took in the living room. Very utilitarian furniture. Sofa with matching chair in wormwood and a Hawaiian print fabric, a coffee table and two end tables, an overstuffed lounge chair, and an assortment of photo blow-ups and numbered prints of the beautiful Hawaiian scenery on the walls. "The pictures are beautiful," Boxer commented.

"They're the only thing of value in the place. They're mostly the work of local artists and photographers. Aleana, my roommate, and I are trying to do our little part in supporting the arts. Other than that, what you see came with the apartment when we leased it." Ona kicked off her shoes. "I'm feeling a bit grungy. I could stand a shower. How about you?"

"Tell you the truth, I feel like I've been run over by a steamroller. A hot shower sounds good."

"Why don't you go ahead. I'll see if I can find something for a nightcap. The bathroom's between the two bedrooms. Towels in the linen closet."

"Thanks, Ona. Vodka will be fine if you've got some."

"Sure," she called out from the kitchen. "Got one of everything — vodka, scotch, bourbon, gin, and three kinds of beer. And a bag of Maui potato chips. Something from each of the basic food groups."

Boxer stripped off his clothes and got the shower going really hot. The steamy shower felt good pounding down on his neck and shoulders, melting away some of the aches and muscle knots caused by his fight with the terrorists earlier. He stood there facing the shower head, letting the hot water do its work, now streaming down his head and face.

The small hands pressing into the flesh of his shoulders came as a surprise to Boxer. "Changed my mind," Ona teased, pressing her naked body against his, wrapping her arms around his chest, sliding one hand down across the muscular ridges of his abdomen, until she found what she wanted. "I'd rather play than drink right now," she said.

"How can a guy resist," Boxer smiled. "Let me finish washing up."

She took the soap from him and began lathering his body, paying special attention to the object of her passion. "There, you ought to be clean as a whistle, now," she said finally. "Why don't we dry off?"

They stepped out of the tub. Ona tossed him a thick towel, and went to him with a second one, blotting the water from his skin while he dried his hair. Then she grabbed another towel and wrapped it around herself. "That's good enough for government work," she said, and tossed her towel in the hamper. She turned provocatively. "Come with me, lover."

Boxer followed her into the far bedroom, slightly favoring his wounded leg. She bent over to turn back the covers, then turned back, looping her arms around his neck.

Boxer lifted her easily, and laid her gently on the bed. Ona slid over and he got in beside her. She put her head back on the pillow, her hair flowing out beneath her. Her beauty reminded him of a Gauguin painting. "I want you inside me, darling. I want you to come in me."

She guided him into her and Boxer closed his eyes, grimacing in delight. Slowly at first they began to rise and fall, coming apart and pressing together, bringing one another to new heights of bliss. After what seemed like forever, Ona's eyes closed, her head tossed backward. "Oh, Jack, now, *now* my darling." And then, totally spent, she fell into his arms. They lay there together, breathing deeply, softly, melding their bodies into one.

Boxer kissed her face tenderly. "I must be in heaven."

She kissed him back, arms holding on tight, the beautiful long black hair covering them both. "Oh, darling. I'm in paradise."

"Paradise." Yoshinobu Tora stood there on the main deck of his pleasure yacht, dressed in black slacks and a black knit shirt with an orange tiger embroidered on the breast pocket, his arms uplifted as if delivering a benediction. "Paradise will be ours once again," said the head of the world's second largest merchant fleet to the small, elite group of his colleagues. "Our comrades have succeeded on all fronts, except in Germany. We are still not quite certain what caused the failure of that mission."

A general raised his voice above the murmurings of the small group, perhaps a dozen in all. "The Germans should have been better trained. Those Beider-Meinhofs," he had trouble with the pronunciation, "are just a band of brigands, undisciplined compared to our own country's heros."

Tora held up a hand for silence. "The German mission was a long-shot at best. Had it succeeded, it would have been a wonderful coup, to pluck a jewel from the breast of our former allies, who have become nothing more than puppet stooges of Americans. But I can assure you, General Okihara, that with the three stolen submarines, and with our land-based forces in place in Hawaii, we shall have no trouble in dealing a death blow to our mortal enemy, the U.S."

A very frail, bent man with a wispy white beard, stood up with the aid of a cane. "It is the only way to lift the yoke of disgrace the Americans have dealt us with the disarmament and occupation after the cowardly surrender."

"Here, here," shouted an elderly gentleman, also dressed in black, with a blazer jacket emblazoned with the Tora tiger insignia. "We would surely have won that war had our leaders not bowed under the threat of still another nuclear devastation. What is a hundred thousand deaths compared to the glory of world domination? We should never have allowed them to humiliate us so."

"Yoshi," Gen. Okihara interrupted, "please expound upon your statement about the three submarines. I count only two."

Tora was all smiles. "Ah, our brothers on the island of Taipan have done us a great service. Their hatred for the government that exiled them to their island home and forced the United Nations to sever relations in favor of the Communists is exceeded only by their greed. They have performed well for us, stealing a diesel powered hunter-killer."

"Not nuclear?" the general asked.

"Alas, no, it is not, my General. Remember though, the significant destruction our non-nuclear subs wrecked upon our enemies during the Great War. The Chinese submarine is fully crewed and is at this moment steaming for Oahu. Soon, the *Ichi-Ban* will return home to escort the NATO sub to the islands just in time to surprise our enemies."

The bent old man once again struggled to his feet. "I must ask you again, Yoshi, why wait so long when an attack now would assure our goals."

"Dear Toshio," Tora said to the former assistant minister of war," "We must show our enemies that we can, and will strike a deathblow to their Pacific fleet today just as we did fifty years ago. And we will do it on the very same day, December seventh. At 0600, our submarines will commence with the torpedoing of the American, Soviet, and British carriers, and as many of the remaining warships as possible until we are stopped.

"At the same time, our small fleet of privately owned jets which have been fitted with contact explosives will dive bomb the largest targets left."

"Kamikaze," someone shouted.

Others picked up the chorus. "Kamikaze, kamikaze, kamikaze."

Tora held up his arms for quiet. When they calmed down he added, "In the next month and half, our agents will have infiltrated the headquarters of the Pacific Fleet and assassinated their leader and many of his high-ranking subordinates."

Cheers went up among the circle of old men.

Yoshinobu Tora went on, "On the Big Island of Hawaii, we will attempt to awaken the sleeping devils that lie within the Kilauea volcano, coaxing it to spew forth its fiery lava on the fools who insist on living and working along its flanks. On Kauai, we shall endeavor to destroy the missile facility at Barking Sands. On Maui, our target will be the Kahului Airport. But remember, our primary goal is the destruction of Pearl Harbor."

A chant of Tora, Tora, Tora went up from the group, building in volume, taking on an almost unearthly sound. Tora, Tora, Tora—the name taken by a war criminal who was hounded underground by the occupying allies after World War II, the man who would build a world-class fleet of merchant ships, become one of Japan's leading citizens, a man who would never forget. He had taken his name from Commander Fuchida's signal to the Japanese Strike Group that they had achieved absolute surprise over the enemy, and that victory was assured. Tora, Tora, Tora.

This time Yoshi let the chanting go on until it died out minutes later. "This meeting of the Shogun Society is concluded," he said. "Now, for some entertainment." At his signal, the bulkhead opening onto the main deck was opened and a dozen geisha girls in traditional dress padded out to greet Tora's guests. They were bearing trays of saki and tea, fruits and sweets for the mostly elderly group. "Don't forget the baths, my friends. The girls will be happy to show you a good time."

Chapter 14

Boxer awakened to the aroma of freshly brewed Kona coffee, the island's finest. He stretched and absentmindedly reached for Ona next to him. She wasn't there, but she had left behind reminders of her presence, her warmth on the bed, and her sweet, musky fragrance.

Just then she walked through the doorway into the bedroom. "Good morning, lover. Fresh coffee and breakfast, compliments of the lady of the house."

Boxer smiled up at her, arms outstretched. She looked beautiful in the early morning sunlight that filtered into the room. Ona stood there barefoot, a floral print skirt wrapped around her waist, and nothing else, her bare breasts jutting out to tease him. She turned back toward the kitchen. "Come and get it," she laughed.

Boxer slipped into his skivvies and padded into the small kitchen. The table was set with the coffee, a freshly sliced pineapple at the peak of flavor, a stack of pancakes garnished with coconut and fresh fruit, and glasses of papaya juice. Boxer scratched his head and made for the chair she beckoned him into.

"The answer is, yes, I can cook, too. I hope you enjoy everything. It's not often I get to prepare breakfast for a man."

He smiled and dug into the food, washing down mouthfuls of pancakes with the delicious coffee. "My compliments to the chef. This sure is a feast, and, I may add, also a feast for my eyes. You look beautiful."

"Flattery will get you nowhere, Jack. We've got lots of work to do today."

They ate together, Boxer helping himself to two more cups of the steaming brew before he finished. He helped her clear the table, standing behind her at the sink, pressing his body into hers, planting little kisses behind her ears.

That was all she needed. She turned around to face him, arms around his neck.

They made love with a vengeance that came of sharing danger together, knowing full well that either or both of them could easily be killed on their next assignment, knowing that this peaceful time together could be their last.

When they were finally spent, they lay there together in a heap, dozing in each other's arms. It was 0830 when they took the Hula Tours van back to the base. Ona escorted Boxer to the circular helicopter pad that bordered Hickam Air Force Base and the Honolulu Airport. She took him to a Bell 206-B Jet Ranger chopper, a five-seater that was the workhorse of the island's helicopter tour companies. This particular one had the same pineapple-rainbow logo as her van, and was also labelled Hula Tours.

"Watch your head, Jack."

Boxer was already crouched low as he made his way to the passenger side door that she held open for him. Ona went around and got into the pilot's seat.

"Where's the skipper?" Boxer shouted over the din.

"You're looking at her." She was pointing to her chest. Here, put on this headset. You'll find it more pleasant than yelling back and forth."

Boxer slipped the headset over his ears and spoke in a

monotone into the mike. "Do you read me?"

Thumbs up. "Read you loud and clear. Ready for take-off?"

"I guess so." He smiled at her. "Is there anything you *can't* do?"

Ona pulled back on the throttle. "If you stick around long enough, you'll find out. There's not much, I'll tell you that. I can also fly a small plane, but this is more fun."

While Boxer buckled himself in with his seat belt, Ona was busy on the radio getting permission from the tower for lift-off. Consent given, she adjusted some controls and pulled back slightly on the steering yoke. The Bell Jet Ranger lifted off, hovered momentarily twenty feet off the ground, and then lunged forward and upward over the lagoon. Once over the ocean, it veered west along the coast over the Barbers Point Naval Station. She pointed out the sites, keeping up a pleasant chatter about the various facilities that they encountered.

"I've never seen Pearl Harbor from the air except on aerial photos. I've always come in by sea. Actually, this is only my second trip. The first was many years ago, before I earned my Dolphins."

"In that case, I'll give you the deluxe tour, a bird's-eye view of all the military locations on the island, plus a free gift from Hilo Hattie's," she smiled, making reference to the creator of the colorful clothing that they wore.

Boxer paid rapt attention as he looked out the side window at the airfield below.

"That's Wheeler Field you're looking at. Up ahead," she pointed to a break in the mountain range that ran parallel to the western shore. "That's Kolekole Pass."

"Oh, yes. That was the route of the Japanese attack on Pearl."

135

They continued through the pass and on over the Schofield Barracks, Boxer making mental notes, as they continued on over the north shore, flew low over the Turtle Bay Hilton, veered easterly and slid down the east coast, taking in the splendor of the mountain range that split the island north to south. Ona set down on peninsula that housed the Marine Corps Naval Station for refueling. "Whenever you're ready," she told him, "we're going to do some island hopping."

"No time like the present." He nodded and Ona took them aloft once more.

"From the looks of the military posts on Oahu, it doesn't look as if a terrorist group would stand much of a chance to do much harm."

"That's what they thought in Nineteen forty-one. Remember," Boxer said, "there will be hundreds of thousands of visitors congregated in a very small area, to say nothing about some of the most expensive warships afloat." He braced himself as the Bell helicopter swooped hard to the west. He continued, "It wouldn't take much to cause a lot of damage, or kill thousands of spectators. A submarine let loose in there, or a light plane, even a chopper like this one, could set off enough explosives to cripple a carrier, or a heavy cruiser, or blow up the airfield. Just think of it."

Ona shivered. "It gives me the chills. Hang on, we're heading out to Kauai. If I wanted to hide a small band of armed men, the Na Pali Coast of Kauai would be just the place. It's almost inaccessible by land, except by hiking trail. You could hole up in there for a month without being noticed."

In fifteen minutes they were passing over the airport at Lihui and swinging south along the coast. "This island has clusters of resorts dotting the coast — north, east and south. The northwest coast consists of steep cliffs jutting into the sea, interspersed with tiny, white sandy beaches which you can only reach by boat or raft. A secluded paradise."

"Or a good hideout, depends on how you look at it," Boxer said.

"I've got to show you Waimea Canyon, Jack. You could put a thousand people in there and no one would ever find them. It looks like the Grand Canyon, only smaller."

Ona followed the flow of a north-south mountain ridge for about five minutes before coming to a sharp precipice. "Hang on tight, Jack and watch this." Ona banked the chopper sharply to the left and seemingly fell down hundreds of feet along the rocky canyon face, levelling off above an almost dry riverbed, and then climbing back up the opposite face, within feet of fern covered rock wall.

Boxer felt queasy. "Hold on, cowboy. I left my stomach down there at the bottom, someplace."

Ona chuckled. "Sorry, lover. You do this often enough, you get used to it. I'll take it a little easier from now on. I'm going to wing out over the Na Pali Coast that I told you about."

And away they soared, down the side of cliff that ran in jagged fingers down to the sea. The chopper hovered over the water a hundred yards offshore, slowly making its way along the rugged, pristine coastline. The shore was dotted with sea caves, lava tubes, rock arches, and secluded sandy beaches, harboring thousands of places to hide.

"I'd like to come back and explore this by sea," Boxer told her. "Another day."

"Roger that, Admiral, as you sailors like to say. Let me show you the crater. It's the wettest spot on earth."

Boxer laughed. "You're really taking this tour guide stuff seriously."

"It's been my cover for almost two years, now. I don't want to blow it. Even some of my close friends think that's what I really do for a living, and I'm not about to disappoint them. On your left. . . ."

Chapter 15

The grey military transport touched down at Hickam Field at 0900 under cloudless skies and bright sunshine. Maj. Roland Jones hefted his seventy-pound pack onto his shoulder and was first off the plane. "Okay," he barked. "Move it out."

Long John Silverman stooped to avoid striking his head on the bulkhead and led his squad of ten men down the boarding ladder, followed by Sgt. Carlos Rivera and his squad. Mean Gene Greene got to his feet and said, "Let's go, men," and he and ten more descended. Noticeably absent was "Snappy" Snappiello, who had lost his life in the Arctic along with twenty-seven other Rangers fighting for the Omega Weather Station.

Rolly and Gene were driven to the headquarters building of the 15th Air Base Wing and presented their orders to the CO. "Morning, Major, Corporal. Welcome to Hickam. I see you have a meeting with CINCPACFLT. Would you care to have breakfast first?"

Jones stood at attention. "No, thank you, Colonel. I'm anxious to get started and I'd like to meet with the old man as soon as possible."

"Right. I'll have a driver take you to headquarters in ten minutes. You know, I've heard a lot about you, Major. You've got quite a reputation."

"Reputations are built on the quality of men who serve under you, Colonel, as you well know. And unfortunately, my reputation cost the lives of many good men. In fact, I'm a squad short. I understand I'm to pick up some replacements at the Marine Corps base here on Oahu."

"I'm sure the admiral will have that worked out for you." At that time, an MP knocked at the door and announced himself. "Private, take these two men to CINCPACFLT Headquarters."

The MP saluted the colonel and Jones. "Yes, sir. Right this way, Major."

Mean Gene shrugged and hoisted his pack onto his shoulders, picked up Rolly's and followed him and the MP to a waiting jeep. They were at headquarters in ten minutes. It was hurry up and wait.

Because of Boxer's sterling recommendation, Willis had wanted to meet the leader of Rolly's Rangers personally. Rolly was to fly over to the Mokapu Peninsula and report to the Kaneohe Marine Corps Base where he was to pick up his reinforcements. "Now, if you'll excuse me. Major, I have an appointment to attend to, also. If you're going my way, we can walk out together."

The admiral's vehicle was an Olds '88 Luxury Edition, painted gray, of course, but with many amenities not found on standard issue. There was a gold Navy seal on the doors, and in black, bold letters, CINCPACFLT. A driver stood at attention holding open the rear door. Willis stepped out under the port-cochere, stopped, looked through his papers, and said, "Damn, but I'm getting forgetful. I've left something on my desk."

Rolly said, "I'd be happy to get it for you, Admiral."

"Quite alright, son. I get so little exercise anymore. You go on ahead."

Rolly and Gene waited in the shade for their jeep to return when Adm. Willis stepped through the doors and walked toward the Olds. They watched the driver suddenly make a face, sniff the air around the car, then stick his head into the interior.

Rolly had a premonition of what might be happening, and shouted, "Admiral, no. Stay back." He raced toward Willis, reaching him just in time. The force of the explosion threw his body crashing into the admiral, blanketing the old man from the blast. The glass entrance doors to the building were shattered, Mean Gene was knocked off his feet, and the car and driver were a twisted remains of charred steel and bones and blood. The Olds lay on its side, a gaping burned out crater marking its former place in the courtyard.

Gene was the first to move. He ran to the supine bodies of Rolly and the admiral and got down on his knees next to them. He gingerly touched Jones's shoulder. "Rolly? Rolly, you okay?"

Rolly Jones moaned and rolled off the body beneath him. He placed his hands over his ears. "Oh, my fucking ears. Yeah, Gene, I'm alright. How's the admiral?"

Willis's facial expression was a blank. Then he blinked, his lips twitched, and he, too, held his ears. "Wha . . . What happened?"

"Your car," Rolly answered hesitantly. "It exploded. Somebody planted a bomb under your car, from the looks of it. Sir, if you hadn't gone back in for those papers, you'd have been in it."

Willis was visibly shaken. They helped him to his feet and brushed off his uniform. "Looks like you saved my life, son," he told Rolly. "I won't forget it." And looking around the courtyard, he asked, "My driver? Has anyone seen Murphy?

"You don't want to look, Admiral," Rolly told him.

"Oh, my god," Willis exclaimed, peering past Jones's body at the twisted wreck. "Who . . . ? How . . . ?"

141

Rolly shook his head. "I don't know, Admiral. Somehow, someone infiltrated your motor pool and placed explosives under the chassis. Whoever these terrorists are they'll stop at nothing."

"My god," Willis said to no one in particular, as swarms of men converged on the scene. "Isn't anything safe around here?"

No one spoke. They just stood there, pondering the admiral's words, and wondering the same thing. Is nothing safe?

Shari and Dave, Vernon, with his coke-bottle thick glasses; fifty-one-year-old Arnie and the two cute black chics; and Buster waited around the campfire for the girl with long blond hair and big boobs, and her Neanderthal boyfriend to return with the fruit. As they sat around munching fish and rice, licking their fingers and casually tossing fishbones over their shoulders into the surf, one couldn't help but notice the diversity of the group, seeming to have absolutely no common ground, save one. They were all naked.

Shari was petite, trim and muscular, and the group's newest member. She had come to Hawaii on a vacation and decided to stay on after meeting Dave. Fun-loving, adventuresome Dave, who told her of wondrous times to be had for free. Food free for the picking in the hidden lush Na Pali valleys, or for the sharing with some friends of his who shed their clothes and came together from time to time in their wilderness hideaway.

Dave had been a football hero at the University of Hawaii, a Greek god's body now gone to pot from too much beer, long, sun-bleached hair reaching to his shoulders, an out-of-shape beach bum who loved the good life in his island paradise.

Vern was thin and darkly tanned all over, showing none of the telltale part-time nudist white patches of Shari and Dave. He didn't contribute much to the group, except to occasionally offer to share a bottle of Thunderbird wine, his constant companion.

No one seemed to know where Arnie came from. The wise old man with salt-and-pepper hair, thin on top, almost gone, pulled back into a short ponytail, and a long, unkempt beard. He was never far from his beat up old Ovation guitar, and led the group in communal singing of the folk songs that built reputations for Pete Seeger, Arlo Guthrie, Peter, Paul and Mary, and others. Arnie, always the old hippie who wouldn't or couldn't change with the times, living on memories and Maui Wowee and Kona Gold.

He was constantly attended by the two black girls who didn't say much, but loved doubling up on Arnie in nocturnal sex romps, and smoking his pot. Some thought they were sisters, but no one ever found out for sure. And Buster, the fat kid, passed out on the beach from too much vodka and pineapple juice, "Breakfast of Champions", as he referred to it when he was sober.

"Hey, Bra, wha' happen to Boobs and Otto? They been gone too long." Vernon liked to adopt the island slang, tried hard to be one of the gang.

"Why don't you go find out? You know, contribute something for a change," Dave challenged.

"Why da hell don't you?" Vern tossed back, then wishing he hadn't.

Dave got up and glared down at Vern, wanting to strike at the skinny leach, really hurt him, but settled for kicking sand at him.

"C'mon, Dave." Shari wrapped her hand around his

143

bulging biceps. "Let's go into the woods and look for them. C'mon okay?" Big smile, flashing white teeth glistening in the moonlight, the sheen of her skin bathed in the glow of the fire—Dave got the idea and an erection at the same time.

"Yeah," still giving the bad eye to Vernon, cowering there behind Arnie, knowing Dave wouldn't dare disturb their guru. Dave watched Shari break for the foliage. "Hey, wait up," he shouted after her. They carefully walked along a hiking trail leading to the dense foliage of the Kalalua Valley, replete with oranges, lemons, bananas, and mangoes—yours for the taking.

"Boobs? Otto?" Shari called.

"Boobs and Otto, where are you?" Dave took up the call.

No answer.

They continued to pick their way along the trail. And then, Shari suddenly stopped short, put her hand over her mouth and pointed up the trail ahead. Two bodies entwined in the age-old missionary position, the Neanderthal hulk of Otto, unmistakable even from the rear, atop a large woman, legs splayed out on their side under him, long, blonde hair cascading out from beneath his large head.

Dave suppressed a giggle. They'd found Boobs and Otto, alright. No wonder they were taking so long. Dave and Shari squatted down on their haunches to watch the show, holding hands just like at the movies. Boobs and Otto didn't move.

Shari whispered in his ear, "Do you think they screwed themselves into a coma?"

Dave smiled, shrugged, and got up. "One way to find out," he whispered.

Shari straightened up and followed him on tiptoes, so

as not to wake the lovers. "Look at all that fruit," she pointed out to Dave.

"There's enough there for everybody. Let's go bring it back to camp, let these two sleep it off."

They gingerly walked up to the fruit laying on the trail alongside the sleeping pair, and began gathering it up. Shari soon had her arms full of mangoes, and as she stood up, her foot slipped. Thinking she'd stepped on a piece of overripe fruit, she turned her head to look. "Uhh," she gasped. "D . . . d . . . Dave? Do you see what I see?"

Dave turned to look, his arms laden with fruit, his eyes squinting to adjust to the shadows on the moonlit trail. "What, Shar?"

"Oh my foot. Oh, Dave!"

There was no doubt. Shari and Dave were staring down at the puddle of coagulating blood oozing out from the blonde girl's head, matting the long, beautiful straw colored hair. Dave moved closer to Shari and put his arm around her, drawing her close. "Oh, my god, look," he said pointing down at the back of Otto's bashed in skull. "Killed where they lay," Dave muttered.

"Do you think . . . ?"

"No sense sticking around to find out," he said, turning to retrace their steps back to the beach.

Shari's voice behind him was a sudden shrill plea. "Dave!"

Dave turned around to see his girlfriend in the grasp of a body clad completely in black, a hand trying to stifle any sound coming from her mouth, the other around her waist, lifting her off the ground, dragging her back into the woods. Dave started towards them. "Hey, you. You can't . . . "

A blade slashed across Dave's face, cutting his words

145

off. Dave stood in shock, his hand to his face, unbelieving. A black clad figure jumped in front of him and delivered a quick kick to Dave's groin.

Dave groaned and doubled up, one hand grasping his throbbing testicles, the other unable to stop the flow of blood down his face. His assailant reached out and grabbed a handful of the thick bleached blond hair, and yanked Dave's head back. Before Dave could react, his throat had been deeply slashed. He wanted to call out to Shari, to anyone, to cry because of the unbelievable pain, but he bled to death before the words could come.

Shari watched the whole thing, knowing what was to come next, kicking and struggling to free herself from the grasp of the man holding her. Dave's killer turned to her and walked slowly closer and closer. The vice-like grip on her tightened. And all she could think of was, What was this Japanese guy dressed in one of those black Ninja costumes doing here in the middle of this tropical wonderland? And why was he killing them?

She never found out.

Vern was throwing little shells at Buster, trying to wake him from his drunken slumber. Arnie was strumming away, singing the refrain of "Puff, the Magic Dragon," about the mystical creature who had lived a few miles away, around the northern coast of Kauai, in the bay of Hanalei.

"Hey, wake up, Buster, I think we got company, Bra."

A shell landed on Buster's nose, waking him. He shook off the drunken stupor and sputtered at Vern. "Hey, screw off asshole, okay? No law against sleepin', is there?"

Vern listened to the sound of the surf lapping against the shore, and something else. Yeah, sure, there it is again. A Zodiak. "Don't you hear it? Listen up, Bra."

Buster sat up and craned his neck towards the surf.

146

"You're fulla it. No, hey, wait. Maybe . . . "

Arnie finished his song. One of the black girls wrapped her arms lovingly around his neck. The other had her face planted in Arnie's lap, oblivious to everything. Arnie smiled at Vern and Buster, held up a fist with pinky and thumb outstretched in the Shaka, or Hawaiian hang loose sign. "Hey, man, no problem. Someone wanna crash, let 'em." He picked up the guitar again. "Anybody know, *If I had a hammer?*"

Sunni Akima was the first out of the Zodiak, and reached his man, Buster, first. Buster was the first to die. Three more of Tora's commandos hit the beach simultaneously, overpowering Vernon, kicking him down and snuffing out his life with their blades.

The black girl around Arnie's neck tried to throw herself in front of him, to offer her body as a shield. It did no good. She was quickly tossed aside and killed. That left Arnie, sitting there, the hippie Budda, guitar in hand, a beautiful black girl with her face in his lap. He gave a halfhearted hang loose sign to the four black-clad commandos converging on him. He watched the guy who killed Buster reach into a waterproof holster and unleash a blued-steel revolver with a long barrel, which turned out to be a silencer. He watched Sunni Akima point the thing at him, standing there point blank, with the girl at his crotch never letting up. He watched the determined Oriental face grimace as his assailant squeezed the trigger, saw the twin flashes of light, heard the muffled thwumps at the same time he felt the searing pain in his chest, the force knocking him backward, his mind still trying to concentrate on the ministerings of his black girl wondering, Why couldn't they have let her finish?

147

Chapter 16

Boxer trotted in a crouch to the Hula Tours helicopter, and took his customary seat next to the pilot. This routine was becoming commonplace for him, and for Ona. Several times a week for the last month he took his maps and charts with him on the aerial tours of the islands, and had Ona swoop low to explore and mark off possible places from which a terrorist gang might launch an attack. Next week, he would begin checking them out on the ground with Rolly Jones.

The Rangers were back up to strength once more, with the acquisition of some Marine volunteers from the mainland and Sgt. Sam Turkell and a squad of Special Forces stationed on Oahu. On Monday, they would begin branching out squad by squad into the valleys and caves, and other natural hiding places to root out any terrorists who might be sheltered there.

When they were airborne, Ona said to Boxer, "This time I'm going to show you where I live on Maui. I've spoken to you often enough about it, but this time I'm going to take you there."

"I'm game."

The chopper flew east southeast for about fifteen minutes, bringing them over the Island of Molokai. "See that finger of land off the northern coast, right there about in the center?"

Boxer nodded.

"That's the Kalaupapa Peninsula, where Father Damien had his famous leper colony." She took the helicopter down lower to give him a better look.

"It's beautiful, and so isolated."

Ona smiled. "That's probably what keeps it looking like what the rest of Hawaii did before the tourist invasion. The only way down from the highlands is by mule. Now I'm going to take us over eastern Maui, where I live, past the town of Hana. That's also pretty remote. Wait until you see the highway to Hana. It's probably the worst roadway in the world."

Boxer unrolled his topographical map of Maui as they flew above the tourist areas on the western shore. "Too many visitors back there for the terrorists to make any use of it. Let's have a look at the north shore again."

"Agreed. There's some mighty rigged coastline running roughly parallel to the highway to Hana. There's deep canyons similar to Kauai's Na Pali coast. It's just as desolate. And the road follows the natural contours of the rock face, with over six hundred hairpin turns and more than fifty one-lane bridges. If two cars passed side by side in opposite directions going too fast, it would be curtains for at least one of them."

Boxer smiled. "Sounds like a suicide run."

"You're not kidding. Believe me, plenty of marriages have split up during that three-hour drive."

In a short while, Ona was setting her chopper down on the tiny Hana airport tarmac. "We'll drive from here. It's not very far."

The ride was short, but not sweet, even for Ona's Suzuki Samurai four-by-four. "I live down near the beach, at the edge of a taro farm. I have a fast boat that I keep under cover so it can't be seen from the sea. And the locals mind their own business. I feel secure way out here,

149

off the beaten path."

Boxer nodded. Ona let him drive, and he was doing his best to keep his eyes on the road ahead, while scanning the many switchbacks and undulations in the road up ahead for oncoming vehicles. Ona was right. This is one mean piece of road. "Hey, look up ahead, down the road apiece. That white car's almost too big for this roadway."

"That's a big, bad-ass Lincoln. The car rentals try to lease them to the tourists with the old bait and switch. You know, like, 'Well, sir, your basic rental pays for this shitty little foreign car, with hardly any room for the missus and the kids, you see. But this here Lincoln, hot damn, it's just your style.' " She sounded like a used car salesman and it gave Boxer a chuckle.

"So the sucker gets in the car back at the airport, no problem. And then someone tells him he's *got* to take the trip to Hana, there's so much to see, you know, the waterfalls, the rainbows, the Seven Sacred Pools, the kids'll just love it. What they don't tell him is that the rental car's much too big for the road. And the missus may divorce him before the ride's over."

Boxer pointed to the big car. "From here, it looks like he's going much too fast. The missus must be giving him hell."

That brought a laugh from Ona. The smile left her face as the Lincoln came closer. "Hey, slow down, jerk," she shouted, though the big car was too far away for the driver to hear her. She turned to Boxer. "Jack, be careful on the turns. That guy doesn't know what he's doing."

Boxer crossed a one lane bridge that began a precarious inside curve in the road. He watched with dismay as the white Lincoln passed a Toyota whose driver was approaching the turn ahead timidly. The Toyota veered into the guard rail and screeched to a halt at the last second before reaching the point of no return and sliding down the mountain face.

"Son-of-a-bitch," Boxer cursed. "Where the hell's he going?"

"Jack, it looks like he's trying to race you to the curve."

"Maybe." Boxer downshifted and floored the Samurai, at the same time switching to four-wheel drive. "We'll see about that."

"That's no family trip, Jack. There's four guys in that Lincoln, and they don't look like they belong here."

There was about a hundred yards between Boxer and the inside of the curve, and an equal distance from there to the Lincoln. "If they get to the corner first, they can block us, or worse. They could take the inside lane and shove us off the cliff. And it's a long way down."

"Jack, please be careful. Hey, the guys in the back have guns."

Boxer shifted up and put the pedal to the metal. "Brace yourself," he shouted. "And don't lean out."

"I have a handgun in my bag."

"Just keep your head down."

A hand holding a gun sprung out of the Lincoln's rear window. Two shots were fired.

"Get down." One slug pinged off the rock face. A second round barely missed Ona, ricochetting off the roll bar over her head.

"Jack, they're driving up the middle of the road."

Boxer's mind clicked with machine-like precision. In the split second before the inevitable happened, he had to decide if they were going for the inside lane and force him off the road, or to turn broadside and shoot them down. Fifty feet, both vehicles heading for the same strip of road, forty miles per hour. Only one could survive.

If the Lincoln took over Boxer's lane, there'd be no way

to avoid a head-on collision. If Boxer swerved to avoid the big car, he'd be dead too. Heads we lose, tails we lose. Fuck it. "Brace," he yelled and took the inside curve close, right up against the rock, pulled on the emergency brake, spun the wheel. The Samurai's rear spun and slammed into the rock, the front angled out. They came to an abrupt halt.

The Lincoln kept on coming. Brakes squealed, rubber burned, the big car skidded broadside to the road. "Keep down," Boxer shouted, released the brake, revved the engine, popped into first. Against a hail of gunfire, the Samurai leaped forward, rammed the Lincoln, caving in the doors, bulldozed it sideways to the precipice, pushing, shoving still; a bull hooking a picador's unwary steed, going for the kill.

The Lincoln teetered on the edge of the road, balanced precariously between the road and disaster, just holding on.

Boxer shifted his vehicle into reverse, backed up a few feet, neutral, revved it up, slipped into first, the bull charging its tormentors one last time.

The Lincoln's driver tried desperately to get out, but his door was jammed. A shot from the back seat, too high. Four terror-stricken men. No place to hide. No place to run.

Boxer's nostrils flared. A crazed look came over his face, a look that told his assailants that they had lost. The Samurai hit the Lincoln with such force that it flipped over on its side, then its roof, over and over, bouncing off the cliff face, rolling, then front to back, head over heals. On the last hop, the Lincoln landed hard on its gas tank, and exploded with a tremendous whump and a fireball that enveloped it.

Boxer watched from the edge of the road, his vehicle

stopping just in time. He wondered whether the fall had killed them before they burned.

Ona sat there next to him in the front seat, arms crisscrossed in front of her, shaking uncontrollably. "Oh, Jack."

He put his arm around her. "Whoever they were, they knew you, Ona. Your cover's been blown. From now on, you'd better stick with me."

She buried her face in his chest, trying to hold back the urge to cry. She mumbled, "You don't have to ask me twice."

Shari Eisenstein's mother was worried when her daughter didn't show up at home as promised one week after the rest of the family. She became frantic when the poor little rich kid from Short Hills, New Jersey, was overdue by two weeks, and called the state police in Honolulu to find her daughter.

The only lead was that Shari Edelstein had linked up with a surfer on the north shore, who was a friend of a friend. And the beach bum, Dave Bollar, a University of Hawaii dropout, had friends on Kauai who liked to camp out in nude.

The prime camping grounds on Kauai were along the Na Pali coast and the lush valleys just inland, part of the state park system. The state police contacted the park ranger, who informed them that the most popular campgrounds were in the Kalalau Valley, a haven for hermits, dropouts, hippies, nudists, druggies, and acid heads, along with the occasional backpacker.

And, yes, to think of it, he had noticed something strange in the past week or so. The "Hole-in-the Wall Gang" seemed to have disappeared. The more-or-less loose group of squatters had along overstayed their camping permits and were living off the land in the valley and on the beach, which was not tolerated. He would see their campfire at night, but when he looked for them the next day they seemed to have disappeared into a hole-in-the-wall. Members would come and go, new ones replacing the brethren who moved on to other things. But this time, the entire band seemed to have disappeared at once. One night he had seen their campfire and then they seemed to have gone for good. But it just hadn't set right with him, glad you asked, he told the state police lieutenant.

The park ranger had made inquiries at the adjacent Barking Sands Missile Range Facility. And the Barking Sands CO mentioned it to CINCPACFLT in report, a copy of which was on Boxer's desk when he arrived Monday morning at 0630.

"Look for some spoiled brat from the mainland when I check out the Na Pali coast today?"

Capt. Ted Lewis, Willis's aide, shrugged. "The old man seems to think it will go a long way in regaining some good will toward the military in Hawaii. Besides, you and your men are going there anyway, and Admiral Willis thinks that maybe there's a connection sitting out there waiting to be connected."

"So now I'm a babysitter?"

"Orders, Admiral Boxer. Sorry. Do the best you can, okay?"

"Sure. Sorry to take it out on you, Ted. I'm just blowing off steam. The big day takes place in three weeks, we finally got the Soviets back in, the Brits don't want to be moored anywhere near the Ruskies, there's two, maybe three hostile submarines out there, and we haven't come close to finding the crazies who are hell bent on destroying Pearl Harbor again. I have enough on my mind

154

without having to find a lost kid who'd rather be here fucking her brains out with the local beach boys than back at school in New Jersey."

Rolly Jones arrived at Boxer's office at 0700, bringing with him his four squad leaders, Rivera, Long John, Mean Gene, and Sam "Turk" Turkell. Looking at Turk, Boxer wondered if this is what our primeval ancestors looked like. Sam was very thick across the shoulders and chest, wide-boned and heavily muscled, and with a big, round head that sported a short brown crewcut. He had been the All-Hawaii karate champ, but was so mean and devastating an opponent that they had asked him to stop competing. Boxer thought he'd do just fine.

Ona joined them momentarily, and marking their maps, they sectioned off the Na Pali area among them. Rolly was to oversee Mean Gene's and Long John's groups. Boxer took Rivera and Turk, and of course, Ona would stay with him, both for her own protection and her local knowledge. They would board four inflatable Zodiaks at Barking Sands and hit the beach at different sites along the coast. The area was being cleared of tourists and the tour companies were ordered to stay clear of Na Pali due to "military maneuvers" in the area.

Boxer, Ona, and Turk's squad landed on a white, sandy stretch of beach that showed signs of having been inhabited regularly until perhaps a week or so ago. There were the remains of a campfire left to burn out on its own, as if the campers couldn't be bothered with dousing the flames and burying the ashes as courtesy would dictate. There were fishbones everywhere, as well as putrefied scraps of meat and rotted fruit. The Rangers immediately quieted down and secured their weapons, M-16s, machetes, knives, and some personal handguns. From this point on, they understood that their lives could depend on their spotting an enemy before being seen or heard by them.

Ona was dressed like the rest of them: Khakis, rubber boots, day pack on her back, and hair under a waterproof slouch hat. She carried only her automatic, and some extra ammo clips.

Ron Sledge would walk point. He was thin and wiry, a hundred and sixty pounds of fury just waiting to be unleashed. He took shit from no man. Turk would follow at a distance, along with Dandy Don Donaldson, known as Triple D, and Will Rockers. Boxer, Ona and two more Rangers would come next, forming the wings of a phalanx, with the remaining five men bringing up the rear. They could be looking for just a bunch of drugged-out hippies trying to keep out of the park ranger's way, but the strike force all treated this exercise as if their lives depended on it.

The beachhead was backed by a tropical forest that made up the valley floor back to the rocky cliff face. A well worn hiking trail cut a path through the foliage, stretched back toward the volcanic cliffs where it began its climb up the steep slopes. A magnificent hundred-foot-high falls cascaded down to form a icy cold stream that dissected the trail and continued its flow out to sea.

Lush foliage prevailed throughout the valley, tall trees interspersed with low-lying ferns and shrubs. A primordial paradise.

After about a quarter mile of progress, Ron Sledge came upon a suspicious area about a dozen feet off to the side of the trail. The underbrush had been trampled, and what appeared to be dried blood was splattered about. An animal slaughtered here? Sledge signalled with a predetermined bird call and made his way back to Turk for a huddle.

156

Turk ordered a halt and went ahead to check out for himself the site that had bothered his point man. He concurred with Sledge. An animal, or animals had undoubtedly been killed here. The question remained, was it the "Hole-in-the-Wall" gang seeking a change in their fish and fruit diet, or were they the prey of someone else? Up to this point, they were merely searching for a band of dropouts living off the land without a permit. Harmless enough. But this discovery certainly changed things.

Turk returned to warn his men. From now on they were on full alert. There was a strong chance that foul play had beset the group. His commandos would go on the assumption that someone armed and dangerous lurked in the valley. Who they were and how many were not known. At best, they were looking for a couple of psychopathic killers, if in fact, any of the hippie band was killed. The group had nothing of value to offer a thief, not even clothing, if the park ranger was correct.

In the worst case, which Boxer suspected, they were up against a terrorist hit-team staking out a place of concealment from which to mount a strike against Pearl Harbor. Either way, Turk realized that his men were walking into danger.

Further on, Sledge came upon a narrow clearing, a natural resting spot where the stream crossed the road before running roughly parallel to it out to sea. There were smooth lava rocks lining both banks of the stream, some low foliage, and a clump of tall trees up ahead and forty yards off the trail to the left. A huge boulder had come to rest long ago to the right of the path, beyond the stream. A nice restful place to hold a picnic before hiking up the slopes. Sledge continued ahead, warily.

He forded the stream, five feet wide at this point, being careful not to slip on the algae covered rocky creek bed.

157

Turk followed at a discreet distance, using the low-lying shrubbery as cover, with Triple D and Rickers slightly behind him, and on either side of the road. By the time Boxer and Ona reached the clearing, Sledge had gotten as far as the clump of trees ahead, Turk had reached the stream crossing, and the remaining commandos straddled the road on either side and to the rear of them. There were four men on the left flank, behind Turk and Rickers, and three more behind Boxer and Ona, closer to the stream. They had formed a loose wedge, fanning out behind Sledge, at point, and Turk, directly behind him.

Suddenly, there was a rustling in the trees ahead. Boxer saw three flashes before he heard the crack of rifle fire, and hurled himself at Ona, taking them both to the ground. They crawled on their bellies for cover behind the boulder. Triple D and Will Rickers were in the line of fire, and were gunned down immediately.

Turk shouted, "Snipers," and dove for cover among the shrubs.

Sledge was out in the open, in clear view of the snipers. He had no chance at all. The second volley caught him with two rounds, smashing through his shoulder and back, tearing up his insides, and lodging against his pelvis and ribs.

The four other men behind Turk on the left flank dropped and ran in a crouch for the cover of the trees to their left. Right into an ambush.

Those trees erupted with the gunfire of at least a half-dozen snipers. Four of Rolly's Rangers went down. Three of them were dead.

The three commandos behind Boxer plunged into the stream, taking cover behind the rocks. Out of the original thirteen, six were killed within one minute.

Turk knew he had to make something happen, or they

were all goners. He removed a grenade from his belt and rolled onto his back. He clutched his M-16 in his left hand, pulled the pin with his teeth, and lobbed the grenade toward the trees up ahead which concealed the snipers. Then, he rolled into a supine position and waited.

The grenade went off, sending bits of turf and shrapnel flying. The startled snipers fired towards the explosion. Turk fired at the flashes. A black-clad figure dropped from a tree.

More shots from the snipers. Turk fired back, inching away from his position on his belly. Boxer pressed Ona to the grounds. "Stay down. Keep your head down," and he rushed for the sniper's position while they were concentrating on Turk. Using the snipers' gun flashes as targets, Boxer set his M-16 on automatic and fired a burst at the treetops. A man screamed.

Turk got up on one knee and emptied a clip at the remaining target. A rifle dropped to the ground. He tumbled forward, keeping to a crouch. He and Boxer converged on the snipers from two directions. One of them was hanging from a rope to a tree bough, where he had tied himself. Turk put two rounds into him for good measure. Boxer found the remaining sniper slumped in a branch of the tree and finished him off too.

Seeing their threat from behind taken out of action, the three commandos who'd taken refuge in the stream regrouped and fired volleys across the trail into the trees where their comarades were gunned down. In a fierce exchange, three of the terrorists were killed. The Rangers rallied and charged across the clearing, firing at the three retreating snipers who survived. Beneath the trees, they found three of their men shot dead, and one man, Larry Kingsly, dazed, but alive. A round had grazed his scalp, leaving him with a pounding headache, but glad to be alive. He'd be known as Lucky Larry from now on.

Turk examined the sniper he'd shot who fell to the ground. Oriental. Japanese, most likely, considering the leads that Boxer had gotten from his Admiral friend. And Boxer's suspicions were panning out. Looked like they'd stumbled onto something big. Turk produced a walkie-talkie from his vest pocket and signalled his remaining men. "Report in, Chico, Thumper, Tony? What's going on?"

The reply began with a cackle of static. "Chico here, Turk. Larry's okay, but the other guys bought it. It looks like the bastards headed upstream, toward the falls. We took three of them out. Chinks, or Gooks, or Japs, looks like."

Boxer looked at Turk, and grimaced. Turk shrugged. "We got three of them over here. Now, listen up. We're going to hit 'em from two sides. It looks like the stream curves on over closer to your position. Keep low, and follow it along. You're bound to run into them up ahead."

"Right, Turk. We copy."

"Roger. Boxer and me will circle around from here, catch them in a pincer. Call me if you see anything."

"Got it, Turk. Out."

Turk tucked the transmitter back into his pocket and said to Boxer, and to Ona, who had moved up to join them. "Let's see if we can catch them in a squeeze play. We'll follow the stream from this bank, but well off the path."

Ona was slightly shaken. She'd been involved in plenty of street action, but this was an all-out combat situation. She'd witnessed a half-dozen men die on each side in a few minutes. Had she and Boxer had the bad luck to walk the left flank instead of the right, they'd be dead right

160

now.

After ten minutes of creeping along close to the ground, Turk got a signal from his men. "Got 'em, Turk. Back against the cliff, just to your side of the falls, there seems to be a cave. We count about five or six of them."

"Good work. Move in as close as you can without being seen. When I get into position, I'll give you three clicks on the 'talkies. When you respond with three clicks, we commence firing. Got it?"

"Got it."

Three terrorists had just left the cover of their cave and were skirting the base of the cliff wall when Turk received his signal. He pointed out the targets to Boxer and said, "Now."

Firing from a kneeling position, Turk and Boxer emptied a clip apiece at the three figures, reloaded, and fired a second burst. Two of the enemy went down immediately. A third took a hit, but tried to crawl back to safety.

Chico's group charged across the stream, firing at will. They finished the job on the guy crawling back to the cave, then shot up one of the remaining three who leaned out past the cave opening to fire at Turk and Boxer.

Boxer said to Turk, "If we can get the others to surrender, I'd like to interrogate them, find out who's behind this whole thing."

Turk shrugged. "Fat chance, but you're calling the shots."

Boxer said, "Cover me." He moved closer to the mouth of the cave, keeping behind the cover of a tree. He shouted into the cave. "You in there. Give yourselves up. You don't stand a chance. If you surrender, I'll see that you're not mistreated."

Silence. Then a loud voice from the cave. "Fuck you, Yankee pig. You want me, you come get me. And you die."

Turk said, "No more Mister Nice Guy. Now, it's my turn." He took another grenade, pulled the pin and lobbed it in a near perfect trajectory into the cave mouth. The raucous boasting ceased. A defeaning explosion reverberated off the cave walls, and debris and smoke spewed out.

There was a moment of silence. Then a voice from within called, "Hold your fire. I'm coming out."

Turk signalled Chico's group. "Hold tight 'til I tell you otherwise."

Sunni Akima walked out from the cave, his black jumpsuit covered with rock dust, and blood oozing from a face wound. He stood there in front of the cave mouth, left hand above his head, holding a carbine. He threw it to the ground in front of him.

Six Rangers never took their eyes or their M-16's off him. They watched him draw a short sword from his belt and hold it in front of him. The commandos expected him to toss it to the ground along with his rifle. Ona knew better. She grasped Boxer's arm and said, "Oh, Jack, no. He's going to . . ."

Before she could finish, before anyone could react, Sunni Akima smiled, turned the sword on himself and said, "Yankee pigs, I will now teach you how to die."

Boxer made a futile dash for the black-clad figure. Ona's hands went up to her mouth. Turk and his men just stood there, weapons at ready, knowing there was nothing they could do.

Sunni Akima pressed the point of the sword against his lower abdomen, glared defiantly at the charging Yankee, and plunged the blade in, deliberately twisted it, and drew it up to his solar plexus. He wretched, his eyes turned up, and he dropped forward onto the hilt.

162

Boxer dropped to his knees and turned the body onto its back. Blood and guts spilled from the wound. Blood trickled from Sunni's mouth, a sardonic smile locked into his death mask. Boxer gasped.

Ona said, "Oh, my god," and went to Boxer's side.

Turk and his men stood there staring. Finally, Turk had the presence of mind to examine the cave, to see who else might be lurking within. He motioned with his head for his men to follow him. They stalked to the mouth of the cave, fired off some covering shots and looked inside. One by one, they stood there staring down, their M-16s hanging at their sides. One commando turned and vomited. Two others walked away.

Boxer got up and walked over to see what could make these seasoned veterans react that way. Ona trailed a step behind him. The stench that hit his nostrils as he approached the cave gave him his first warning. There, laid out in neat rows at the rear of the cave lay nine bloated, decomposing, maggot infested, naked bodies.

Boxer closed his eyes and walked away. Someone was going to have to tell Mrs. Edelstein that they'd found her daughter.

Chapter 17

Yoshi Tora lay face down on a padded massage table, naked except for a black towel with orange logo draped across his ancient backside. A young woman was kneading the muscles of his back and shoulders, her skillful fingers seeking out the knots in the deep tissue and applying Shiatsu fingertip massage to these pressure points. Tora moaned his pleasure. At his age, he felt, this was even better than getting laid.

The masseuse was also naked except for the familiar black towel around her hips, fastened low on one side. Sweat glistened off her bare breasts while she ministered to the old man, his hand caressing her bare thighs from time-to-time. She didn't seem to mind; he paid well for his pleasures.

And one of his great pleasures was the Tora Princess, his two-hundred eighty foot private pleasure yacht, rumored to be worth over one hundred million dollars. It was on this yacht that Yoshi Tora was now being attended to. In a few minutes, he would preside over a meeting of the Shogun Society, whose venerable members were now starting to file into the twenty-by-thirty foot dining salon to wait for their leader.

Yoshi ran his hand up the young woman's leg, slid it up under the towel, and squeezed the firm, muscular flesh of her buttock. She continued her massage. "Let us finish up, Midori, my dear. They will be waiting for me before long."

She helped him off the table, wrapped his towel around his waist, and fastened it with a tucked-in knot. They walked off the sun deck, past his private pool and entered the sauna and shower reserved for his exclusive use. She adjusted the temperature controls to 115 degrees. They were soon dripping with sweat, relieving the body of its poisons, he liked to think.

Yoshi nodded to her, and Midori took down a split bamboo switch from its place on the wall and wordlessly proceeded to lightly swat the old man's back, chest, and shoulders. He began to moan once again with pleasure, and rolled over face down on the bench. She tugged off his towel and continued whipping his skin down the back, onto the behind, and the backs of his legs. The extreme heat and flicking bamboo switch had turned his skin bright red.

Yoshi Tora rolled over on his back, his eyes closed, his face a mask of serenity. The masseuse swatted his chest and belly, then his thighs, causing the exquisite pain to amplify all his senses. Then, with no more preamble, she knelt beside him and began massaging his genitals, delicately at first, then with more and more pressure, and with consummate skill, she brought the dead back to life, teasing, squeezing, plying her trade while Tora's head rolled from side to side, his moanings increased in tempo with her strokes until he could contain himself no longer. He erupted with the gusto of a young man, which for the moment, he was.

She deftly wiped him off, helped him to his feet, and walked him into the adjacent stall shower. Tossing her towel out behind her, Midori turned the water on very cold, increased the spray until it stung the skin, and moved under the shower head alongside him.

The icy spray invigorated Yoshi, shocking his system back to total alertness. He patted the young woman's behind, and she shut off the water, towelled him dry, then herself, and helped him into a black terry robe. They rode the private elevator down two decks and entered Tora's personal suite of rooms. There, she helped him dress in black slacks and a turtleneck cashmere sweater, with still another orange tiger logo. He slipped into sandals and walked down a short passageway to join his guests. As for the young woman, her work for the afternoon was completed. Midori was finding life at sea quite enjoyable, not very taxing, and far more rewarding than life on the Ginza. She was quite pleased with herself, as was Yoshi Tora.

Tora strode through the double doors to the dining saloon: His face all smiles, his complexion, the healthy pink of radiant good health. All rose as he entered, toasting him with little cups of warmed saki, and remarking that he looked exceptionally fit.

Tora held up his arms, and the assemblage quieted down. "Please be seated, my old and dear friends. Let us first eat, and then we shall discuss the final preparations for our own little celebration."

As if out of nowhere, six uniformed sushi chefs appeared to serve the dozen guests. With dazzling displays of artistry, they served up succulent strips of fresh fish and various types of other seafood, including shrimps and octopus, while serving wenches kept up with the demand for green tea and saki. When everyone's appetites had been satiated, the low table was cleared, and everyone settled back on their mats and pillows.

Yoshi stood at the head of the table. "I would now

like to bring you all up to date on our master plan. What we want most is to foil the Yankee's Pearl Harbor Day event. To have them treat our Empire's finest hour as a heinous crime is personally repugnant, as I'm sure it is with everyone assembled here."

Cheers went up around the table. "As things are in war," he continued, "the victors write the history books, and had our cowardly leaders not surrendered to the Western allies, the complete, utter destruction of the American forces at Pearl Harbor would have gone down as the single greatest moment in the history of warfare."

More cheers from the group, and a low murmuring of Tora, Tora, Tora. Yoshi held up a hand for quiet. "What we shall do, what we must do is prevent the Americans from holding their damning ceremony. To this end, we have a two-pronged offensive. One," he held a forefinger aloft for emphasis, "we shall use the threat of nuclear attack on the island to coerce the Yankees to cancel their celebration. And, of course, we have the capacity to do this, with the possession of a Chinese SBLN, a submarine capable of launching a nuclear armed ballistic missile to a destination as far as five thousand miles away. A technology, by the way," he went on, "stolen from the American Navy."

This time, Tora let the chanting go on for a few minutes. "Of course, we wouldn't really devastate the island of Oahu. We couldn't afford that. Most of us have considerable holdings on the island. And we wouldn't want to go cutting off our own noses, would we?"

Many of the elderly men chuckled. They knew all too well that collectively, they and their organizations owned perhaps twenty per cent of the real estate on Oahu, with additional holdings on the neighboring islands.

"However," Tora continued, "they shall not go unpunished if they fail to heed our threat. Our ultimatum shall be to cancel the ceremony or as many as five major cities within a five thousand mile radius of Pearl Harbor will be destroyed by our nuclear bombs. Our list will include San Francisco, Sydney, Beijing, Vladivostok, Manila, and Singapore."

A thin man with a wispy white beard cleared his throat and raised his hand. Tora acknowledged him. "General Okihara?"

"I beg of you, Yoshi, find another American target. My cartel has major holdings in San Francisco."

"Well taken, General. We can easily destroy the American naval base at San Diego. And in addition, we shall selectively destroy targets in and around Pearl Harbor. There will be three major carrier groups present for the ceremony, the British, the Soviets, and of course, the American Third Fleet. And as history teaches us, there are many other military targets throughout Oahu and the other islands. We also have an experiment to try on the Big Island of Hawaii. We will attempt to awaken the sleeping devils in the Kilauea volcano with a sizable bomb explosion. And," he continued to the assemblage, "we shall demand a ransom of one billion dollars in gold and diamonds for our troubles, in exchange for not destroying the cities I've mentioned."

The old men began to stand offer toasts to their leader. However, one voice called out, "But Yoshi, what if they find out that we are responsible for the attack?"

Tora's voice was cold, harsh. "What of it? Are you afraid to die?"

The man backed down, ashamed.

"Is anyone here afraid to die for the glory that is rightfully ours?"

The room fell silent. No one man dared to answer. Yoshi Tora now held them mesmerized. He held up a fist overhead and shouted, *"Banzai! Banzai!"*

A solitary voice replied, *"Banzai."*

Several more men repeated the salute, *"Banzai, Banzai"*

Finally, with one collective voice, they began chanting, "Tora, Tora, Tora."

Yoshi Tora stood there proudly, fist raised in salute, the sound of his name resounding in his ears, and he smiled, for he loved every minute of it. Surely, he was the cat that licked the cream.

Boxer stepped out of the Hula Tours van and proceeded directly to the entrance to the CINCPACFLT Headquarters. The MPs guarding the doorway had long since become accustomed to the head of security for the upcoming event in his colorful Hawaiian print clothing. They snapped to attention and held the doors open for him. At Willis' private office, Boxer was directed to a small conference room down the hall. "The Admiral and his guests, Mr. Mako and Admiral Stark, are just finishing lunch, sir. Can I bring you something to eat?"

Boxer hadn't eaten since 0530 and it was almost 2:00 P.M., but food was not one of the things on his mind, now. "Just coffee will be fine, Marie. Thanks."

Willis's secretary knocked on the meeting room door and nodded. "I think you can go right in, now, Admiral Boxer. They're expecting you."

As Boxer entered the richly panelled room, stewards

were removing lunch dishes, and bringing in trays of coffee and tea. They set another place for Boxer. Willis said, "Jack, I think you've already met Mr. Hoshi Mako?" Boxer nodded. "Mr. Mako, Admiral Jack Boxer."

The old man dressed in a black pinstripe business suit started to rise.

"Please, sir, don't get up on my account. It's a pleasure to meet with you again." He turned to the two Navy men and saluted. "Admiral Stark. Admiral Willis."

CINCPACFLT said, "Sit, son. Mr. Mako and Admiral Stark have been filling me in on their theory about what's been going on with all these terrorist raids around the globe."

"Not theory, Admiral Willis. I do not take pleasure in contradicting you, sir, but my own intelligence people have shown me that it is one of my own countrymen, Yoshinobu Tora, who is the mastermind behind all the troubles."

Stark said, "I'm inclined to agree with Mako, Charlie. The evidence seems to point to this Tora fellow. Hoshi here tells me there's a lot of scuttlebutt going on in Japan about a secret organization of old military men, mostly, called the Shogun Society. The old boys didn't take it very well when their Empire lost the war."

Willis was shaking his head. "Dick, Mr. Mako, look, I can't go on hearsay with this. There's too much at stake. I need solid proof before I can go arresting a man of Tora's stature, just as I would had the situation been reversed, and it was Tora who knew Admiral Stark and claimed it was you looking to start World War III."

Mako's face reddened. He was a man who was not used to having his word doubted. "By that time, it may

170

prove too late, Admiral." Mako put down his teacup, still half full, and stood up. "Now, if you'll excuse me, Admiral," Mako put a hand on Stark's shoulder. "I shall be leaving. We have nothing more to discuss."

Willis stood up, as did the others. Mako bowed perfunctorily and strode out of the room.

After a few moment's pause, Stark said, "Now we got him pissed. He could have been a powerful ally. Hoshi's even got his own little private army. I've seen part of it training on his estate."

Willis sat back down, tapped out a filter cigarette and lit up. "This isn't easy for me, Dick. I know Mako's an old friend of yours. But that's just it. Everything he's given us is based upon his revelations to an old friend. And he expects us to believe him on faith."

Stark said, "I believe him."

"I'm convinced of that much, Admiral Stark. I don't mean to offend you. You're my former CNO, and I've always respected your advice. I just can't let personal friendship cloud the issues here. Without hard evidence to the contrary, I have to treat Mako's story as just that. Unsubstantiated."

"Well, then, I too, have nothing more to add. Good afternoon, gentlemen."

Boxer rose and shook hands with his mentor. He had been silent during the exchange. Willis was his boss, after all. But he tended to go along with Stark's gut feeling that Mako was telling the true story. "I suppose I won't see you again until after the big event, Jack. I'd guess you're going to be tied up solid for the next week."

"I'm afraid so, Admiral Stark. And if Mako comes up with anything solid, I'd like to know about it."

After Stark had left the room, Willis lit another cigarette, his ashtray now overflowing with butts. "Light up if you care to, Jack. I'm going to have an after-dinner brandy. Join me?"

Boxer fished his pipe out of a pocket and tamped a sweet-smelling tobacco into the bowl. He nodded, yes, while touching a flame to the tobacco plug. "Thanks, Admiral. It may be my last drink for a while, what with Pearl Harbor Day just a week away. November thirtieth already. It's hard to believe that time's gone by so quickly."

Willis nodded. He went to the dry bar against the far wall and produced two snifters and a bottle of Remy Martin VSOP. He poured them each two fingers and recorked the bottle. He handed Boxer his drink and touched glasses. "Here's to the success of Pearl Harbor Day."

"I'll certainly drink to that."

Willis said, "Have a seat, Jack. I'd like to clear the air about something."

Well, here it finally comes. Boxer got back into his comfortable chair, swirled the amber liquor around, and savored its aroma before taking a long pull. Willis sat across the narrow table from him and lay his hands palms upward on the table. "Look, Jack, I know you care a lot about Admiral Stark, and that you disapprove of the way I handled him and his friend Mako."

Boxer drew on his pipe, let the smoke waft towards the ceiling, but said nothing.

"I want to believe them, too. But in the back of my mind is the treachery of the Japanese ambassadors to the U.S. back in December Nineteen forty-one, when they were still discussing peace, while their task force was steaming toward Pearl Harbor. And, mind you,

172

Hoshi Mako was one of the aviators who attacked our bases."

Boxer still held his tongue. He had a lot more respect for Willis than the current CNO, Mason. Yet, he tended to go along with Stark's assessment of his friend Mako.

"Look," Willis continued. "Here we have this shipping magnate telling us that his chief rival is behind the terrorist activities lately and that Tora's ultimate goal is to repeat the devastation of Pearl Harbor. Conceivably, it could be the other way around. Stark admits that Mako has a private army."

"I still don't trust Tora, sir. That incident upon leaving San Diego left me with the feeling that Tora could have been behind it."

"Because the *Ichi-Ban* tanker was in the vicinity?"

"That, and the fact that the *Ichi-Ban* was a larger target than the tanker that was sunk, and yet its captain wasn't even aware that there was an incident, or that a hostile sub was in the area. Surely, it was close enough to have received radio warnings, or to have picked up the Mayday. It was a lot closer to the incident than the *Manta* was."

Willis asked, "Isn't it possible that the hostile sub beat it out of there without being detected by the *Ichi-Ban?*"

Boxer took another pull on his brandy. "I chased the *Murmansk,* and I'm assuming that it was the stolen Soviet *Alfa,* in the direction of the *Ichi-Ban.* My gut feeling is that they would have had knowledge of that sub."

"But how . . . ?"

"At the time of its inception, my very first super-sub, the *Shark,* was kept top secret. And to hide it from predators, we transported it in a special compartment in the belly of the *Tecumseh,* a supertanker roughly the size of the *Ichi-Ban.* There are too many similarities, here, too many coincidences to suit me, Admiral Willis."

"Well, then we shouldn't rule out either premise, Jack. We each have to go with our own gut feelings."

Boxer nodded, and took another puff on his pipe. Then, there was a knock on the door. Willis said, "Enter."

Marie opened the door, and Capt. Ted Lewis entered, holding a video tape in his hand. "Bad news, Admiral," Willis's aide said, while two ranks wheeled in a TV and VCR unit on a cart. "This was just coped off the television. All the networks carried it. I think it's something you should see."

Chapter 18

Capt. Lewis popped the cassette into the VCR. The fuzzy black-and-white static soon gave way to color bars, then bars and tone, then fade to black. Finally, fade up to an announcer wearing a camel hair blazer and red tie. He had been professionally made up and his hair had the plastered-on look of many of the networks' top anchormen. He said, "I am Marty Krebs at Station KXLR in Burbank, California. I have been ordered to read to you the following message under penalty of death. Off-camera are two machine-gun armed men who wish to remain anonymous. This, now, is their message."

Boxer and Willis sat there staring at the screen, giving the announcer their rapt attention. Krebs went on giving the two ultimatums: One, that the Pearl Harbor Day ceremony not be held; and that, two, the United States, U.S.S.R., Australia, China, and a few others chip in to pay a billion dollar ransom. A similar video has been transmitted to the other major powers, in their native languages. There would be exactly one week to comply, the final day being December seventh. If the celebration did go on as planned, and, if the ransom was not paid, the penalty would be the destruction of a major city in each of these nations."

Krebs concluded with, "I am pressed to assure you that this is not a prank, that I am reading a statement prepared by these people not of my own free will, and that they are deadly serious."

As the camera pulled back to a medium shot of Krebs, the barrel of a Soviet AK-47 assault rifle came into view, pointing directly at the announcer's head. Then, in full view, flames shot from the gun and almost immediately, Krebs' head burst apart on camera, blood and bits of bone and grey matter spewing out, followed by the announcers' body lurching sideways out of the chair. There were screams, and then the screen went fuzzy again. No fade to black. The ending was unexpected, and unrehearsed.

"Shee-it," Willis looked at Boxer incredulously.

Boxer grimaced. "They wanted us to take them seriously."

"Well," Willis added, "They sure succeeded. And they didn't say who they were. Usually, these bastards are publicity hungry, will go out of their way to take responsibility."

Boxer nodded his head. "Which goes to show that we're not dealing with a band of loonies out to make a name for themselves. They have a much higher goal."

"Geez," CINCPACFLT said, "I could use another stiff one. More brandy, Jack? Ted?" Willis didn't wait for an answer, he returned with the third snifter and the bottle of Remy. He handed the glasses around and said, "Gentlemen, we have a war to avert."

Boxer had trouble sleeping that night, the image of Marty Krebs's life being snuffed out just to make a point, coming back over and over in his mind. Boxer was also bothered by the logistics involved in the terror-

176

ist's threat. They simply couldn't be a large enough organization to launch nuclear warheads at such diverse targets from any other country. Unless the missiles were launched by a SLBN from a central location, somewhere equidistant, somewhere midway. Midway Island would be ideal, but so would Hawaii. Although it was only 0200, Boxer got out of bed, being careful not to disturb Ona, gathered up his maps and charts and took them into the spare bedroom, which the two of them had converted into an office of sorts. Then, with a pair of dividers, he measured the distance to each of the target cities using Oahu as the center. Close enough. Son-of-a-Bitch. The boomer is right here in our midst, where they can keep a close eye on what happens at Pearl. If we can get the Chinese to confirm that they lost a boomer.

He was startled by the opening of the bedroom door. A narrow band of light from the room illuminated Ona's scantily clad body in the doorway. "I should have known," she smiled at him. "When I rolled over and you weren't there, I figured your mind wasn't on sleep." She blew him a kiss. "I'll go put on some coffee."

Boxer smiled. Ona was always there for him when he needed her. That set the occasional thoughts of his fiancée, Francine, deeper into the back of his mind. He'd deal with that if and when the time ever came.

Boxer devoured the full breakfast Ona had prepared for him, washing it down with three cups of black coffee.

He then waited a half-hour before Willis finished with his early morning briefing.

"I think we have to go on the assumption that the enemy is in our midst, Admiral Willis. We know they've got a Soviet *Alfa,* and one of our old diesel jobs that we

177

lent to NATO. And if the Chinese sub that intel has word of being stolen comes up as being a boomer, we'll send out an ASW patrol to look for her. Do you think the People's Republic will cooperate?"

"No harm in asking," Willis told him. "I'll see what I can do. Meanwhile, it wouldn't hurt for you to have a look around in the *Manta*."

The *Tora Princess,* steaming at eighteen knots, finally caught up with the *Ichi-Ban* at a spot approximately two hundred miles north of Oahu, roughly the same area from which the Japanese Imperial Navy had launched their infamous attack fifty years ago. A thirty-foot motor launch was winched down over the stern with a quorum of the Shogun Society aboard. From there, it was a short sail to the supertanker, where they were hoisted aboard. From now on, until their demands were met, and until they consummated the destruction that they intended, it would be all work and no more play, regardless of the compliance of the Americans and their allies. From the moment the elderly group left the amenities of the *Princess,* they knew they had to get down to serious business.

The owner's bridge on the *Ichi-Ban* wasn't exactly spartan, except by comparison to the *Tora Princess.* The staterooms were lavishly appointed, and laid out with large double berths. The bathrooms were quite large and stylish, though not embellished with gold and marble. And the conference room was more than adequate for the most prestigious corporate body.

Here, everyone wore black, the entire crew, the staff, and, of course, the venerable heads of the Shogun Society. On every chest was the orange embroidered leaping tiger that was the corporate symbol of the Tora Line, and personal icon of its master, Yoshi Tora.

The crew of the *Ichi-Ban* worked with military precision, and, in truth, they were a military unit that had replaced the normal mercantile crew of the super-tanker. And the huge ship had undergone some modifications of its original design. First of all, the watertight compartment was large enough to house any of the three submarines in their fleet. The deck had been converted to a carrier deck, complete with elevators and catapult, though of somewhat primitive design in order to retain its cover as a commercial vessel.

Below deck were stored a half-dozen Lear jets, armed with a single bomb capable of sinking anything afloat. Their pilots didn't stand a chance of survival, but as far as Tora was concerned, it was worth the risk for a chance to destroy a carrier.

It was from this modified tanker that the three stolen subs had been fully crewed and provisioned. The Italian and Chinese crews that had pilfered them had been replaced by the Society's own secret navy, and locked in a holding cell within the vast confines of the ship. They had been treated well, but were not free to leave until Tora's plan had been executed. No sense taking a chance on having security blown by a gang of fanatics seeking world-wide recognition for their feats.

Yoshi Tora called the ship's captain to his quarters. "Captain Kiyota, please explain to us our current status."

"Yes, sir. We are currently two hundred and thirty miles due north of Oahu. We shall maintain this position as long as possible, keeping in mind we do not want to arouse suspicion. Then, at midnight, seven December, we

179

shall circle the island clockwise and come up due south of our current position, 157° 58', about fifty miles offshore, in order to give our submarines some room to maneuver."

"Very good, Captain. That is as instructed. And what of our submarines?"

Kiyota replied, "The Chinese boomer, the SSBN, if you will, has been renamed the *Akagi*."

"Ahh, a wise choice, Captain. I was aboard the carrier, *Akagi* when it was the flagship of our fleet on the original campaign against Pearl Harbor. How fitting that the missile submarine will carry her name."

Kiyota smiled. "Thank you, sir. At this moment, the *Akagi* is laying several hundred miles off the coast in one of these four grids. For security reasons, the exact location is unknown even to myself."

"What?" Tora blustered.

"It is best, sir. That way, even if there were traitors aboard, even if the Americans were to somehow capture the *Ichi-Ban* in an attempt to stop our intended bombings, they couldn't get the location of the *Akagi* from us. She will return to the mother ship only in a case of extreme danger of being found and sunk before shooting off her missiles."

Tora thought a moment. "I don't like the idea of not having absolute control of this mission, Captain. But, yes, you may be correct. They could never torture information from us that we do not know."

Kiyota realized he had almost overstepped his authority. Even still, if he were wrong about this, there would be hell to pay. He continued, "The Soviet *Alfa,* now named the *Kaga,* is well to the north and west of Kauai, so." He was pointing to a spot on a nautical chart that he was glad he'd remembered to bring along with him. "Also at midnight, she will take up position south of us, with the hope that we can screen for her against any allied return fire. Personally, I think we will catch the Yankees napping again. History has a way of repeating itself."

Yoshi Tora laughed. He liked Kiyota's spirit. "And what of the NATO diesel sub?" Tora knew that was their weakest link.

"Ah, yes, sir. The *Yokohama*. We shall mother her in our womb until the time comes, and at the right moment, we shall give birth to her and send her to her destiny."

Tora knew what that meant. The *Yokohama* was going to be sent on a suicide run, with little or no chance of survival. Without the long range capacity of the two nuclear subs, and lacking long range cruise missiles, the *Yokohama's* job was to take herself right into the harbor and torpedo as many ships as she could. As long as her captain believed that he could ultimately escape, Tora felt that he would carry out his mission. "And where is the baby now, Captain?" Tora smiled as he continued with the analogy.

"She is on a final practice run, sir. She is somewhere east of the Big Island, checking her newly fitted fire control computers. When she has acquired firing solutions on enough sea traffic to satisfy her captain that the computers are working properly, she will retire to the *Ichi-Ban* until seven December."

At that very moment, the *Yokohama* was stalking a group of merchantmen steaming for Oahu from California. The closest was a bulk carrier, the bold white block letters SUGARCO evident on the bow, and again on the smokestack. Perfect. Capt. Sukiyama moved the search scope through an arc of one hundred eighty degrees, sighting two more bulk carriers and a freighter, all separated from each other by about two miles of ocean. He slapped up the periscope handles and barked, "Down scope."

Immediately, the periscope slid down into its well. "FCO, prepare firing solution for the closest target."

"Aye, aye, Captain." FCO tapped in coordinates into his console and watched the triangulation appear on the monitor. "Very well, Captain, we have a solution."

Sukiyama left his post and walked to the rear of the control center to check his officer's figures. FCO pointed to the screen and boasted triumphantly, "I can assure you, Captain, that we would have scored a bulls-eye had you chosen to fire."

Sukiyama put a hand on his subordinate's shoulder. "Good work, Toki. There are three more merchantmen in that convoy. Apparently, the Americans are so cowed by our recent successes that they are afraid to send their merchant ships into the Pacific alone. Just as well, Toki. It will give us more targets to practice on. Choose the freighter, on the far right."

"Aye, aye, Captain."

"SO, fire up the active sonar. I want a better picture to work from."

The sonar man cringed, for he knew they would be giving away their position to any ship that happened to be listening. He also knew better than to argue with his captain, a capital offense. Commander Tora demanded strict discipline, and rigid adherence to protocol. "Aye,

182

aye, Captain. I have an active sonar fix on the freighter. Target bearing zero five zero . . . Range eight thousand meters . . . Speed one two knots and closing."

Sukiyama decided to play his game a little more boldly. He keyed his torpedo room. "TO, load one and two. Set them for acoustic homing." And to the FCO, he added, "Slave those two fish in on the sonar reading." He pounded a fist into his palm. He was tired of playing children's games, and this exercise would make the simulation more genuine.

"Up scope," he commanded. He wanted to see for himself what was obvious on the sonar display. He had the freighter in his sights. An easy target. The blue and white logo was easily visible on the bow. It simply read FORD. So . . . an auto transport. The American car maker's sub-compacts had been seriously competing with his own motherland's vehicles. Here would be the opportunity to even the score. But alas, he had his orders, don't fire unless fired upon.

"Captain," SO called out. "I'm picking up pinging. Someone has us on their own sonar."

Sukiyama did a sweep of the horizon. No change. Then he turned the scope's eye skyward. Damn, a helicopter. One of those merchantmen must be carrying a chopper. And why not? he mused. The *Ichi-Ban* carried several helicopters, in addition to the dive bombers.

"Sonobuoys in the water, Captain."

The pinging was beginning to annoy Sukiyama. And now he was had by the chopper. Well, he could always claim he was fired upon. What the hell. "FCO, fire one."

"What? But, Captain, you know . . . "

Sukiyama had his automatic pistol, the only one in the

183

boat, aimed at the fire control officer's head. He would not tolerate having his authority questioned. "I order you to fire tube number one."

FCO knew that he was a dead man if he disobeyed. "Aye, aye, Captain." He turned a dial and pulled down a lever. The whoosh of compressed air forcing the fish out could be heard throughout the sub.

Captain Sukiyama watched through the scope as the torpedo closed in on the freighter. He saw the car carrier's bow erupt into a fountain of seawater before bursting into a ball of flame that shot two hundred feet skyward. Before he could order a second, killing shot, the sonar officer's voice crackled over the intercom. "Target bearing two four zero, Captain. Range twenty five hundred meters . . . Speed three zero . . . That's no merchantman, Captain."

Sukiyama spun the scope directly behind him and found himself staring down the bow of a destroyer raging towards his sub. "Shit," he muttered to himself as he slapped the scopes handles closed. "Down scope," he demanded. "Dive . . . Dive . . . Dive."

Chapter 19

Capt. I.W. Harper steamed his destroyer, *U.S.S. Camden,* ahead full speed, intent on bagging his first submarine. "Son-of-a-bitch. That was cold-blooded, premeditated murder," he cursed. "Free the ASROC launcher," he ordered into his mike. "Sonar, have you got that fix, yet?"

"Aye, aye, skipper. We're locked right on the bastard."

"Fire ASROC."

With a roar, the missile took off from the deck of the *Camden,* soared a thousand yards through the air before separating in two parts. The torpedo that was the forward half plunged into the sea and homed in on the hostile sub, its active sonar pinging away, picking up cavitation noises made by the fleeing submarine. "I think we've got him, skipper," the sonar chief reported.

"Stick with it, Sam. And keep the chopper in the air 'til we make sure."

The helicopter swooped in low over the projected course of the diving sub, a passive sonobuoy trailing from a long cable from its belly. The chopper, in turn, transmitted its data back to the destroyer for consumption by the ship's sensitive hearing systems. "Bridge, sonar. The chopper has him diving deep below the convoy, skipper."

Harper was worried. "Stand by to abort if necessary, Sam. We can't risk damaging another merchantman."

The captain could see the Ford carrier listing to starboard, and settling slightly at the bows. He needed to get a tug out here fast, but not with an unknown hostile sub in these waters.

"Skipper, the target's beyond the convoy now. He's trying to outrun the torp, but I think we've got 'em."

Before Harper could respond, there was a thunderous underwater explosion about a mile past the SUGARCO cargo vessel, followed by a hundred foot geyser. "Good shooting, chief." He immediately brought his binoculars to his eyes and studied the sea in the vicinity of the explosion. "Stand by the five inch gun in case we didn't finish him off."

"Aye, aye, Captain."

"I'd sure like some prisoners to take back to Admiral Boxer. Let's go have a closer look."

He ordered the engines slowed two thirds and let the forward momentum bring them slowly upon their target. His forward lookout pointed to a ripple in the surface and shouted, "Submarine breaking surface, Skipper. Off the starboard bow."

Harper grabbed an electric bullhorn. The forward gunnery team already had the five-incher aimed at the prospective target. Come on up to papa, the captain said aloud to no one. Nice and easy does it.

The *Yokohama*'s bow broke the surface and rose about twenty feet before being dragged back under by the weight of the sea pouring into the ruptured stern quarter. "Quick, get some lines over," Harper shouted. "Try to get a line to them before they go under."

The captain's pleas were to no avail. The *Yokohama* rose at the bows one last time, spiralled backward and went into a death dive almost four miles below the sea.

On the destroyer's sensitive sonar, the crew could hear the screams and cries of the submariners who hadn't died immediately from the explosion. Harper himself felt a knot in his stomach. It was a horrible way to go.

"That fool." Yoshi Tora was livid. Captain Kiyota, the *Ichi-Ban*'s skipper backed up a step, trying to keep out of range of the wrath of his commander in chief. Sukiyama had violated a cardinal rule and turned a simple practice run into a debacle that cost Tora one-third of his navy.

"I made myself perfectly clear," Tora continued his tirade. "He was not to engage the enemy. Period. His mission was to slip into the harbor and destroy as many enemy warships as he could. Not to bring attention to himself by firing on civilians." The old man looked around at the few men standing in attendance with him in the combat information center. Kiyota's luck had just run out. Tora noticed him trying to back away.

"Didn't I make myself clear? Answer me, dammit."

"Yes, sir. Perfectly. Sukiyama is a fool, not deserving of his command."

"The weak link. Not that I had much choice. There was barely time to fully train three submarine captains. Sukiyama was the least of them, to command the most expendable of our boats." Tora was pacing back and forth behind the chart table. One part of his master plan had already gone awry without having completed so much as an iota of its designated goal. "Now the *Kaga* must do double duty," he said aloud. All eyes were upon him now. "Not only must she stand guard over the ballistic sub, but at the last moment she must launch an attack on the targets inside the harbor."

Kiyota cleared his throat. "Permit me to say, sir, that Captain Tomi Saburo is capable of the task."

Yoshi Tora growled something unintelligible.

The wispy old man who was the former Minister of War piped in with, "Yoshi, it is time to put this in the past and concentrate on renewing our commitment to Operation Z." Operation Z was the code name for the attack on Pearl Harbor in 1941, and Tora had chosen it as the buzzword for his current offensive.

Tora seemed to have calmed down. "You are correct, of course, Hijiki. We still have to strike at the airports, to close them down to tourist traffic. We will do whatever we can to ruin the ceremony. The people will stay away in droves."

"And the Big Bang," the general interjected. "Let us not forget that." A thin smile creased his face.

"And the raid on the memorial, itself," Hijiki said. "That was a brilliant plan of yours, Yoshi. When is that set for?"

Yoshi Tora looked over his hard core advisors, and smiled faintly, the countdown was about to begin. "Tomorrow," he said. The time had come to take the initiative, to begin his offensive in earnest, instead of reacting to the enemy's tactics. "Tomorrow."

Turk felt a bit silly dressed in the park ranger's uniform, but orders were orders. Acting on a tip from Admiral Stark and his friend Mako, Boxer had assigned two squads to protect the Arizona Memorial. Turk's squad had replaced the official crew of park rangers and U.S. Navy personnel assigned as tour guides and shuttle operators. Mean Gene and his men posed as tourists, splitting up and making repeated trips through the introductory movie program and the short hop on the shuttle to the somber white memorial, itself.

The first three days went uneventfully. But on this overcast morning of December 4, that was about to change.

The forty-seat Blue Line tour bus pulled into the visitor's parking lot and disgorged its full load of passengers, mostly Japanese tourists in their dark slacks and white dress shirts, some wearing dark business suits. There was a preponderance of men in the group, the half-dozen or so women with them seemingly detached.

In another part of the parking area a third force was present, part of a small, private army under the hand of Hoshi Mako. A pair of eyes looking through the tinted glass of a Rolls Royce noticed that this group of tourists didn't quite fit the mold of the others. The men all reminded him of soldiers, the women of something else. Paid window dressing, mused Yoni, Mako's grandson, from the concealment of the black Rolls. This was the group he and his men were waiting patiently for, unbeknown to either Tora's assassins, or to Admiral Boxer. Even grandfather's friend, Admiral Stark, was kept in the dark for fear of tipping off the authorities, Mako had been forbidden by Admiral Willis to interfere.

Although this tour group was acting just as expected, snapping pictures and buying souvenirs, Yoni was not fooled. He hoped that the American commandos were not fooled, either.

Niki Nikimora secured the fourth tour of the day for his party, and lined them all up for a group picture. The bewildered women, whom Niki had paid a madame four hundred dollars apiece for a day's services as "companions," were shifted into the front row. Dress up the photo, Niki figured. He held up a hand for silence. "Okay," he said. "Everybody smile. Say Lichee."

That brought laughs from some of Niki's men, and giggles from most of the "ladies." Showmanship was one of Nikimora's strong points.

The P.A. system announced, "Group Four is now ready to enter the theater. Please line up at the entrance door, proceed through the auditorium and begin seating along the right-hand wall."

Niki ushered his contingent into the auditorium, making sure they all took seats together, close to the exit door leading to the shuttle. Unknown to him, Mean Gene Greene and four of his men followed them in, and took seats in the two rows directly behind them. Gene was playing the percentages. This bunch was large enough to cause problems if that were their intention. And the bimbos with them looked out of place with the otherwise all male group. But not to put all his eggs in one basket, five more of Mean Gene's squad would go through with the next group of tourists.

Niki Nikimora endured the twenty-minute film portraying the bombing of Pearl Harbor, some of it actual footage captured from the Japanese. A smile came over his face as he watched the awesome spectacle of the destruction of the *U.S.S. Arizona,* the huge fireball soaring heavenward. The movie went on to say that the *Arizona* had been damaged so severely that she had sunk in about nine minutes, trapping her skipper and a ranking admiral, plus over eleven hundred sailors and marines. The moderator said the men probably died instantly. Niki personally doubted it.

190

The film ended, and the exit door opened to the outside. The haze was beginning to break up, with sunlight shining through the cloud cover. A typical Oahu morning, to be followed by the usual bright sunshine and eighty degree temperatures that Hawaii was noted for. Niki hustled his group through the exit and to the front of the queue lining up for the shuttle ferry over to the memorial.

Two of Turk's men, familiar with boat handling, replaced the pair of Navy personnel, an ensign and an E-3, as shuttle operator and crew. When the launch was full, they pulled away from the dock in a wide arch and made for the memorial, standing alone, awesome, at the site of the former Battleship Row.

Gene was beginning to feel uneasy about this bunch that they'd followed in. They were carrying too many totes and bags, and the six women clearly didn't belong with these men. From the looks of them, Gene figured, they were probably wondering why they were spending so much time sitting on their asses instead of lying on their backs.

With the shuttle launch tied up alongside the structure, people began pouring off the vessel and lining up inside the assembly area of the memorial. Last to leave, Gene alerted Turk's men to possible trouble. They, in turn, hustled the previous tour group onto the other, return boat, but remained on the boarding dock adjacent to the white concrete edifice, themselves.

Mean Gene felt the prickle of hairs at the back of his neck, a bad sign. So this was going to be it. From inside the semi-open central assembly area in the center of the building, he checked out his surroundings. The hundred and eighty-four foot long structure straddled the wreck of the *Arizona,* which lay just beneath the surface of the harbor, fore and aft. Behind it was Ford Island, so that was one less thing to worry about. Looking east, he saw the visitor center, with the *U.S.S. Bowfin,* a landlocked World War II submarine and the adjacent Bowfin Park to the left. Beyond that was the Pearl Harbor Yacht Club, a private marina.

Gene strolled back to the shrine chamber with its white marble wall insribed with the names of the dead, finally spotting Turk. Gene feigned a clumsy stumble, and Turk rushed to his aid, a tourist in distress. A brief mumbled warning put Turk on guard. He quickly took stock of his position. He had three of his men aboard dressed as park rangers, like himself. Two shuttle operators for each launch, make that only two, the return shuttle had already cast off. So that was six, and perhaps a half-dozen with Gene. Against how many? And, who, exactly? There were at least sixty Orientals on the monument right now. He wouldn't really find out til the shooting started.

Niki Nikimora timed his actions so that the return launch was well on its way back to the visitor's center. That left only the two sailors from the remaining shuttle and a handful of park police to deal with. He reached behind his back, beneath his suit jacket, and felt the handle of the twelve-shot automatic pistol tucked into his belt. He ticked off a checklist in his mind: Kill the tour guides, kill the sailors and secure the launch, kill as many civilians as possible, including the whores they had brought with them, and finally, but most importantly, blow up the Memorial itself. Then, execute their escape. Yes, he mused, some of us might escape.

Niki bared his gun and shouted to his men, "Ichi."

192

Thirty-two of Niki's commandos dug into pockets and tote bags and produced weapons.

Good, Niki thought. So far, so good. "Ni," he counted. He watched his men turn their guns on the . . . what? "Shit," he muttered. They'd been had. "Fire at will," he shouted, looking for the nearest target. One of his bimbos became Niki's first victim.

Turk and his men pulled hammerless, 38° two-inch barrel revolvers from pockets and fired point blank at the startled terrorists. The short-barrelled guns had a dual purpose: concealment, and the lack of firepower to bore through an intended target and hit innocent bystanders. In spite of these precautions, the unprepared civilians took heavy losses.

The shuttle crew retrieved heavier caliber automatics from their launch and cut down the squad running out to take over their boat.

Niki knew he'd been set up. His hit-team was being decimated by a few park rangers and what . . . a half-dozen civilians shooting at them. Civilians? Like hell. Niki fired off a shot that struck one of Mean Gene's men.

Got to abort, Niki thought. Get the hell out of here, to fight again somewhere else. And where was his backup speedboat? He thought about that, as well as how he could get something out of this mission. The speedboat driver was waiting at the yacht club for an explosion to signal his run for the memorial to pick up his survivors. "Let's go," he shouted to his men. "Fire off your explosives and get out."

Niki charged towards the entranceway, firing at anything in his path. He dove to the floor just inside the doorway, to avoid a fusillade from the shuttle's crew. He

193

dug into his jacket pocket and withdrew a grenade. He pulled the pin and lobbed it in the direction of the fire directed at him. The grenade exploded on the floating dock a few feet from the shuttle, sending shards of shrapnel and debris flailing at the two crewmen. The firing ceased momentarily.

Niki removed the grenade from his other pocket and sent that one hurtling in the same direction. The second explosion silenced his opposition from the launch drivers. He ran down the gangplank and took up a position covering the entrance. Two of his own men came running out, followed by two civilians firing at them. Niki yelled for his men to drop, and cut down their adversaries.

A roar of engines heralded the arrival of a twin-Merc powered speedboat heading their way. Niki coached it to the landing just past the sinking hulk of the shuttle launch. "What took you so long?" he shouted, and jumped into the cushioned open interior. "Let's get the hell out of here."

His two remaining henchmen barely made it into the speedboat before it thundered off towards the parking lot of the visitor center. If his backup squad were in place there, then escape was possible, Niki felt.

Turk took too long to realize what was going on outside. When it finally hit him, he raced to one of the wide openings in the side of the memorial, and fired off several shots at the fleeing speedboat. His undersized gun wasn't intended for long-range shooting, and his shots were off the mark. He ran to phone ahead to warn of the danger.

Too late. The speedboat touched against the tarmac of the parking area, and Niki and the others jumped out with the twin engines still running. The boat ran amok like a dog chasing its tail.

Niki led the others across the parking lot in the direction his backup crew was to meet him. Good, there they are. Niki waved his arms over his head, and an Audi 4000 led two white vans speeding to meet him. He hopped into the back seat of the Audi while his accomplices found room in the vans. Tires screeched as they veered towards the exit. Terrified visitors dove for cover for fear of being run down. Niki would stop for nothing. "Go faster," he ordered his driver.

Yoni Mako had noticed the suspicious looking getaway squad when they arrived an hour earlier, disdaining the visitor's center to sit in their vehicles. He had commandeered an Dole Pineapple Tour bus and at exactly that moment, his driver dashed for the entrance, effectively blocking it.

The Audi swung away at the last moment, avoiding a collision. The van following them wasn't as agile and crashed headfirst into the heavy bus. The second van barely missed, skidding to a halt a few feet from its sister vehicle.

Now. Yoni Mako unleashed an UZI automatic assault gun and aimed at the getaway vehicles. At his signal, two dozen more of his men, all dressed in dark blue coveralls for easy identification of one another, fired up their cars and tour vans and surrounded the terrorists.

Niki Nikimora pointed to the only way for them to escape. He told his driver, "Go around the bus. I'll take care of covering up."

The Audi lurched for the front of the bus, which was now stalled from the impact of the crash. As his driver maneuvered around the tight curve to the exit, two of

Yoni's men sped up in a sedan to cut them off. Niki leaned out the back window and fired off an entire clip through the windshield of the sedan. Both driver and passenger died instantly, their car smashing into the bus, barely missing the fleeing Audi.

Niki could hear that the weapons fire was dying down on the other side of the bus. His men were being wiped out. But at least he had thwarted the bastards trying to get him. Their own disabled vehicles locked them in the parking lot. He chanced a peek out of the window at the men in blue jumpsuits trying frantically to catch him. Mako, he thought. He caught a glimpse of the young man standing with an UZI alongside a black Rolls Royce. He was sure, now. Yoni Mako. Grandson of his leader, Tora's mortal enemy. Revenge will be sweet, he sneered. He said to the driver, "Let's get the hell out of here."

Chapter 20

"That attack on the Arizona Memorial was an outrage. An insult." Admiral Willis was livid. An unprovoked attack upon one of the nation's most cherished war memorials almost destroyed by a band of terrorists, and within shooting distance of his headquarters? "Those responsible for that reprehensible act have declared war on the U.S.A. They are to be flushed out and brought to justice as war criminals."

Boxer sat there in CINCPACFLT headquarters, feeling the enormity of Willis' declaration. Ona was at his side. The message being given him was clear. Seek and destroy the enemy. Find them and kill on sight. No more Mr. Nice Guy. Before he could reply, Willis continued, "By the way, Jack, your men did a bang-up job out there stopping those bastards. They are to be commended."

"Thank you, Admiral." Boxer knew that their patience and training had paid off. But they had help, he told the old man. "The tip we got from Mr. Mako via Admiral Stark helped us set it up. And some of Mako's men were there on their own, and broke up the terrorists' escape. I'm told only one or two of them got away."

Admiral Willis cleared his throat. "Yes, well, that's another thing. I don't want to seem ungrateful, but I don't like the idea of civilians meddling in military affairs. If they get hurt, there'll be hell to pay. And I still have to feel that Mako's got a vested interest in this thing. The man he's accusing is a major business rival of his. Putting Tora out of business would establish the Mako Lines as the largest shipping company in Japan by a wide margin, and possibly even number one in the world. I don't like that."

Number one, Boxer thought, digging back into his limited knowledge of the Japanese language. *Ichi-Ban.* So who's trying for world hegemony? Sounds like our old friend Tora. "Well, his intelligence is good, Admiral."

Willis scowled at Boxer. "Go ahead and say it. Better than ours," he growled. "And now he's warning us about an air threat. They wouldn't dare attack Oahu by air. With all the military bases on the island on full alert, an air raid against us wouldn't stand a chance."

Boxer looked at Ona, then back at his superior. "Probably not, sir, though we wouldn't rule it out. Ona and I figure that if they want to wreck our ceremony, and keep the tourists home, all they'd have to do is give the impression that it would be unsafe to come to Hawaii at all. If you remember back a half dozen years or so, a major terrorist offensive at the airports in Italy, Germany, and France kept the tourists out of Europe in record numbers. The same thing could happen here. Hit the neighboring islands and close down the airports."

Willis didn't like being disagreed with. Yet, Boxer did have a point. "Of course, I remember the Da Vinci Airport bombing, and the others. Okay, take a look around. Set up a defensive perimeter, then report back here. We have a big event ahead of us in just three days." Adm. Willis rose from his seat, signifying the end of their meeting. "Anything else?"

Boxer got up, thought about it for a moment, then said, "Yes, sir, there is one thing." Ona and Willis stared at him. "I'd like some close surveillance on Tora's tanker, the *Ichi-Ban*. She's sitting a couple hundred miles to the north, hoping we won't notice her. I'd put at least a patrol boat in her lap, and round the clock chopper overflights."

Willis shook his head. "Can't do it. We're not at war with Japan. Their consul would be all over our case. My guess, the politicos would just love it. The media would eat it up. The answer is no."

Boxer stood his ground. "We could at least have the choppers pass overhead from time to time, sir. Just routine stuff. And there'll be Orion spy in the sky flying over the harbor from now on. It wouldn't hurt if they'd give a listen for us."

"Get out of here, Boxer," CINCPACFLT barked. "You're really testing my patience."

As Boxer grabbed Ona by the hand and departed, Willis chuckled to himself, and made the necessary phone calls. He ordered the Navy's Orion high altitude surveillance plane to key in on the supertanker *Ichi-Ban*. And the Third Fleet would begin holding helicopter ASW maneuvers two hundred miles north of the island.

"Mako is a filthy traitor. He must be destroyed." Yoshi Tora was red-faced when Niki reported back on the failure of his mission. Tora was furious. Never mind the American security forces were waiting for them. It had to be Mako, his arch-rival. Mako, whose forgive-and-forget pleas to the Japanese Parliament persuaded them not to boycott the American Pearl Harbor Day ceremony. Mako, who had to tip off the United States Navy on Oahu of his plan to destroy them. Mako, who sent

199

his own grandson and henchmen to play a role in Tora's aborted attempt to destroy the very symbol that stood guard over the American rallying point of the last big war.

Tora sneered. The Americans were big on that. Once it had been, "Remember the Alamo," until it was replaced by, "Remember the *Arizona*." And Mako was helping the wrong side. For that, he must die. Mako . . . Mako . . . Mako. The name alone made his blood boil.

Yoshi Tora slammed his fist hard on the black lacquered conference table. "Mistakes like this will not be tolerated," he barked at his council of war. He glared at his hard-core group of followers: Niki Nikimora, Kiyota, the captain of the *Ichi-Ban,* the generals, the former assistant minister of war of the Imperial Empire, and the others, mostly old men. "There is much work yet to be done. Tomorrow morning, we will proceed with our air raid on the lesser islands. Then, on Saturday, we will have some surprises for the Yankees." Tora stared down each man in the room. Then a thin smile creased his face. "And for that traitor, Mako."

The room was silent for what seemed an eternity. No one dared speak. Finally, Yoshi Tora said, "Tonight, under cover of darkness, I am changing my command post to the Soviet submarine. I want to be closer to the action. Meanwhile, Captain Kiyota, prepare our little fleet of jets below for the air action tomorrow."

Kiyota was afraid to speak up, for fear of incurring Tora's wrath. But to send those Learjets up under the current circumstances would be total folly. "Pardon me for saying so, sir, but the American fleet seems to be holding helicopter search maneuvers in the near vicinity of our ship. One of them manages to fly over us about every half hour or so. To send up the Lear jets with that kind of cover would be suicide."

Yoshi Tora stomped his foot. He looked like he wanted to kill someone, and Kiyota could almost feel it coming. Instead, the old man said, "Damn them. They seem to anticipate our every move. Almost as if one of us is telling them our plans." He looked them all over. "No, of course not. There is only the one who vowed to stop us, the man whom I stood alongside of before the Emperor, to be decorated for valor and dedication to the Empire near the end of the Great War. The very man who built a shipping consortium to rival my own, and who now seeks to destroy me. Mako."

All eyes were upon Tora. He gave them the *Banzai* salute, and turned to exit. Over his shoulder he said, "I go now. There is a tender standing by to take me to the *Kaga*. Captain Saburo is waiting close by to pick me up."

Boxer and Ona arrived at the circular helicopter pad. "What's this?" he whistled. He walked around the familiar chopper, examining the new addition strung across the landing struts. On the otherwise benign Bell Jet Ranger, there was attached a pod of six rockets in their launch tubes.

"I had the chopper beefed up a bit, considering what we learned from Mako. The firepower could come in handy. Those are air-to-air rockets, in case we meet up with the opposition."

Boxer was studying the flying machine which almost looked too delicate for its newly acquired arsenal. "Shouldn't we leave the shooting to the Air Force and

201

the Navy?" He climbed aboard.

"Oh, please take the back seat, Jack. It'll be easier to use the M-16 there if you need to."

Boxer ducked his head below the whirling rotors, and climbed into the seat behind the pilot. That gave him access to both sides of the craft.

"To answer your question, Jack, we'll be patrolling over heavily populated areas. It's much too risky to use the big guns unless the terrorists come in on military fighters. But I really doubt that they will. It would be easy enough for them to do their damage with light, civilian planes, alike the kind that take the tourists on sightseeing excursions." She smiled broadly. "Personally, I wouldn't fly in anything that couldn't go backwards."

Boxer strapped himself into his seat and lay the M-16 across his lap. "Okay, skipper," he chided, "your tail gunner is ready. Take 'er up."

"Okay, Jack." Ona gave a thumbs up and pulled back on the controls, the chopper lifted off and veered out over the Pacific. "I'm going to head southeast, and hope they leave Kauai alone. We'll fly over Molokai and Lanai on our way to Maui, stop to refuel and head over the Big Island."

"Right." Boxer consulted his charts. If their intelligence was correct, that would be the logical course for them to follow.

In fifteen minutes, Ona spotted an Aloha Airlines passenger jet flying overhead on its short hop to Maui, judging by its altitude and trajectory. It was heading over the north shore of Molokai for a landing at Kahului Airport, Maui's airlink to the other islands and to the world. The air traffic controllers had been alerted to watch for anything unusual.

Most commercial flights came into Kahului airport from the north, either from the northeast if from the Big Island, or the mainland, or from the northwest if coming from Kauai or from Honolulu Airport in Oahu. Instead, she opted to split the two smaller islands and approach Maui's airport from the southeast. Her approach would be over the former whaling town of Lahaina, around the mountain range that formed the western half of the island and use Highway 380 as a guide into the airport. She figured that would supplement the coverage from the control tower.

After a few more minutes went by, they were flying over land once more. Boxer pointed out the four brightly painted Cessnas that had just taken off below them.

"Damn!" Jack, that's Lanai, and it doesn't have an airport to accommodate tour planes. It's almost privately owned, and covered with pineapple fields. I don't trust those four. I'm going to hang back just a bit and see what they're up to."

Boxer could feel it in his gut, too. He released the safety on his M-16, and opened the side windows of the chopper.

The four airplanes flew in a swept wing formation, two planes taking the lead, with their wingmen outside to the rear. They banked sharply and lined up with Highway 380. "That's it," Ona said into her headset. "I'm going in after them. She radioed an alert to the tower. Airport passengers were herded back inside the terminal buildings. Commercial traffic was diverted away. Coming from the south, the attack gave them little time to prepare.

Ona keyed her radio. "Red and white Cessnas, you are flying over a restricted area. Identify yourselves."

No response.

Ona repeated her call three times. On the last, when they were dangerously close to the airport, she heard a dialogue in Japanese between the airplanes, but they had still not responded to her inquiry. She swooped low, in an effort to read their numbers and possibly company names on the bottom sides of their aircraft. She had to make certain before firing on unknown civilian light aircraft.

"Jack, look. Between the landing wheels."

Each of the Cessnas carried a single bomb below their belly. That was good enough for Ona. "I'm going to fire a warning shot, Jack."

He wanted to tell her to shoot to kill, but he was too late. She fired off a rocket that came perilously close to one of the lead airplanes, passing just overhead, and continuing off. It fell harmlessly out to sea. She again warned, "Turn away, you are over a restricted area."

More shouting from the pilots. The leftmost plane in the formation rolled away and circled back behind Ona. The other three continued their bearing towards Kahului. Suddenly, a bomb separated from the lead plane.

Ona fired. Her rocket exploded the bomb before it dropped fifty feet from Cessna. Her second shot hit the Cessna in the center of its fuselage, adding its two broken sections to the debris raining down onto the cane fields around the airport.

There was shooting at them from behind. A round glanced off the chopper's door to Boxer's right. Too close for comfort. He shouldered the M-16 and leaned out the window on his left. The plane that had dropped behind was almost upon them now. Two men were firing at him from the cockpit. He said to Ona, "Can you do something to give me a better shot at them?"

Ona responded, and the chopper swooped down the airplane and to the left. Very quickly the Bell Ranger seemed to slide backward, coming up almost alongside the Cessna. Boxer fired off a burst from his weapon, shattering the cockpit window, and killing the two gunmen. The pilot climbed to avoid Boxer's gunfire.

Ona followed the airplane up, lurching ahead to give Boxer a better shot at the pilot. "Quickly, Jack. The others."

Boxer fired off another burst at the plane just behind him now. He watched the prop disintegrate and the windshield shatter. The plane spun out of control and spiralled down toward the mountains to the west.

"Damn," Ona shouted. She pointed to a fireburst on the tarmac at the outskirts of the airport. One bomb had landed. There was still one more armed Cessna to deal with, and it was heading towards the control tower. She fired off a rocket which blew the light plane to oblivion. A jeep-mounted SAM missile fired from the edge of the airport below finished off the one plane that had successfully bombed the airfield. Fiery fragments showered down to the sea.

"Good work, Ona. That was great shooting."

"I think we took a hit on the fuselage. I'd better set down and take a look."

The hit proved to be a gouge torn out of the aluminum skin covering the starboard door. Ona patched it with silvery duct tape. "That ought to hold it till we get back to the base. I want to top off the fuel tank and see what's happening on the Big Island." She smiled, "You still game?"

Boxer held up the M-16. There were several more full

ammo clips left inside the chopper. "Ready when you are."

On the island of Hawaii, somewhere on the Kona coast, a red and white Mitsubishi MU-2 twin-turboprop aircraft took off over the ocean, looked back around in a big arch and headed down around the tip of the island, the southernmost point in the United States, and headed up the east coast. Suspended from the MU-2's underside was an huge black bomb, giving the appearance of an enormous phallus hanging from the plane's crotch.

In fact, that was what caught Ona's attention when her Bell Jet Ranger swept over General Lyman field at the town of Hilo and continued on to almost collide with the twin-engine plane at the outskirts of Hawaii Volcanoes National Park. The chopper chased the unaware airplane up the sloping sides of the Kilauea volcano almost four thousand feet before Ona tuned in on the MU-2's radio frequency and warned it off.

The sight of the crater below was awesome. For the third time this year, the still-active volcano was showing signs of life, a cauldron of molten lava waiting for a push from the bowels of the earth to unleash its fury. It was the aim of the Mitsubishi's pilot to help Mother Nature along by dropping the monster bomb into its midst, set to detonate below the surface. Ona's task was to stop it.

She was down to two rockets. She fired the first one as a warning as the plane circled around and headed back to its target. A reply in broken English sputtered, "Stay back, fool." This was punctuated by a burst of gunfire from the airplane's cabin. The red and white aircraft made a daring run for the center of the crater.

206

Boxer put a hand on Ona's shoulder. "Do it," he said.

Ona touched the firing mechanism that had been installed on the control yoke and the remaining rocket surged toward the MU-2. The pilot dove into the crater in an effort to lose the projectile homing in on his craft. He almost made it. He had armed his bomb and touched the launch button at the very moment Ona's rocket tore off the tail of his plane. He tumbled ass overhead into the fiery broth below him, screaming in anguish as the molten lava devoured the remains of the airplane, crushing the burning the hulk and its contents.

Fifteen seconds later, as Ona lifted her chopper up and away from the crater, they heard a muffled roar, followed by a volcanic eruption of molten lava and ash over seventy feet in the air. The time-delayed bomb had woken the spirit of the ancient god, Pele, and he had spoken.

Chapter 21

They were seated in Boxer's stateroom at the submarine base. Stark had a current chart of the harbor unrolled on a table. Matchsticks and coins served as ships. He was explaining to Boxer what it was like on December 7, 1941. "I was a young ensign aboard old CL-48, the *U.S.S. Honolulu,* a light cruiser. We were moored just across the southeast loch from the sub base here. At 0755 that morning, I was in the officer's mess having breakfast when the skies opened up with the first wave of torpedo bombers sweeping in from two directions. They hit every outboard ship on Battleship Row. Those tin cans got beaten up pretty bad.

"By this time, we realized that we were being attacked, and we all ran like hell to man the anti-aircraft guns on deck. The sky was filled with Japanese *Kate* torpedo bombers, and we tried like hell to shoot them down. Didn't do much good." Stark was getting very animated. It seemed to Boxer that the admiral was reliving the moment as if it were yesterday.

"Then came the dive bombers and horizontal bombers, fighters. *Vals* and *Zeros* everywhere. One of 'em dropped a bomb on the *Honolulu,* and knocked out a gun turret. Try as we did, we couldn't seem to stop the bombardment." Stark's eyes were beginning to well up.

"Let me get you a drink, Admiral Stark. Scotch still good?"

"Thanks, son. I'd appreciate that. My throat is getting a little dry." Boxer poured the retired CNO two fingers of Chivas and a Stoli straight up for himself.

"To Pearl Harbor Day," Boxer toasted his mentor.

"Pearl Harbor Day," Stark said, and drained half the mellow liquor. "Well, the big boys were sitting ducks. We couldn't do much more than watch when the bombs started to fall. The gun crews were caught off guard, and didn't score many hits.

"Anyway, from my vantage point, I could see the pounding the battleships were taking. From right across the harbor I could see the *Arizona* take a hit, and then a secondary explosion blew it to hell. I'll never forget that moment as long as I live." He took another sip of his drink.

Stark began moving matchsticks around, snapping them in two to punctuate his story. Boxer watched the rage build in the man, the white knuckles of his hands as he balled them into fists, and the reddening of his face. "Then they got the *Oklahoma*," Stark continued. "Destroyed. The *West Virginia,* the *Raleigh,* the *Utah* . . . Hell, that was just an old stripped down target ship, but they thought it was a carrier.

"Then they hit the *California,* another battleship, putting her out of action. Then the *Nevada,* the *Maryland,* the *Tennessee.* You couldn't see through the smoke and flames. There were anti-aircraft rounds everywhere. It was a miracle for the Japanese that they lost so few aircraft."

Stark sat down. He was drained, as was his glass of scotch. "They say war is hell, Jack, and I mean to tell you that it's true." He reached over and put a hand on Boxer's shoulder. "Go on out there, son. Leave this desk jockeying to someone else and take the *Manta* out yourself. Go find those bastards intent on starting things up all over again." The old man looked Boxer straight in the eye. "Destroy them, Jack. Get them before they destroy everything those brave souls died for fifty years ago."

The retired admiral sat back in his seat then, just sat there, very quiet. In a few minutes, Boxer noticed the old man's eyes were closed, and he was breathing deeply and regularly. Boxer put a light blanket over Stark, turned out the lights, and headed for CINCPACFLT headquarters. He had work to do.

It was almost midnight when Boxer entered the war room, to find Admiral Willis pacing the floor. He was studying a Plexiglas map of the Pacific theater which took up almost the entire right-hand side of the room, with young officers plotting the whereabouts of all United States ships, and the suspected locations of the other nation's fleets. The mass of red markers in the Russian Sea of Okhotsk portrayed the formidable Soviet submarine bastion. Other concentrations of red dots were in the Sea of Japan and off the coast of Viet Nam, especially at Da Nang and Haiphong.

The United States was represented by blue indicators, which were heavily massed around the Hawaiian chain, throughout the other United States oriented islands, the Philippines and Japan. And, of course, many other colored markers dotted the Pacific.

Behind the admiral was an eight-by-eight glass model of the Hawaiian Islands, major and minor, and also a blowup of Oahu. It was here that Willis tapped the plexiglas and said, "You're right Jack. They've got to be right out here. And it looks like you've been right on the money about Tora and his gang. The *Ichi-Ban* had been sitting up here for the past week, and now they've changed their position to just south of the harbor, about a hundred and fifty miles off the coast. I know they're up to something, but my hands are tied as far as arresting them or searching their vessel. Diplomacy," he spat.

Willis turned abruptly. "Jack, those terrorists are prepared for a first strike nuclear offensive against any or all of eight major world cities unless we pay the billion they've demanded." He glanced at his chronometer. "The deadline is less than six hours away. The ceremony is at noon. I have to be there with the President while he delivers a speech for the cameras, and hope that the crazies don't try something stupid."

"What about the ransom, Admiral? I've heard on the news that the major powers have agreed to pay."

Willis walked over to his desk and tapped out a cigarette. He was consuming one every ten to fifteen minutes. He lit up and took a deep drag, letting the smoke punish him for what he was about to say. "That was for the media, Jack. And hopefully to forestall the terrorists. The involved nations couldn't come to an agreement on who should pay what. The Soviets felt that they could handle any threat, and to hell with the smaller nations. Besides, most of them are our allies, anyway."

Boxer stared at him in disbelief. The future of the world at stake and the governments were arguing about paying for its ransom. He let out a long breath and shook his head.

"Jack, I want you to go out there in your submarine and find the boomer. Find it and destroy it."

Boxer smiled. This was beginning to sound like a

broken record. "You've got half the fleet out looking for that nuke, Admiral. What makes you sure that the *Manta* will succeed where all the others have failed?"

"I can't be sure of anything, Jack, but you're our best hope by now. At 0400 we start sending messages through all the major networks, and all the available military frequencies. We're not sure how they're listening, but we feel satisfied that they are, somehow. The terrorists will be informed that we've capitulated to their demands. A phony ransom of mock diamonds had been prepared for delivery any way they want it."

"Think it will work?"

"Not a chance. But we're hoping it will stall them, buy us a few extra hours to find them and neutralize their threat."

Boxer knew what that meant. Blow them the fuck out of the sea before they had a chance to arm their missiles. "Very well, Admiral. I'll round up my men and get going."

Willis's face softened somewhat. The beginnings of a grin? "Your men are on board, waiting for you. Your boat is ready to sail, skipper."

The use of the term, skipper, made Boxer smile. He saluted the commander in chief of the Pacific Fleet. "Thank you, sir. I'm on my way."

Clemens brought the *Manta* through the channels of Pearl Harbor, and headed due south at ten knots. After an hour, Boxer took the conn. "Mark," he said to his EXO, "I still feel I'm right about Tora using the *Ichi-Ban* to hide his boomer from us. When I drove the *Shark*, years ago, I'd slip into the false tanker hull of the

212

Tecumseh, our mother ship. A tricky maneuver in those days. Crude, but it worked."

Clemens said, "You wrote that chapter of the book, skipper. It would explain why that nuke has been so hard to find."

"Right," Boxer said. He was studying the UWIS screen, programmed to show them a radius of two hundred and fifty miles. Not very accurate at that distance, nonetheless it showed the position of any large ship that made noise or threw off a heat signature. Boxer even noted a school of whales heading east northeast at twelve knots. Probably headed for Maui, where whale watching had been reported good, lately. He tapped his finger at two bright blips approximately one hundred miles south of them.

"Mark, what's the last known position of the *Ichi-Ban?*"

Clemens checked his log. "Twenty-one south, One-fifty-five fifty six west, that puts her right about . . . here." His finger came to rest on the very spot his skipper had targeted moments ago.

"I think they might be using the tanker as a picket to hide the boomer behind. I think we'll go take a look for ourselves." He lifted his microphone and keyed his diving officer. "Whitey, take us down to four zero zero feet."

Chief White pushed forward on the diving yoke while repeating, "Diving to four zero, zero, aye, aye, sir."

"Helmsman, come to one two zero. EO ahead two-thirds."

"Aye, aye, skipper, coming to one two zero," Mahoney replied.

"All ahead two-thirds, Skipper," noted the Engineering

Officer.

The *Manta* surged forward at twenty-five knots on a circuitous route around the supertanker. Boxer was in a hurry to find the missile sub, and this seemed his best shot. Time was indeed running out on him. If his hunch wasn't correct, he might not get a second chance.

After an hour, "Mahoney, left rudder. Come to two seven five."

"Aye, aye, skipper."

"EO, ahead full for the next half hour. Bring us up to flank speed."

"Going to flank speed. Engines ahead all full."

Clem followed their progress on the monitor. They were circling behind the *Ichi-Ban*, hoping to catch the Chinese missile sub napping. They would drive south, then come up behind the boomer, hoping to sneak up and nail them before they got a chance to unleash their nuclear payload on the world.

When Boxer had narrowed the gap sufficiently, he ordered the *Manta* slowed to five knots and set the UWIS for a fifty mile radius. Immediately, the area of ocean represented on the console was greatly reduced, but the details were that much larger and sharper. He studied the screen carefully. Yes, he was sure he had found his boomer. Now, to get into killing range before being detected.

The *Manta* drifted west to east at five knots, finally coming up ten miles due south of the Chinese sub, making her fourteen miles south of the supertanker. Boxer consulted the chronometer on the bulkhead. The red LED timepiece showed 0530. What normally would be a patient, waiting game would now, of necessity, become a race against the clock.

214

"FTO, set up one and two."

"Aye, aye, skipper. Loading one and two." The torpedo officer supervised the fitting of two Mark 48's into the two outer forward tubes.

Boxer said to Clemens, set up a firing solution on one and two. I can't take a chance of missing the shot." The tremendous amount of destruction at stake was almost too much for the mind to accept.

Boxer crept up closer, inching his way forward at a painstakingly slow three knots, producing as little sound as possible. "Sonar, give me range to the target."

"Aye, aye, skipper." Then Hi Fi Freedman made a fatal mistake. He toggled his active sonar, emitting two pings that bounced off the target and echoed back to the *Manta* "Range four thousand two hundred yards, skipper."

The return ping was obvious. If they heard it aboard the *Manta,* then the Chinese boomer did too. Boxer ordered, "FCO, slave those fish into the coordinates."

"Conn, sonar. I have two targets now, say again, two targets."

Boxer watched the shadowy figure of a submarine at two miles seem to split apart into two.

"Torp in the water, skipper. Bearing zero one five . . . Range three five zero zero . . . Speed six five and closing." Hi Fi's voice became excited. "Correction . . . correction, skipper. Make that two torps coming in."

He'd been ambushed by a gang of amateurs. The boomer was practically sitting over the *Alfa,* quiet as can be. So that explains why only one sub showed on his long range sonar and UWIS. "Fire one and two. Helmsman, hard right rudder. Come to zero nine five. Whitey, bring us up to one zero zero."

215

The two fish swam off on a reciprocal bearing. There was a terrible collision as one torpedo from each sub collided head on. The percussion trigged off the *Manta's* second fish, and it exploded harmlessly.

The *Manta* veered hard right and surge ahead at flank speed. Chief White blew some forward ballast and the sub rose sharply at the bows. Boxer hung onto the COMCOMP console handrail. The inclinemeter read forty-five degrees.

The *Alfa's* fish kept coming, pinging hard at them. Damn, Boxer cursed to himself, that *Alfa* skipper is good.

The Soviet hunter-killer sub held its ground, guiding her remaining wire-guided torpedo from the sonar image that the fleeing American sub was producing. The *Manta's* cavitation sounds seemed to scream their position to the enemy.

Boxer maneuvered hard left and dove, trying to dislodge the enemy fish from his tail, but the torpedo was too fast, and it had happened all to quickly. Clemens was wide-eyed watching the blip closing in on the UWIS.

"Prepare to take a hit," Boxer said into the MC. His voice was tinged with anxiety. As the blip closed in, he looked at his exec. "Brace yourself, Clem."

At that moment, Boxer tried one last desperate maneuver, jinking his sub upwards. The torpedo exploded against the sensitive shaft plates, contorting the propeller and bending the shaft at an odd angle. The shaft housing was the *Manta's* most vulnerable area, and the *Alfa* had exploited it.

The *Manta* spiralled downward, the diving officer trying desperately to hold her under control. There followed a hull popping sound, from the stern, and the sea began forcing its way in. Boxer shouted, "Damage control, get the pumps going aft."

"Aye, aye, skipper. Already on my way."

The *Manta* touched bottom with a crash, bouncing once before settling on its keel. They were under two thousand feet of ocean, and it was all the super alloy hull and turtle shell outer skin could do to maintain the integrity of the hull. Already there were screeching and popping noises heard throughout the boat.

"DCO, report on damages and injuries." Boxer was pissed with himself for getting bushwhacked by the Soviet sub. It should never have happened. He shouldn't have assumed that Hi Fi wouldn't hit the active search sonar, when he could get his bearings from the UWIS. Hell, he was only a kid, not yet twenty-one.

DCO fed data into his console, giving Boxer the picture he needed on his main computer screen. The stern was in bad shape. He'd have to suggest major changes there if he ever got out of this one alive.

The second torpedo exploded against the top of the sail, the ten feet or so that protruded when the tower was retracted into its well to streamline the hull shape. It is also very vulnerable, as was any area where there was a flange or seal, rather than a weld.

The *Manta* shook mightily with the hit. It shuddered against the sea bottom when the explosion gouged a chunk out of the outer hull, and caved the topmost part of the sail in on itself. Bodies were thrown to the deck and into bulkheads. Priceless electronics modules were smashed beyond repair as sailors careened off them. An acrid smell soon permeated the sub.

Boxer pulled himself up. He was bleeding profusely from a head wound. He wiped the blood away with his sleeve and tried to regain control of the situation. Half his crew appeared to be dead or injured. "Oh, my god," he muttered before slipping back to the deck.

"Well done, Captain. The second torpedo finished her off."

Tomi Saburo looked down at the elderly man dressed in black with the orange tiger logo on his chest. "It was your brilliant strategy that not only saved us, sir, but caught the Americans with their pants down and killed their sub. And, judging from the hull shape, they sent one of their best against us. That looks to be a *Barracuda* class to me."

Yoshi Tora smiled. Yes, it had been a good kill. And it had been wise to chase the wounded sub and go for the *coup de grace,* while the missile sub escaped to disappear once more, keeping their threat alive. No sense taking chances. "It seems to be a modification of the *Barracuda* type. Note the pinched bow and flare amidships?" From their short distance to the stricken *Manta,* the computer enhanced sonar image was incredible. "And yes, Tomi, the strategy was a good one. Goes way back to the Big War. After all, I was driving subs long before that skipper was even a gleam in his parents' eyes."

Captain Saburo glanced at the bulkhead-mounted clock. It was 0630, a half-hour past the deadline. It was not missed on Tora. He verified the time on his watch. "Yes, Tomi, we have given the dogs more time than we agreed upon. Our dilemma is now, do we fire off the ballistic missiles, or do we collect our billion dollar ransom, and then wreck havoc anyway?"

Tomi Saburo smiled. Of course, the old man was right. "Yes, take the diamonds and then go on with our plan anyway."

Yoshi Tora smiled back. "Now, let us give them something to remember for the next time they send a boy to do a man's job. They shall pay dearly for trying to sink us. It is time to begin our assault."

Chapter 22

Admiral Stark awakened with a start after dozing fitfully for an hour. He was startled by a knock at the door to Boxer's quarters at the sub base. It was Ona, in to report for the night and coordinate plans for the big day tomorrow. She left herself in. "Oh, hi, Admiral Stark. Sorry if I woke you. Where's Jack?"

"Jack? Stark struggled to clear his head. "Went off in the *Manta* to look for the Boomer and sink it before the deadline this morning."

"Oh. Well, I guess I'm on my own, then, until he gets back. I'll deal with Major Jones and his men, myself. We've got every available gun battery and SAM missile launcher in the vicinity set up for anti-aircraft activity. Also, Admiral Willis has the frigate, *Philadelphia,* blocking the harbor. She's the best ASW ship we've got. They won't get through, Admiral. I'm confident of that."

Stark got up from the sofa. "You can be sure they'll try, young lady. They're a clever bunch. Very clever."

Ona shrugged. "Well, if everything's okay here, I'll be on my way."

The admiral checked the time. It was after 1:00 A.M. "Do you think you could give me a lift to Diamond Head? I promised Mr. Mako that I'd join him this morning."

"Rather late for that, don't you think?"

Admiral Stark headed for the bathroom. "I don't

220

think he ever sleeps, if you want my opinion. Mind if I take five minutes to wash up?"

"Take all the time you need, Admiral. By the way, the President will be addressing the nation from the harbor at noon. Do you think you can make it?"

The old man came back into the living room wiping his face with a small white towel. "We'll see, Ona. I'll do the best I can."

"Well, here, then." She handed him a three-by-five card. "It's by invitation only. You might as well take this."

The ride to Diamond Head only took a half hour, due to the late hour and lack of traffic. It was a beautiful, clear night, with a delightful breeze, and the temperature had cooled to seventy. She arrived at the gate of Mako's estate, and waited with Stark until a servant came to get him. He looks very weary, Ona noticed. This whole thing is getting to him. She put the government issue auto into gear and headed back to the naval base. Gone was the familiar Hula Tours van and the colorful clothing. She was dressed in a conservative suit, white shirt, and neckerchief. It was time to get down to business.

"Welcome, my dear friend." Hoshi Mako took Stark by the hand and sat him down on a divan. He had a map with the layout of his villa on a low table before them. His granddaughter brought over the ever-present pot of tea.

"How are the preparations going at the naval base?" he asked the Admiral.

"They seem ready, but I wouldn't rule out an enemy attack, anyway. There is a real dilemma." Stark took a

221

sip of tea. "The world's finest interceptor planes are located right there at Hickam Air Force Base. Surface to air missiles galore. But, if you recall, during the bombing of Pearl Harbor in '41, most of the destruction to Honolulu was caused by our own shells missing their targets and landing in the city. And it's ten times more populated today."

"Yes, you have a distinct disadvantage. While the terrorists feel free to do whatever they please, your government has to hold back on its main armament for fear of causing more devastation."

It was now 3:00 A.M. Mako clapped his hands and a servant appeared, seemingly from out of nowhere. "It is time for my breakfast," the elderly man said. The servant left and quickly returned with a bowl of steaming white rice, and a small plate filled with delicately sliced strips of raw fish. "Care to join me?"

Stark sipped his tea and shook his head, no.

"It's better for you than bacon and eggs," he said, popping a sliver into his mouth with a pair of ivory chopsticks.

When he had finished, the servant reappeared silently and cleared the table. Mako pointed to his map. "I have taken measures to protect my family from a terrorist raid. Surely, they will come for me if they find out that I have been instrumental in targeting them. And I'm quite certain that they are aware."

"Here are my defenses," he showed Stark. "These gazebos out in the garden, and here again, the tea house. Under the beautiful cupolas are the finest miniaturized radar units available. And the tool shed, and the workers' quarters—here and here—conceal mobile SAM missile batteries. And my men are well-armed. They are at

222

platoon strength. Come, I will show you."

Stark donned a light cardigan sweater to ward off the early morning chill. Mako was wrapped in his robe. He led the admiral out the back of the main building and they strolled along a garden path. Mako pointed out his strategic defenses.

"I'm really surprised, Hoshi. This is my second visit through your grounds. On first inspection, everything appeared normal. You've done a beautiful job of camouflage."

Mako took Stark by the arm. "I have something else that might interest you, old friend." They walked down a path that led to the water's edge. The property ended with an abrupt drop of a dozen feet down a cliff of lava rock. A wooden bridge took them to a boat house on stilts over the water. Just inside its double overhead doors, there was a thirty-two foot luxury yacht tied up to a pier, further cutting off the view inside from any boats that might be passing by too closely while the boathouse was open.

"Be careful now," Mako implored. He led Stark inside through a rear door and very carefully made his way forward along a catwalk dividing the structure. Some kind of vessel was visible in the leftmost berth, although it was covered with a custom-fitted tarp.

An armed man dressed in dark blue coveralls appeared. Mako gave him directions in Japanese, and the guard unfastened the tarpaulin. Stark sucked in a long deep breath. An electric winch lifted the cover to reveal the sail and upper portion of a mini-submarine, also dark blue with white Japanese characters, and underneath, in English, the word *IOTA*. "A submarine," Stark exclaimed.

"A two-man submersible," Mako explained. "The prototype of the Iota Electric Boat Company of Japan. Officially, it belongs to my shipping company, Mako Lines. It is used for surveillance, salvage work, underwater repair, and the like. Here, it is at my personal disposal. Would you care to come below?"

Stark nodded, "You bet."

What appeared to be a thirty-five foot long cigar-shaped vessel, very sleek and streamlined, proved below decks to consist of a pressure hull made of two very thick steel spheres joined together by a short tunnel. This, in turn, was covered by a fiberglass reinforced plastic outer hull giving it fine lines and easy maneuverability.

There was more than enough room for two men to work comfortably, with sufficient space for a third if conditions warranted it. There was standing headroom under the sail, with excellent visibility. Stark noticed a lot of electronic equipment and made mention of it to Mako.

Mako smiled. "I have had the *Iota* retrofit with radar and sonar gear. There is a sonar receiver dish and a set of pingers mounted to the nose."

Stark nodded his head. "And this?"

"Ah, that is the firing controls."

"Firing controls for what?"

Mako said, "The *Iota*, as I have had her modified, carries a Mark-46 torpedo in her keel. A crude torpedo by today's standards, but nonetheless, effective at close range."

Admiral Stark couldn't believe it. "You've got yourself a real fighting boat here, Hoshi."

Mako agreed. "I have many enemies, Admiral, some

with a lot more firepower at their command than this. I figured I might need an escape vessel if Yoshi Tora tries to seek revenge against me for my part in thwarting his efforts. A shame that your military leaders didn't heed my warnings sooner."

That lesson was becoming all the more painful. There was a deadline only hours away before Tora fired his SLBMs against the world, with only Boxer in the *Manta* standing in his way.

"You should be safe here with me, Admiral Stark, in the event there is an air raid on Pearl Harbor. There is an underground shelter below the main building. It is protected by solid lava rock."

Stark followed Mako's lead walking out of the boathouse and back over the wooden bridge. "Then we shall watch the day's proceedings from here, together."

"Mayday, Mayday," Boxer's desperate call for help was picked up by the destroyer, *Patrick Henry,* which had been in charge of the Third Fleet's ASW maneuvers in the vicinity of the *Ichi-Ban.* Anti-submarine choppers homed in on the *Manta's* weak radio signals, quickly locating the wreckage and dropping radio marker buoys. One of the helicopter pilots tried to raise somebody aboard the sub.

"This is *Tango Henry One,* we have your position, over."

Boxer's weak voice came back, *"Tango Henry,* acknowledge. This is Capt. Jack Boxer aboard the *Manta.* Have you located the *Alfa?"*

"Negative, *Manta."*

"Suggest you flush him out, *Tango Henry.* We sailed

right into a trap. The *Alfa* torpedoed us twice. The first damaged our stern. The second hit us when we lay helpless on the ocean floor."

"Roger that, Captain. I'll relay that back to my commander."

"Thanks."

"*Manta,* please state your current situation, over."

There was a squawking sound, then silence for a minute. "We are immobile on the bottom, with fifty percent casualties. We are taking on water faster than we can pump it out, and something is wrong with the air scrubber. It's getting hard to breathe down here."

"Roger that, *Manta,* I'll try to get a DSRV down to you. Try and hang on a little longer."

Boxer didn't reply to that. Almost immediately, a cacophony of sonar pinging bounced off the *Manta.* The ASW force must be blasting the ocean for the *Alfa,* Boxer thought. Now if we can only hold up long enough to be rescued.

By 0900, the *Patrick Henry* was lowering a fifty-foot-long black cylinder, eight feet in diameter, onto the escape hatch on the Manta's foredeck. The deep submergence rescue vehicle had a bell-shaped flange which fit over the hatch, forming a perfect seal, so when the trapped seawater was expelled, the three-man DSRV crew could transfer the *Manta*'s sailors out under normal atmospheric pressure. It would be a slow procedure, with room for only a dozen men besides the crew.

Boxer insisted on being the last to leave his boat, but Admiral Willis had already thought of that and countermanded him. Willis wanted Boxer and any able-bodied officers taken out in the first pass along with the most seriously wounded. Boxer was fuming when he stepped

226

out of the rescue device aboard the *Patrick Henry*. He demanded to see the ship's captain.

Capt. Harold Fisher had Boxer's orders in hand when he strode onto the copter pad on the rear deck to meet him. Boxer snarled, "I demand to know why my wounded weren't taken aboard first. I'll . . ."

"Save it, sir. This is directly from CINCPACFLT himself. The old man wants you back at headquarters ASAP. There's a chopper ready now to take you, Admiral. How many officers going with you?"

Boxer snatched the papers from the ship's captain and cursed aloud. He looked behind him. There was Chief Amos White, the DO, Clem and Mahoney, his helmsman. "My EXO and two chiefs, Captain. And myself. The others are either dead or injured."

The big Sikorski had them back at headquarters in forty minutes, sweaty and miserable in their light blue jumpsuits. Boxer's arm hung at a funny angle, a fact he could no longer hide. I ached too much to hold in the normal position.

"You look all beat up, Jack. I'm sorry. I was going to send you back out aboard another sub, but you're hurt too bad."

"I'll be fine, Admiral. Just get me patched up. I can handle the conn with one arm."

"How about your men?"

Clem, Whitey, and Mahoney could scarcely hold themselves upright, but that did not deter them. "Ready to go, Admiral," they almost chorused in unison.

"Well, men, your fighting spirit is still good, so I'm putting you aboard an LA class nuke. Sorry it's not as fancy as yours . . ." Willis watched Boxer's face sag. "Sorry about the *Manta*, Jack. I'll see what I can do to

227

have her put back in shape, too."

"Admiral," Boxer was suddenly aware that he'd lost all track of time. "How is it that we're all not blown to hell? There was an 0600 deadline. Did they . . ."

"We stalled them off with some fake diamonds, Jack. They just made the pickup, say . . ." he checked his watch, "an hour ago. It's just a matter of time until they catch on. Meanwhile, it's going to be up to you to find them again and stop them."

Boxer's body seemed to sag. "You sure you've got the right man for the job, sir. I really blew it this time."

"But you lived through it, son. There's nothing like learning from your mistakes."

Chapter 23

"Captain Kiyota, we have been timing the intervals between passes by the Yankee helicopters. They have been very consistent. About one every half-hour, give or take five minutes."

"Very good, Lieutenant."

"There is one due any minute, now, Captain."

Kiyota picked up the intercom mike. "Get ready. The chopper will be here momentarily. You know what you have to do?"

"Aye, aye, Captain."

He keyed his flight technicians on the deck below. "Get the planes ready. You will have less than an hour to launch all six."

"Yes, Captain. We're ready."

Two crewmen stepped out onto the deck alongside the rail. One hefted a missile launcher onto his shoulder. The other checked to make sure the SAM missile was seated properly, and that the ignition wires were connected. Satisfied, he slapped the gunner on his helmet and stepped out of the way.

The Navy helicopter was on time. It flew over the *Ichi-Ban,* circled once and hovered overhead while the copilot had a look around with his binoculars. The gunner waited with his officer until the chopper crew were in direct line with the morning sun, making their visibility difficult. "Now," the officer said. The SAM operator stepped out from behind his cover, sighted and fired his missile.

The chopper pilot didn't have time to respond. The rocket smashed its way into the cockpit where it detonated against the rear of the cabin. The explosion ignited the fuel tank behind the cabin and the helicopter burst apart. The pilot and his crew died instantly, and fell to the sea amid the burning debris.

Kiyota was elated. "Now," he called down the deck immediately below. "The chopper is down. Quickly, quickly."

In twenty minutes, six new Lear jets were lined up in two rows on the *Ichi-Ban*'s deck. Originally designed as fast transportation for the business executive, these beauties had been modified by Tora into innocent looking, but deadly dive bombers. Their mission: Fly into Honolulu airport, but instead of landing as expected, loop around to the mouth of adjacent Pearl Harbor and hit the largest targets afloat. Those were the orders for five of the jet pilots. The sixth was to initiate a personal vendetta for Hishi Tora. This aviator was to head east, to Diamond Head.

The captain and entire crew of the *Ichi-Ban* stood on the deck to give the flyers a *Banzai* salute to see them off. For some of the flyers, they realized, it would be their last.

The Lear jets never had a chance. Tora must have known all along that this was to be a Kamikaze attack. The first jet, T-1, bluffed a landing at Honolulu International Airport, then suddenly flipped over and headed straight for the harbor. The air traffic controller warned T-1 away, but the jet simply ignored the tower and flew in at five hundred knots.

230

An alarm sounded at Hickam Field, adjacent to the commercial airport. The SAM battery which was standing by was alerted. Ona had done her job well.

The Soviet carrier, *Kiev*, was laying at anchor just outside the harbor. An alert machine gunner fired on the fast approaching jet as it closed in on the Russian's flagship. The SAM missile struck the tail of the Lear jet just as the first machine-gun rounds found their mark. T-1 was blown to oblivion.

The next four of Tora's tiny air force fared even worse. They were blown from the sky before they got close to the harbor. Hickam's guns were merciless. Only T-6 escaped their wrath, as it continued east along the coast, its twin bombs and wing-mounted machine guns armed and ready.

A siren went off in the garden of Mako's estate. "Air Raid, Grandfather, get down." Yoni Mako hustled the two old men into the basement, the three of them crawling on hands and knees as fast as they could. The young man sent them down another level, to the bomb shelter below the house. As soon as they left him, he found a headset and listened to his radar operators.

"We are tracking a private jet onto the estate, now. He's . . ."

Yoni could hear the staccato rat-a-tat of a machine gun and the screams of his radar operator. A bomb crashed through the roof of the very building he was in. The explosion blew out the livingroom, and even shook him up in the reinforced basement below ground.

T-6 streaked out over the ocean to regroup before going in for another attack. He never got the chance. Two SAM missiles vectored in on the jet and it exploded over the sea.

Yoni waited a full ten minutes before going downstairs and telling his grandfather all was safe once again.

Boxer and Clemens shared a jeep for the ride from CINCPACFLT headquarters to the submarine base a short distance away. Whitey and Mahoney rode in a following vehicle. They walked up the brow of the *Los Angeles* class sub, *Newport,* looking like the losers of a bar brawl. Boxer's arm was heavily bandaged and in a sling strapped close to his side.

Clemens had a bloody bandage wrapped around his forhead. Whitey's bruises were invisible, but still very real. Mahoney walked with a limp.

They had been expected. The captain and his officers were present to greet them, officially. The exec barked, "Admiral on board," and they all stood at attention and saluted.

Boxer and his men returned the salute. "At ease, gentlemen," Boxer said. "From now on we'll dispense with the saluting, if you don't mind." He removed an envelope that had been tucked under his broken arm and handed it to the captain. "I'm Adm. Jack Boxer. This is my EXO, Capt. Mark Clemens, Chiefs White and Mahoney, my DO and helmsman, respectively."

The captain of the *Newport* was about to salute again, but Boxer's look cut him off. "Capt. James Beam, Admiral." He went on to introduce his staff. "Where are the rest of your people, sir? We were expecting to be replaced by your officers and CPOs."

Boxer said, "We're all that's left standing, Captain. I'd appreciate it if you and your men stay on to help us run the boat."

Some of Beam's officer cadre looked at him with smiles on their faces. So they were not going to get kicked off their own sub after all. Beam stood at attention. "We'd be honored to serve under you, Admiral Boxer. Why don't we go below and I'll show you around."

Boxer and his men, accompanied by Capt. Beam, made a tour of the *Newport*. This was the Navy's hot sub before the introduction of the *Shark* class. He was very familiar with it. He asked his men, "Any questions?"

Clemens shook his head, no. Mahoney shrugged. Whitey said, "I cut my teeth on diesels, twenty-five years ago, sir, and I've worked on everything that's come up since then, right on up to the *Manta*." He ran his hand along the top of an overhead pipe, checking it for dust, out of habit. There was none. "This one's a beaut," he said.

They walked back to the control center. Boxer said, "Capt. Beam, I've got the conn because I've fought with these bastards already. I've seen what they can do. The skipper of the *Alfa*'s a good one. Real good. And time is running out. I'd like to get going. Have your men cast off."

"Yes, sir," Beam said, glad to share the command. He ordered the sub cast off from its mooring and piloted it out of the harbor. When they'd cleared the last of the ships at anchor off the coast he said, "We're in open water, Admiral."

"I've got the conn, Captain. Thanks for your help. "And please, my men call me skipper."

Beam started to salute, then stopped himself. "Yes, sir, skipper."

Boxer checked his instrumentation, noted his depth and bearing, and ordered a dive. "Okay, Captain, let's go hunting."

Mako's intelligence people told him about the sinking of the *Manta*. Stark said, "Why won't they listen to reason?"

Mako shook his head. "I'm afraid they are committed to not harassing the *Ichi-Ban,* because of the diplomatic considerations. I have no such restrictions. It is time for me to take direct action."

"Meaning?"

"I will set off in the *Iota* and keep an eye on the super tanker, myself."

"I'm going with you."

Mako said, "Very well. I cannot argue with an old friend."

Stark accompanied Mako down the path to the boat-house. At the foot of the wooden bridge, Mako said, "Oh, I am such a fool. I have left my navigation equipment behind at the main house. Would you be so kind as to go back and ask my grandson to get for me? He will bring you and the equipment back on an electric cart. Meanwhile, I'll get the boat ready."

Well, it as a long walk back for an old man, but Stark agreed. It took him fifteen minutes to cover the mostly uphill climb back to the house. When he told Yoni what his grandfather wanted, the young man couldn't find it promptly. In all, three-quarters of an hour had gone by before Yoni stood before him with a filled duffle bag. That was okay, Stark figured. He could use the rest after all that exertion.

"Well, son, ready to go?"

Yoni stood before him, head down. He said, "I'm sorry to have had to deceive you, sir, but my grandfather is already gone."

Stark looked up, surprised.

"He instructed me to delay you as long as possible so he could slip away in the *Iota* alone."

"But . . ."

"He did not wish for you to be injured if things went wrong."

Stark was not happy about this. "But what about him? He's my friend. What if . . .?"

"My grandfather is his own man. He knows exactly what he is doing."

So do I, Stark thought to himself.

The Japanese delegation was seated around a long low red lacquered table having their mid-morning tea before venturing forth to their reserved seats at the Pearl Harbor Day ceremony. The mood was festive. Why shouldn't it be? Fifty years ago their fathers were at war with the United States. And having lost that war, their nation was now a staunch ally and major trading party, and they were to be honored guests at the commemoration. One of them remarked about how time heals all wounds, and the others agreed.

The pretty serving girls were pouring tea and making a big fuss over the senior member of the group, Gufi Okido. Gufi was all smiles, for today was also his fiftieth birthday. He was born the very day of the attack. While they were singing a birthday song in his honor, the door to the teahouse opened and a young Japanese man with shoulder-length hair swished into the room. He was carrying a long, white box bearing the name, Bonsai Florists.

As the singing faded, the young man worked his way to the head of the table, hips undulating, his arms waving effeminately. He placed the box in front of Okido and opened it. "Surprise. Free flowers for your lapels. Compliments of my boss at Bonsai Florists." He reached in and took out a beautiful tropical flower tied up with a wisp of fern. "This one's for you. Here, let me help you."

The young man finished and showed the boutonniere off to the group. He glowed at their applause. "Please sign here, sir. There's no charge. This is just to show my boss that you received the flowers."

Okido took a pair of glasses from his breast pocket and slid them up his nose. The florist handed him a pen, and he bent over the receipt to sign it.

The long-haired young man reached in his pocket while Okido was busy signing for the gift, and withdrew a long, silenced handgun. Before anyone realized what was going on, he placed the end of the barrel against Okido's temple and fired off a shot.

Okido was blown off the chair by the force of the slug. It traveled through his brain and exited the other side with a spew of blood and gray matter. The women screamed. The men tried to regain composure and shouted at the young man. Some wisely ducked for cover.

The exit door opened again and three similarly dressed men entered with their silenced revolvers drawn. The florist said, "All of you, get on your feet. Do as I say or you will be killed. Does anyone here doubt what I say?"

236

Nobody did. One by one, the delegates got up and stood behind their places at the table. The florist motioned with his head and an accomplice went to check out the kitchen. He came out dragging a terrified serving girl by her kimono. "Look what I found in the kitchen — this little chickie here." He put the barrel of the gun to her face, and she closed her eyes.

"Women up against that wall. Turn around. If you move, I'll kill you. Understand?"

They did. Five waitresses stood face against the wall, as rigid as could be, not daring to move a muscle.

"Now, I want each of you men to remove your clothes, down to your underwear."

No one moved.

The florist put the tip of his gun barrel into the ear of the nearest man. "Take off your clothes right now, or you are a dead man."

The man's hands were shaking almost too hard for him to open his buttons. The florist removed the revolver, and the shaking subsided. The man removed his jacket, then his tie and shirt.

"Pants, too." The florist prodded him with the gun, the pants fell to the floor and the man stepped out of them. All of their shoes were already lined up against the near wall.

As the other members of the party removed their clothing, two of the intruders gathered them up and piled them by the door.

"Good. Now I want you all to face that wall, no there, away from the women." The florist kicked one straggler in the behind. "You, too, lard-ass. You need a special invitation?"

Now, they had all complied.

237

"Everybody down on his knees. If you want to live through this, do what I say."

When the florist had them all on their knees facing the wall, he nodded to his men. They quickly stepped behind the row of delegates and pumped one silenced bullet into each head.

The serving women screamed. The florist turned to face them, and shot each of them in the head or chest. Then he said to his cohorts, "Make sure."

One more round was expended on each victim. Then the assailants threw the clothing and shoes into large cloth sacks they'd brought with them, and backed out the exit.

"Wait a minute," the florist told them. He walked to the head of the table and plucked a flower from the box. He brought it to his lips and kissed it. Then he threw it on the table and left.

Chapter 24

Bleachers had been set up in the courtyard of Third Fleet's headquarters on Ford Island, facing the podium where the President would soon be delivering his address. The newly-trimmed lawn was already being trampled by the TV camera crews setting up shop in front of the VIP seats. Cables were run from microphones and Sony video camcorders back to vans parked behind and aft of the podium. Secret Servicemen and women were on rooftops and walking the perimeter, warily eyeing the arriving dignitaries and support personnel filing into their seats.

Ona stood discretely behind the rostrum. Her job was to supplement the Secret Service, and to secure the entire island, limiting access to invitees only. It was she who had chosen Ford Island for the Presidential visit, considering it easier to defend than the surrounding areas of Pearl Harbor. And it was Ona who decided that it wouldn't hurt to have Maj. Rolly Jones and two squads of his Rangers nearby as additional protection.

Jones deployed his men in several innocent looking television studio vans interspersed among the genuine ones. As long as all went well, almost no one would realize their presence.

At 1115 hours, a Blackhawk helicopter touched down on a landing pad behind the headquarters building, and President Spooner walked the short distance to the stage. He was accompanied by Admiral Willis and his personal contingency of Secret Service agents. One of them carried the emergency medical kit in the event the President should be injured. At least one of them wielded a compact UZI submachine gun. At one minute to noon, everyone rose while the Marine band played "Hail to the Chief."

Spooner took the podium and held both hands aloft in a V-for-Victory salute amid cheers from the audience. He thanked the emissaries of the more than twenty nations present for supporting the ceremony, and went on with a ten-minute speech invoking world peace and harmony. The President concluded, "And it my sincere hope and prayer that the nations of this fragile planet of ours have truly learned the lessons born out of that fateful day, fifty years ago today, December seven Nineteen forty-one."

As the crowd rose to give Spooner a standing ovation, Niki Nikimora jumped up and shouted to the so far docile Japanese contingent, "Now."

Twenty terrorists rose as one. Concealed on them were high-tech plastic handguns, the kind meant to fool airport metal detectors. They had gotten through the Ford Island security force as well. Each automatic carried a fourteen-round clip, and each man carried a spare.

Nikimora yelled, "Fire at will." He rushed the stage, firing at the President and Willis, while his men cut down the Secret Servicemen.

Three rounds smashed into the wooden podium, sending splinters of wood and lead fragments. Before he could react, Willis was grazed by a bit of shrapnel, and ducked behind the rostrum. President Spooner just stood there, dumbfounded.

Ona dashed to his rescue from ten yards back. She took him down with a flying tackle around his chest, and covered his body with hers. Meanwhile, his bodyguard was being wiped out. The terrorists advanced with surprising little resistance.

Niki Nikimora took out the UZI wielding defender with three well placed shots and lurched to the stage. He kicked away the podium and took point blank aim at Admiral Willis. "Death to you, swine."

Rolly Jones stood twelve feet away, pointing an M-16 at Nikimora. He shouted, "Drop it, motherfucker!"

Niki looked up. Who would shoot first? He raised his automatic at Jones, but his split second decision took too long and cost him his life.

Rolly fired a short burst, then another. Niki's body twitched and jerked, and stumbled backward. He was bleeding all over.

"Let's go, Rangers," Jones ordered. His men responded on the double. The terrorists were no match for the well-armed Rangers. They fought furiously, but leaderless, their drive fell apart. A third of Rolly's men died before the last of the terrorists took his own life rather than risk capture.

President Spooner lay under the weight of the woman who saved his life. He was thinking, I guess they didn't learn the lessons history taught us fifty years ago. Will they every learn?

When the firing stopped, Ona rolled off Spooner, feeling slightly embarrassed. She was bleeding on the President. He got up and helped her to her feet. "You're hurt."

Ona managed a smile. "It's nothing, Mr. President. I'll be alright." And she collapsed.

It was 1300 hours aboard the Soviet *Alfa* class submarine, renamed the *Kaga* by Tora's crew. The radioman interrupted a tense conversation between Yoshi Tora and the sub's captain, Tomi Saburo. "Still no word from Nikimora, sir."

Tora said, "Then we must assume that he is dead."

"Or captured," the captain shot back.

Tora's face reddened. "There is no place in our plans for capture, Captain. You would be wise to keep that in mind. There is only success or failure. And failure carries the death penalty." He regained his composure now, and spoke more quietly. "Death is sometimes the reward even with victory."

"How will we know, then, if Niki succeeded in killing the leader of the U.S. Pacific Fleet and their President?"

Tora smiled. "When we read about it in the newspapers tomorrow. Now enough of this. We have our own objective to attend to."

"Yes, of course."

Tora told the radioman, "Contact the captain of the *Akagi* on the ship-to-ship radio." Tora accompanied him back to the listening station.

In a moment, the radio operator handed him a spare headset. "The *Akagi,* Sir."

"Captain, I order you to prepare to launch your missiles. The targets I have chosen are San Diego, Vladivostok and Beijing. You will commence firing at exactly 1400 hours at those three cities. You will then withdraw and await my orders to bomb the secondary targets. Do you understand?"

"Yes, sir. I understand my orders perfectly. *Banzai.*"

Yoshi Tora put down the radio headset and returned to the attack center. "Well, Captain, we have our ransom now in a Swiss bank that I control. My experts are checking them out at this moment. Now, to punish our enemies for the defeat in Nineteen forty-one. Stand by to launch your cruise missiles."

"Aye, aye, sir." Tomi Saburo was now a happy man. For a terrorist to work for a man such as this was a great honor. The bombings at airports, the indiscriminate killings of innocent women and children in train stations or shopping malls, the destruction of United Sates servicemen's hangouts, all of that paled in comparison with this. The complete devastation of three major cities. Revenge has never been so sweet, the sub captain thought.

Saburo picked up his intercom mike. "Forward torpedo room, lead all six tubes with cruise missiles."

"Aye, aye, Captain. Loading one through six with SLCMs."

"Firing sequence is one-three-two-four-five-six," he told the fire control officer.

"Choose your targets well, Captain," Tora told him.

Capt. Saburo gave six sets of coordinates to the fire control team. "Prepare fire solutions on all six targets," he ordered.

In five minutes, "Set, Captain."

Tomi Saburo looked at Tora, who nodded.

Saburo stood at the fire control module, directly behind the firing apparatus. He put a hand on his officer's shoulder and said, "Fire."

The *U.S.S. Newport* was working one hundred eighty

miles offshore, running sprint and drift patterns to allow the mile long towed array cable they trailed to search for the *Alfa*. Boxer dashed at forty knots for ten minutes to close the gap between his sub and the *Alfa*, but at that speed, the sonar gear was useless. To compensate, the *Newport* was made to drift at five knots to allow the sensitive array to listen.

Boxer ordered a three-sixty sweep to check behind the sub, and continued to sprint ahead again. The *Newport* was in the drift phase when the *Kaga* fired off its cruise missiles.

"Conn, sonar. Target bearing one seven five degrees. A sub, Admiral, too far to get an accurate range. At least twenty miles, sir."

Boxer raced back to the sonar room, followed by Captain Beam, leaving Clem with the conn. "Show me," Boxer ordered.

"Right here, sir." The sonar display showed a large bright blip at the fringes of the screen. "She made a lot of noise. My guess was she fired off some torps against something, but now I'm more inclined to think they were missiles."

"If you're right, let's hope that it's the *Alfa* and not the boomer." Boxer and Beam looked at each other. Both men feared the Soviet *Alfa*, but its destruction capacity was limited. The ballistic missile sub was another thing. The threat of nuclear devastation hung heavy over both skippers.

Boxer keyed the bridge on the MC mike. "Clem, let's close the gap."

Clemens ordered the new course while Boxer and Beam returned to the attack center. "Helmsman come to course one seven five degrees."

"Aye, aye, sir. Coming to one seven five."

"EO, ahead two thirds."

"Aye, aye, sir. All ahead two-thirds."

The *Newport* turned left and lunged ahead at thirty knots.

Boxer said, "Take us deep, Clem. Eight hundred feet." There would be less interference with the sonar at that depth.

The *Newport* angled downward at a sharp incline. Whitey was calling off their descent. "Passing through four hundred feet . . . passing through five hundred . . . Finally, "We are at eight zero zero. Diving planes are now at null."

Boxer took over the conn. He chased the *Alfa* east past Diamond Head and up the east coast, before heading around to Oahu's north shore. The *Kaga* was making a lot of noise, figuring she could outrun anything on the sea, or below.

Patience. Mako had put the *Iota* down into a rift in the ocean floor, not far from the gigantic underbelly of the supertanker *Ichi-Ban*. The passive sonar dome in the tail of the submersible almost went wild when the Chinese missile sub appeared below the stern of the mother ship, and slipped out into the ocean below.

Mako kept the *Iota* in the wake of the giant sub, the *Akagi*'s cavitation noises and the submersible's small electric motor combining to make the tiny craft almost invisible to the boomer. For almost a half-hour, the *Iota* followed the supersub southwest, away from Oahu, when suddenly, it reversed course. Mako figured that the Chinese submarine was headed off to fire its ballistic missiles, as Tora had threatened. Something had happened to cause its captain to change his plans.

Mako had no sophisticated equipment aboard to help him plan his objective. All he had to rely on were sonar soundings and common sense. And his common sense told him that the boomer was heading back to the *Ichi-Ban*. For what, though, he wondered. Well, if she didn't fire her missiles, then something spooked her into running home.

Her captain must be a coward, Mako thought. If Yoshi Tora, himself were in command, he would have fired off his missiles even under the immediate threat of annihilation. Thank God, then, that this captain was not his arch-enemy. He followed the larger sub back to the *Ichi-Ban,* having difficulty keeping up with the behemoth at ten knots.

As they reacquired the supertanker, Mako hid the *Iota* behind one of the outcroppings of coral in the area, this one the size of a small house. He sat there and waited in the tiny underwater vessel, wondering about the conversation that must be taking place between the captains of the submarine and the tanker. No doubt it wasn't a very cordial exchange.

In fact, Mako was correct. The boomer's captain argued and pleaded with Kiyota to open the hydraulic hatch in the false bottom of the tanker and allow the submarine to enter.

"You are not authorized to do so," Captain Kiyota screamed into the radio. "You were ordered to launch your missiles. Now do so."

"But our sonar picked up an enemy hunter sub out there, very close to our launch position. We could not risk being destroyed before we got our missiles away."

"You fool," Kiyota spat. "I shall have a word with Master Tora about you." He tried to reach the *Alfa,* but Saburo and Mako were too occupied to answer, even had they received the message. As it was, the *Kaga* was doing close to fifty knots on a zig-zag course, trying to find a way to rid itself of the fast submarine on its tail.

The captain of the missile sub became belligerent. "I order you to open the hatch and allow us to reenter, he told Kiyota. Unless you want me to create my own opening in your hull."

The man has gone mad, Kiyota reasoned. Better to do what he asks and have Tora deal with him later than risk damage to both the *Ichi-Ban* and the sub. "Very well, Captain. Stand by to enter." Kiyota operated the hydraulic hatch mechanism and the supertanker opened it cavernous mouth to the boomer.

Ah, Mako thought. Just what I've been waiting for. He waited until the Chinese submarine was halfway into the mother ship when he brought the *Iota* into position. The boomer seemed to be swallowed up by the tanker. Mako sent a brief message to a receiver mounted in his estate on Diamond Head, and followed the giant sub into the bowels of the Ichi-Ban. He waited until the hydraulic hatch was closed. Then he fired his single torpedo.

The explosion that followed was visible as far away as Pearl Harbor.

Tora was running out of options. There was no longer anyplace to hide except the depths of the sea. Circling helicopters were constantly hammering him with active sonar and passing his location to the submarine chasing him. He guessed they wouldn't try to torpedo him, themselves, for fear of sinking the wrong sub.

He guessed right. He circled the island, his superior speed keeping the following boat at an ever-widening distance. The *Kaga* was now fifty miles off the westernmost point on Oahu, a prominence of land known as Kaena Point. Following the chart, Captain Saburo pointed out to his boss that legend had it that this was the point of departure for the souls of dead Hawaiians.

"Ha," Tora laughed, derisively. "Those fools didn't know what they were talking about. Let's shake that bugger on our tails."

Tomi Saburo said, "Right." He held the intercom mike to his lips. "Helmsman, hard left rudder. Come to course one eight zero."

"Aye, aye, Captain. Coming to course one eight zero." They were now driving due south.

"Diving Officer, to go one thousand feet."

"Diving to one thousand feet. Aye, aye, sir."

Captain Saburo nodded. "Engines all ahead one third."

The submarine slowed appreciably, until they were doing five knots, and hardly making any noise at all. Saburo continued, "All hands, rig for quiet."

Immediately, everyone not specifically assigned to a task in running the ship climbed into their bunks and just lay there. Tora was supremely confident, now. No one could find him now, No one."

"We've lost her, skipper."

Captain Beam asked, "Just like that?"

Boxer strode to the sonar station. "Let me have a

"look, son."

"Here's where we lost her, Admiral." The sonarman's finger was on the screen. "We had her going due west, sir, when the cavitation sounds died."

Boxer turned to Captain Beam. "Very clever, this skipper. He's drawn us out here, only to disappear on us. We're supposed to think he's still heading west, and hurry to catch up to him. But I don't think that's where that *Alfa* is heading."

Beam touched a faint blip on the screen. "What's that?" he asked his SO.

"Whale, sir. Very distinct sound."

Boxer took the phones and placed them over one ear. "I think he's right, Captain. Let's circle to see if we can pick him up on passive."

Beam gave the orders and the *Newport* described a sphere.

"No dice, sir."

The monitor was empty except for the lonely whale.

Boxer told the sonar officer, "Use the thermographic display. Let's see if we can pick up a heat signature."

"Aye, aye, sir." The SO fiddled with an adjoining terminal. "All clear for five miles, Admiral."

"Go to fifty."

"Yes, Sir. Here's something, Admiral. Very faint, down here twenty miles to the south."

Boxer tapped the screen. "Let's go have a look, Captain," he told Beam.

"Roger that, sir." He gave the necessary commands and the *Newport* changed course to south. In twenty minutes they were near the sight of the reported contact. "Lost her again, skipper."

Boxer turned to Captain Beam. "Four knots."

Beam ordered his EO, "Four knots."

"Four knots, aye, aye, Captain." The *Newport* slowed.

"Torpedo in the water," the sonar man said. He pressed his phones to his ears. "Make that two torpedos, bearing zero six five and zero six three, Sir. Range five thousand feet . . . Speed six zero knots . . . Depth one thousand."

Boxer grabbed the MC mike. "All ahead full. Helmsman, full-right rudder, come to zero nine zero. Whitey, up to two hundred. Clem, fire off a noisemaker."

The *Newport* veered sharply to the right, picked up speed and shot upward. This created a disturbance in the water, which, along with the noisemaker, fooled one of the torpedoes. There was a loud explosion at the spot the *Newport* just vacated. The second torpedo, however, continued tracking Boxer's sub.

"The torp's actively pinging us, now, skipper."

Boxer acknowledged with a nod of his head. That was very obvious from the sound waves echoing throughout the sub's hull.

"Torp's closing on us, sir."

"Roger that, sonar. Whitey, dive. Take it down to fifty feet from the bottom."

"Where the hell'd that come from, Admiral. Why did we lose the *Alfa,* but he still nailed us?"

"He must have been hiding behind a pressure ridge back there. That skipper really knows his stuff."

Sonar reported, "The torp's still gaining, sir."

"Whitey, at fifty feet, take us back up, sharply."

"Aye, aye, sir. We're passing through one hundred now. Fifty, okay, brace yourselves." Whitey pulled back hard on the diving yoke, at the same time blowing forward ballast. The *Newport* shot up abruptly, almost knocking anyone standing into each other.

The torpedo sped past their stern and exploded on the bottom.

"Load one and two," Boxer ordered. "Mark-48's"

"Torpedo in the water, off the port bow, sir."

"Fire one and the reciprocal bearing," Boxer said. "Hard-left rudder. Come to two four five."

Captain Beam watched the sonar monitor. "He's running, Skipper. You've got 'em on the run."

"Fire two." As the torpedo left its tube with a whoosh of compressed air, Boxer ordered, "Load three and four."

The *Alfa* set off a noisemaker as well. The Mark-48 didn't go for it. It exploded one hundred feet off the *Kaga*'s stern. The sonar man got excited. "You got 'em, skipper. She's faltering."

Boxer keyed the fire control officer. "Solution on three and four."

"Set," FCO replied.

"Fire three and four."

There was silence as they listened to the fish leave their tubes, and watched the two smaller, faster blips converge on the one larger blip on the sonar screen. There was a flash, and all three blips disappeared. The sonar operator pulled his phones off at the last moment, his head a little shaky from the blast. "Bulls-eye. That's a hit." He forced himself to calm down. "Repeat, that's a hit on the *Alfa*. Both torps."

A cheer went up in the attack center. Boxer cut it off with a look. "Keep monitoring. Follow it to the surface."

Aboard the *Alfa,* Captain Tomi Saburo clutched the periscope pedestal, a nasty gash on his forehead bleed-

251

ing profusely. He looked at Tora. "I must surface. Got to get my people off."

Yoshi Tora looked around the command center. The computer consoles were smashed. Sailors had been battered by the twin impacts, and lay strewn around the deck. The hull was screeching under the pressure of the sea, and he could hear the sounds of water rushing into the engine compartment. He stared at Captain Saburo, and shook his head. "No, Captain. You have fought valiantly, but we have lost. Now it is time to die like men."

Saburo let out a deep breath and hung his head. Together, they waited there, hearing the twisting of the bulkheads, and the hull popping noises as the sea closed in around them, crushing the pressure hull, rushing in and taking its due.

"They're not surfacing, skipper. I just heard the hull crush. I think . . . they're gone."

Boxer looked at Captain Beam. "Brave souls, Captain. But for the wrong cause."

Ona lay on her back in an awkwardly shaped hospital bed in Tripler Hospital, not far from Pearl Harbor. She beamed from ear-to-ear when Boxer entered her room with a huge bouquet of tropical flowers. "Thanks, Jack. Please put it over there on the counter."

Boxer set the flowers down next to the floral piece that dwarfed the one he'd brought. It was from President Spooner. The card on it read, "To the bravest of them all."

Boxer walked over and kissed her, gently lifting a wisp of her long, black hair off of her face. "I'll be back to see you tonight, darling. I have to drop Admiral Stark off someplace."

Ona blew him a kiss and watched him leave her hospital room. Admiral Stark was waiting in the downstairs lobby.

The two men drove the few miles to Pearl Harbor, and pulled into the visitor's center. Boxer had called ahead, and the shuttle launch was reserved just for the two of them. They were ferried across to the Arizona Memorial, which was also empty of visitors. Boxer led Stark over the gangplank into the Memorial; two Admirals in full dress whites, the younger one bearing a long flower box.

Boxer held the box open for Admiral Stark, who removed a beautiful lei made of hibiscus petals. He held it up and tossed it into the water. "To my dear friend, Hoshi Mako," he said. "He gave his life to save millions of others."

Boxer removed a second lei, and accompanied Stark to the rear of the Memorial. The old man knelt down and placed the lei at the base of the marble wall, inscribed with the names of those who died fifty years ago to the day. He couldn't speak. A tear welled up in his eye and he wiped it away.

Boxer helped him up, put his arm around his old friend and mentor, and they walked away.

THE END

ASHES
by William W. Johnstone

OUT OF THE ASHES   (1137, $3.50)

Ben Raines hadn't looked forward to the War, but he knew it was coming. After the balloons went up, Ben was one of the survivors, fighting his way across the country, searching for his family, and leading a band of new pioneers attempting to bring American OUT OF THE ASHES.

FIRE IN THE ASHES   (2669, $3.95)

It's 1999 and the world as we know it no longer exists. Ben Raines, leader of the Resistance, must regroup his rebels and prep them for bloody guerrilla war. But are they ready to face an even fiercer foe—the human mutants threatening to overpower the world!

ANARCHY IN THE ASHES   (2592, $3.95)

Out of the smoldering nuclear wreckage of World War III, Ben Raines has emerged as the strong leader the Resistance needs. When Sam Hartline, the mercenary, joins forces with an invading army of Russians, Ben and his people raise a bloody banner of defiance to defend earth's last bastion of freedom.

SMOKE FROM THE ASHES   (2191, $3.50)

Swarming across America's Southern tier march the avenging soldiers of Libyan blood terrorist Khamsin. Lurking in the blackened ruins of once-great cities are the mutant Night People, crazed killers of all who dare enter their domain. Only Ben Raines, his son Buddy, and a handful of Ben's Rebel Army remain to strike a blow for the survival of America and the future of the free world!

ALONE IN THE ASHES   (2591, $3.95)

In this hellish new world there are human animals and Ben Raines—famed soldier and survival expert—soon becomes their hunted prey. He desperately tries to stay one step ahead of death, but no one can survive ALONE IN THE ASHES.

Available wherever paperbacks are sold, or order direct from the Publisher. Send cover price plus 50¢ per copy for mailing and handling to Zebra Books, Dept. 2628, 475 Park Avenue South, New York, N.Y. 10016. Residents of New York, New Jersey and Pennsylvania must include sales tax. DO NOT SEND CASH.

TURN TO RICHARD P. HENRICK
FOR THE BEST IN UNDERSEA ACTION!

SILENT WARRIORS   (1675, $3.95)

The RED STAR, Russia's newest, most technically advanced submarine, has been dispatched to spearhead a massive nuclear first strike against the U.S. Cut off from all radio contact, the crew of an American attack sub must engage the deadly enemy alone, or witness the explosive end of the world above!

THE PHOENIX ODYSSEY   (1789, $3.95)

During a routine War Alert drill, all communications to the U.S.S. PHOENIX suddenly and mysteriously vanish. Deaf to orders cancelling the exercise, in six short hours the PHOENIX will unleash its nuclear arsenal against the Russian mainland!

COUNTERFORCE   (2013, $3.95)

In an era of U.S.-Soviet cooperation, a deadly trio of Kremlin war mongers unleashes their ultimate secret weapon: a lone Russian submarine armed with enough nuclear firepower to obliterate the entire U.S. defensive system. As an unsuspecting world races towards the apocalypse, the U.S.S. TRITON must seek out and destroy the undersea killer!

FLIGHT OF THE CONDOR   (2139, $3.95)

America's most advanced defensive surveillance satelllite is abandoning its orbit, leaving the U.S. blind and defenseless to a Soviet missile attack. From the depths of the ocean to the threshold of outer space, the stage is set for mankind's ultimate confrontation with nuclear doom!

WHEN DUTY CALLS   (2256, $3.95)

An awesome new laser defense system will render the U.S.S.R. untouchable in the event of nuclear attack. Faced with total devastation, America's last hope lies onboard a captured Soviet submarine, as U.S. SEAL team Alpha prepares for a daring assault on Russian soil!

Available wherever paperbacks are sold, or order direct from the Publisher. Send cover price plus 50¢ per copy for mailing and handling to Zebra Books, Dept. 2628, 475 Park Avenue South, New York, N.Y. 10016. Residents of New York, New Jersey and Pennsylvania must include sales tax. DO NOT SEND CASH.